Those '67 Blues
A Novel

by
B.K. Bryans

Those '67 Blues

by
B.K. Bryans

First Edition
© 2011 Brian K. Bryans
Moonlight Intruders © 1988 Craig Kodera
& The Greenwich Workshop
All rights reserved.

No portion of this book may be reproduced or transmitted in any form, or by any means, electronic or mechanical, including photocopying, recording or by information storage and retrieval systems, without the expressed written permission of the author.

ISBN: 978-0-9845777-7-4

Technical Review Editor: Nelson O. Ottenhausen
Managing Editor: Dari Bradley
Sr. Editor: Doris Littlefield
Cover Painting: Craig Kodera
Cover Arrangement: Dari Bradley

This is a fictional story: Use or mention of events, places, names of anyone, or any similarity of the story line to actual persons, places or events, is purely coincidental.

Published by Patriot Media, Inc.
Publishing America's Patriots
P.O. Box 5414
Niceville, FL 32578
United States of America
www.patriotmediainc.com

Reviews

'I loved *Those '67 Blues,* but it touched nerves that I thought were long buried. It has the authentic feel of someone who has actually flown combat missions in that war that I've found missing in most of the books I've read on the subject. The emotion conveys so well.'

Tony Tambini, *Vietnam War A-4 / A-7 pilot.*

'*Those '67 Blues* is my kind of book. It has the accurate detail that satisfies the guy who's "been there and done that" and intrigues the guy who wishes he could have. *Blues* takes you through virtually every aspect of the carrier war in 1967 and does it so precisely you feel as if you are right there getting shot at. Those readers who flew into the flak, missile, and MIG mess in North Vietnam will relive the adrenalin rush that comes from dodging SAMs, and feel the heartbreak of seeing our guys going down in flames or swinging under a chute (if they're lucky). To the curious readers, you can't get any closer to being there than *Those '67 Blues.*'

Phil Waters, *Vietnam-era A-6 Bombardier/Navigator*

Acknowledgements

Thank you to my wife Pat, for her understanding, patience, and support during the writing of this book.

Special thanks to Craig Kodera for capturing in *Moonlight Intruders* the feeling one felt when slipping quietly into enemy territory under cover of darkness. His painting makes a significant contribution to this novel, and his generosity in allowing us to use it is appreciated.

B.K. Bryans

Introduction

Some years seem in retrospect to have been inflection points in the course of national character and events. Like the shifting of tectonic plates, huge and lasting changes occur. The year 1967 was such a year for the United States of America.

The nation's nuclear arsenal peaked in 1967 with an estimated thirty-two thousand nukes, four times what the Soviet Union possessed. In January of that year, the Green Bay Packers defeated the Kansas City Chiefs 35-10 in Super Bowl I. Sports, news broadcasting, and television advertising have never been the same.

April brought large anti-war demonstrations to New York. At this point, U.S. ground forces had been in South Vietnam for six years, and *Rolling Thunder*, the military title for the gradual and sustained aerial bombardment of North Vietnam, had been going on for a little more than two years.

In June, Israel defeated its Arab neighbors in what came to be called the Six-Day War, thus gaining control of the West Bank, the Gaza Strip, the Sinai Peninsula, and the Golan Heights. The American military forces, shackled and frustrated in Vietnam, looked with envy at the Israelis and said, 'See what could be done if we were turned loose.'

That summer, the drug culture took the spotlight and focused on the Haight-Ashbury section of San Francisco. About a hundred thousand hippies, druggies, and *love-children* partook of music with drugs and *free love* at its height.

A good time was had by all, or so it's been reported.

Meanwhile, women were beginning to flex their freedom muscles with the National Organization for Women (NOW) staging its first convention. The meetings focused on the Equal Rights Amendment, publicly funded child care, and repeal of abortion laws. At the time, all fifty states banned abortion, but California and Arizona soon liberalized their abortion laws and thirteen other states followed suit during the next three years.

Roe v. Wade was low on the horizon.

Long-festering racial issues turned violent. On July 12th, a black Newark, New Jersey cab driver was arrested on a traffic violation and then beaten by the arresting officers. A crowd gathered outside police headquarters. Thinking the cabbie had been killed, they rioted. By July 17th, when state police and National Guard troops gained control, there were twenty-three dead, seventy-five injured, and over fifteen hundred arrested.

Six days later, on the night of July 23rd, Detroit police raided an after-hours drinking club in a black neighborhood. They expected to roust a few regulars, but they encountered more than eighty patrons holding a welcome-home party for two returning Vietnam veterans. A brawl ensued; it was followed by five days of racial rioting that left forty-three dead, almost twelve hundred injured, and more than seven thousand arrested.

On October 21st, an estimated fifty thousand war protestors stormed the Pentagon, and an all-night riot occurred. Almost seven hundred were arrested.

Concurrently, President Lyndon Johnson and Secretary of Defense Robert McNamara ordered increased air strikes into North Vietnam even as they placed additional restrictions on targets and tactics. Sortie rates and aircraft losses surged throughout the autumn months. Major multi-aircraft *alpha* strikes were sent daily into the Iron Triangle delineated by Hanoi, Haiphong, and Nam Dinh.

At night, Navy all-weather A-6 Intruders went in low and alone.

'Tell the Vietnamese they've got to draw in their horns or we're going to bomb them back into the Stone Age.'

Gen. Curtis LeMay, May 1964

Those '67 Blues

Chapter 1
Day One

Yankee Station

The flight deck tilted, and what had been a gentle afternoon breeze across the Tonkin Gulf stiffened into a gale as USS *Valiant* turned into the wind. The ship's OOD (officer of the deck) glanced at the clock, then back at the moving compass heading. He intended to roll the big ship out onto its launch course precisely as the bridge clock's sweep-second hand indicated 1300 hours.

This was no game to the OOD. While the *brown shoe* naval aviators aboard the massive aircraft carrier were judged on their airmanship and precision flying, the *black shoe* surface warfare officers were rated on their ship-handling abilities. And the captain, the ultimate judge, lounged in his tall leather chair on the port wing of the bridge, not twenty feet away, watching.

Valiant's size, with a flight deck eleven hundred feet long and two hundred fifty feet wide, was a major factor in the OOD's calculations, of course. So were the subtle effects of wind and wave. The flight deck stood sixty feet above the waterline, and the ship's *island* soared another sixty into the air. The wind's affect against the carrier's side could be substantial, and it would change throughout the turn. The sea's long, rolling swells could affect the turn in other more subtle ways.

Then there was the helmsman. Some were better than others; this one tended to respond a bit slower than most. The OOD compensated by giving his orders a tad early.

The OOD smiled in satisfaction as the ship's bow marched past the scattered rain clouds perched low on the horizon. Any fool could give orders to turn the ship; it took a real seaman to do it with precision.

And the captain would notice. He always did.

Below on the flight deck, unaware of the melee swirling around him, Lieutenant Mike Roamer pushed his A-6 Intruder's twin throttles forward then focused on the plane director a dozen feet away.

The director, a teenager with a wispy mustache that almost matched the color of his yellow jersey, moved his extended hands in short, precise strokes as he leaned back into the freshening wind and willed the bulky plane onto its assigned catapult: cat one, forward on the starboard side.

Lieutenant Roamer's feet stabbed at alternate brake pedals, and his left hand tweaked the plane's throttles in response to the steady stream of urgent signals. Three other aircraft also moved in the immediate vicinity and margins for error were slight.

Roamer's A-6 appeared to waddle as it zigzagged up the deck. The outboard sections of the folded wings, the tips almost meeting above the aft fuselage, trembled in the changing air currents. Once on the catapult, the director made fists and crossed his wrists—*stop*.

Mike jammed on both brakes and pulled the twin throttles back to idle. The Intruder, heavy with twenty thousand pounds of JP-5 fuel plus twenty-two 500-pound bombs slung under its thick wings, shuddered to a stop.

Rocking in the wind, the plane waited.

Wisps of steam curled up from the cat track below and rolled down the deck to oblivion. A jet blast deflector, a steel slab referred to merely as the JBD, rose from the deck a few feet behind the aircraft.

A pair of young men in faded green jerseys scampered under the plane. Mike couldn't see what they were doing, but he knew their routine. They would lower a T-bar attached to the front of the nose landing gear strut and hook the plane to the catapult's shuttle. Then they would lower a similar bar from the strut's back side and fasten it to the holdback fitting.

The director raised both arms over his head with fingers touching then spread his arms out to shoulder height.

Mike moved a lever on the center console. The outer sections of the plane's broad wings swung down into horizontal position and locked. With its fifty-three feet of wingspan in place, the bird was ready to fly.

A bearded aviation ordnanceman in a sweat-stained red jersey ducked under the plane and emerged a few seconds later with four steel pins attached to red banners. He held them up for Mike's approval. The four MERs (multiple ejector racks) cradling the bombs could now be jettisoned in an emergency.

With a vigorous thumbs-up, Mike signaled his approval, then watched the ordnanceman move off to prepare the A-6 on the port catapult. Satisfied with his half of the cockpit, Mike turned his attention to the man on his right.

Lieutenant Terry Anders, the bombardier/navigator, leaned over the aircraft's built-in computer keyboard entering a series of geographic coordinates. The radarscope mounted in front of the B/N's face and the rugged computer situated between his knees were evidence of the A-6's identity as the premier all-weather attack aircraft in anyone's Navy or Air Force.

Finished, Lieutenant Anders pushed his body back in the ejection seat, locked his shoulder harness, and crossed himself.

Mike looked back to the director; then he keyed the ICS (intercom system) and said, "It's a cakewalk today. You think you need that?"

"I fly with you," Terry said. "I cross myself every time."

On deck, the director held up both fists and opened them.

Mike released the brakes, and the A-6 squatted as the catapult shuttle inched forward, placing tension between the airplane's nose gear and the holdback fitting. In effect, the catapult launched the nose strut and the rest of the airplane followed—hopefully.

A lanky young man in a green jersey held up a slate board on Terry's side of the aircraft. The number 58,600 was scrawled across it.

Terry responded with a thumbs-up.

Over the ICS, Mike asked, "That board ever wrong?"

"Not so far, but I'm waiting."

The man turned the slate board to face the crew manning the catapult controls in the starboard catwalk. The cat's end speed would be set to accommodate wind across the deck, air density, and the airplane's weight: 58,600 pounds.

Now the director swept both hands toward another man in a yellow jersey, the catapult officer, who stood midway between the two bow cats, leaning backward into the wind.

With control passed, Mike shifted his attention to the new boss, the cat officer, a senior pilot now serving time as ship's company. He glanced at his watch and moved to stand in front of Mike's port wing, the time-honored signal that the catapult would not be fired until both he and the pilot were ready. He twirled two fingers over his head.

Mike pushed both throttles all the way forward to the stops. His eyes scanned the engine instruments, looking for anything that might defy normal. The twin Pratt & Whitney J52 jet engines spewed out eighteen thousand pounds of thrust against the JBD. The airplane pulled at its metal tether.

With the heel of his left hand pressed against both throttle heads, Mike wrapped his fingers around a short metal bar that extended out from the left side of the cockpit. This prevented the throttles from being thrown back to idle during a cat shot.

Satisfied with the gauges, Mike faced the cat officer and saluted, the *ready* signal. When Mike's right arm came down, he gripped the control stick and tucked his elbow into his hip to keep the stick from slamming back into his gut during launch.

At full power, the A-6 waited on the cat, trembling—its crew impatient.

USS *Valiant* rolled out onto the launch course, flight deck suddenly level, as the sweep-second hand of the ship's clock clicked past the numeral twelve. On the bow, the cat officer swept his arm forward as if lunging against an opponent with an epee—the starboard catapult fired.

WHAM.

A pulse of steam shoved Mike's body back against his ejection seat and accelerated the A-6 down the cat track to 165 knots. Even at that speed, the heavy plane settled a few feet as it left the bow at the end of the cat stroke.

Mike steadied the aircraft then turned a few degrees right to ensure separation from the A-6 coming off the port cat. He raised the landing gear, felt the *thumps* as the big wheels seated in their wells, then raised the flaps.

FIRE.

The starboard fire-warning light on the instrument panel flashed bright red. A *de-de-de-de-de* warning tone warbled over the intercom.

Mike yanked the starboard throttle back to the fuel-cut-off position, hoping to starve the flames.

As the heavy plane settled toward the water, Terry yelled, "Oh shit!" He pushed the radar hood out of the way and raised his hands to the primary ejection handle at the top of his seat.

Reaching forward, Mike stabbed the button that jettisoned the MERs and their attached ordnance then rotated the aircraft's nose to the max-lift position on the angle-of-attack indicator, trying for a single-engine climb out. The knuckles of his left hand turned pale as he forced the left throttle forward against its stop; his leg muscles tightened as he used rudder pressure to compensate for asymmetric thrust.

Something unfamiliar sucked the moisture out of Mike's mouth.

Sheets of trailing flame appeared in the rear-view mirrors.

A warning blasted over the UHF radio on *Valiant*'s launch channel: "A-Six off cat one, you're on fire. Eject! Eject! Eject!"

The canopy blew off and Terry's ejection seat shot up the rails.

Mike gave one split-second thought to trying to save the airplane then reached up with both hands and pulled the face curtain mounted on top of his Martin-Baker GRU5 ejection seat. That triggered escape technology derived from decades of American R&D.

One of three cartridges in the eighty-feet-per-second ejection gun that comprised the seat's spine fired, and the seat bucket started its rocket ride up guide rails attached to the aircraft. Radio and oxygen connections to the airframe snapped. Emergency oxygen from a bottle in Mike's seat pack flowed to his mask.

When the nylon restraint line running through metal rings in the garters strapped around Mike's calves, snapped taut, they yanked his legs back against the ejection seat, and kept his feet from striking the instrument panel and canopy bow.

A static line between the seat and the airframe reached its full extension and triggered timers before it broke. A half-second later, a gun embedded in the seat bucket fired to deploy two small drogue parachutes that stabilized the ejection seat. One second later, scissor shackles cut everything that connected Mike to the seat, and yet another drogue deployed. This one yanked the parachute out of its backpack and rolled Mike out of the ejection seat. The face curtain, still clutched in his hands, came free.

Three seconds after he initiated the ejection sequence, Mike's upward ride peaked with his parachute deployed in full blossom two hundred feet above the doomed airplane. His first coherent thought as the parachute yanked him upright was, *I'm alive.*

The A-6 slammed into the water, and a large fireball raced to engulf Mike, interrupting his joy at being alive. He yanked the parachute riser farthest from the flames and slipped away. The heat was—

He was underwater, sinking.

His parachute's nylon lines reached for him, entangling his arms like tentacles. He pushed them away and fought to release the two Koch fittings that attached his torso harness to the parachute risers. One came free, but the other stuck as the wind pushed the billowing canopy across the water's surface. He pulled on that riser with one hand and squeezed the fitting with the other hand.

It released.

Relieved, Mike let himself sink for a couple of seconds to let the surface wind move the parachute away. The water felt warm, a pleasant surprise. Then—

Thud. Thud. Thud. Thud.

Four giant screws pounding the water.

Damn. The ship. Close.

Mike pulled the toggles on the donut-shaped life preserver around his waist and popped to the surface. He ripped off his oxygen mask and gulped in warm, sweet air as he twisted to face the ship's sound.

The steel monster slid past just two hundred feet away, but passed by. Now in the clear, Mike waved both arms, and several crewmen on deck pointed at him. One man cheered.

A roar close overhead drowned out all other sounds as one of the ship's UH-2A plane-guard helicopters came to a hover thirty feet overhead. Rotor wash rifled stinging drops of water at Mike's head, and he yanked down his helmet visor to protect his face.

A *horse collar* rescue sling at the end of a steel cable plopped into the water four yards away. Mike did a clumsy breaststroke over to it. He lifted the collar over his head and swam through it, then twisted around so the collar was under his arms with the cable attachment in front of his face. He tried to look up, but the spray defeated him, so he ducked his head, gave a thumbs-up signal, and wrapped his arms around the collar. The cable snapped taut, plucking Mike out of the ocean like a limp sea bass.

Seven seconds later Mike dangled outside the helicopter's large hatch. A hairy hand reached out, grabbed the cable, and swung him into the helo. He landed in a wet pile on the helo's deck and looked up into the smiling face of the chopper's enlisted crewman.

"My B/N," Mike shouted over the helo's roar. "Did they get him?"

"Don't know," the sailor said as he helped Mike out of the rescue collar. "Hang on, sir, I'll find out." He cupped his hand over a boom mike attached to the side of his hardhat and said something Mike couldn't hear. Then the sailor leaned close to Mike's ear and said, "The destroyer's picking him up. He appears to be okay."

Mike laughed and stuck his right thumb up in the air.

The sailor laughed with him.

Aboard *Valiant*, Commander Harold (Dutch) Jansen, commanding officer of Attack Squadron Sixty-Six (VA-66), navigated through the warren of cubicles and metal dividers that made up the ship's sickbay two levels below the hangar deck. He turned a corner and found Terry Anders seated on a steel table with a blue, Navy-issue bathrobe wrapped around his thin body. A pile of wet flight gear lay in the corner next to the B/N's soaked boots.

Terry looked very vulnerable.

Commander Jansen put a hand on Terry's shoulder. "You okay?"

"Yes, sir." Terry coughed and swallowed. "I got tangled in my chute and sucked in some saltwater, but doc says I'm in good shape."

"Outstanding. Where's Mike?"

Terry pointed. "Through that door."

"Thanks. I'll be back."

Jansen knocked once on the door and jerked it open.

Mike stood in the middle of a small room, an ill-fitting Navy bathrobe hanging from his shoulders. A sodden flight suit lay in one corner on top of his torso harness, boots, and survival gear. A small puddle of seawater formed on the deck around the pile. Mike's wet skivvy shorts, featuring multiple red hearts, lay atop everything else.

Jansen suppressed a smile.

Lieutenant Commander Phil Jewett, the air wing's flight surgeon, had a stethoscope pressed against Mike's bare chest. Doctor Jewett ignored Jansen, moved the instrument to a new spot, and listened.

Mike grinned at his commanding officer and winked.

The doctor stepped back, draped the stethoscope around his neck, and said, "He's fine, Commander. So is Anders. But keep both of them out of the air for a couple of days, just in case. Ejections put a strain on the upper cervical spine, and they don't help the brain stem either."

"I'll see to it, Doc. You finished with him?"

"He's all yours."

Turning to his pilot, Jansen said, "Okay, Mike ... what happened?"

"Beats the hell out of me, Skipper. Normal cat shot. Wheels came up as advertised. When I moved the flap handle everything turned to shit."

"No vibration? No strange noises?"

"Not a thing. The starboard fire warning light came on ... I chopped the right throttle and blew off the ordnance. I heard the call to eject and saw fire in the mirrors."

"You initiate the ejection?"

"Terry beat me to it. The canopy blew and up he went. I got lonesome, so I went too."

"Looks like a couple of good decisions."

Jansen turned back to the doctor, now busy making notes at a small metal shelf attached to the bulkhead across the room. "These lads look cold. You prescribing medicinal whiskey?"

The doctor looked up and grinned. "I've got a call in to the captain. He likes to do the honors himself. I suspect he tastes the stuff first to make sure it hasn't gone bad. I'll see that these two each get a shot."

"Thanks. That should warm them up."

Jansen turned to Mike. "I've got to check out the film of your cat shot and see if there's anything of interest on it. After you and Terry get dressed, come on down to the ready room. You'll both have to write up statements for the accident investigation, and it's best if you start while everything is still fresh in your minds."

"Yes, sir. You know how I love paperwork."

"So I've heard."

Chapter 2
Day One Continued

Yankee Station

The two bow cats fired together and the ship shuddered in response as Mike stepped into his two-man stateroom still clad in the bathrobe and flip-flops issued to him in sickbay. The flip-flops squeaked as he walked on the tiled deck.

Lieutenant Matthew (Cherokee) Ridge set aside the book he was reading and peered down at Mike from the top bunk. "Have a nice swim?"

"Yeah. The water's warm."

"I watched your little adventure from the deck. Those Martin-Baker seats give you a hell of a ride, don't they? You hurt anyplace?"

"Back's a bit sore, but that's about it."

"Well, glad you made it. Now that I've got you housebroke, I'd hate to have to train another roomie."

"You're all heart," Mike said as he pulled clean underwear from a metal drawer and proceeded to get dressed in his short-sleeve khaki uniform.

Cherokee Ridge slung his bare legs over the edge of his bunk and perched there like a giant owl in underwear. "How's Terry doing?"

"He's okay. But you can bet those worry beads he carries are going to get a workout."

"He does seem a little nervous in the service."

"That's understandable," Mike said. "New wife, baby on the way, and he's over here fighting a war."

"Yeah ... you know, he always struck me as the serious type, a school teacher maybe. Religious as hell to boot. What's he doing out here in this world-class goat screw?"

"His dad flew Corsairs in the big war and all he ever wanted to do was fly for the Navy. He failed the vision test so now he's a B/N."

"Happy?"

"Sort of. Terry loves the Navy and the flying, but he hates what we're doing over here. And while he feels a duty to fight America's war, he also takes his family responsibilities back home real serious. He's conflicted."

"Conflicted? What in hell does that mean? We didn't use big words back on the rez."

"Torn in opposite directions," Mike said, then asked, "You ever been in that condition?"

Cherokee thought on that for a second. "Nah. Sounds complicated. He gonna bail out on us?"

"Don't know. Terry says he wants to stay in, but I think he wants to go home and play with the baby's mama. Writes her every day."

"I saw the lady. The urge is understandable. Where'd he find her?"

"Kansas. One of those corn-fed girls. She doesn't know squat about the war, even less about the Navy, so she worries a lot … and that gets to Terry. She's got the guy in a real box. Like I said, conflicted."

Hawaii

Tiny bubbles ... in the wine.

The words drifted over the barroom's speaker system, each syllable round and full, almost chubby. They overcame the sound of a jet engine turning up somewhere in the distance.

Roger Brackett paused in the doorway while he attempted to connect a face or a name to the singer's voice.

Makes me feel happy ... makes me feel fine.

Has to be Don Ho. Who the hell else would you expect to hear in the lower level of the Honolulu airline terminal, especially in a palm-frond-infested bistro named the Aloha Bar & Grill?

Roger glanced around the darkened room. Four young men in Army uniforms huddled in a corner booth nursing beers. Their somber demeanor meant they were headed west—to Nam. *Sorry 'bout that.*

All the stools at the bar were empty, so Roger picked one arbitrarily. He dropped his canvas travel bag onto the floor next to the chosen spot and settled in.

The aging bartender took some time to recognize the new customer, but he finally set aside the well-polished glass he was fondling. He came over, flashed some teeth and said, "Aloha."

"You're kidding."

"Yeah. They pay me to say that. What'll you have?"

Roger glanced at the overhead clock; twenty minutes before his flight to Manila was due to board. "My entire Hawaiian experience is going to be this one drink. What do you recommend?"

"A mai tai."

"What's in it?"

"Mostly rum."

"I'll try one."

Roger refolded his wrinkled copy of the *Honolulu Star-Bulletin* in order to fit the newspaper into his allotted space at the bar. He didn't like to take more than his share of anything.

The bartender set down a dark-colored drink with a cherry on top, grinned again and said, *"Okole maluna."*

"What's that mean?"

"Same as cheers or bottoms up. We want you to have the full Hawaiian experience."

"Thank you so much."

Dropping the mai-tai's cherry into a nearby ashtray, Roger sipped his drink and scanned the newspaper's front page. The inch-high headline shrieked, *Pentagon Surrounded.*

Bending over, the bartender tried to read the paper upside down. "That is one real ring-ding pisser, ain't it? How many of those assholes were there?"

"The demonstrators?"

"Yeah."

"The paper says up to fifty thousand. Protesting the Vietnam War. They rallied at the Lincoln Memorial then marched to the Pentagon."

The bartender straightened up and moved his rag around the already-clean bar top. "The cops should have put some buckshot into 'em. That would've broken it up. Anyway, I think the whole damn thing's a communist plot. Did the law bust any of 'em or just turn the other cheek?"

Roger made a major dent in his drink while he scanned the column. "Says here almost seven hundred people were arrested." He looked up and grinned. "Doesn't say how many were communists."

The bartender eased back a bit. "You in the military?"

"Nope ... reporter."

"A reporter, huh? Why ain't you in uniform? You look to be about the right age."

"I'm Four-F. Slight heart arrhythmia."

"Lucky you. Keeps you out of the draft. Away from Nam."

"Yeah. Lucky me."

Roger tossed down the last of his mai-tai, put two dollars on the bar and stood up.

The bartender scooped up the money. "Thanks. You ever been there? Vietnam?"

"Yeah. Saigon. Three months ago."

"Saigon, huh? Where you headed now?"

"A ship off the coast of North Vietnam on a patch of water called Yankee Station."

"What in hell's out there?"

"The Navy's air war."

"Well, good luck, fella. You might need it. Aloha."

"Yeah … aloha." Roger grabbed his travel bag and headed for the Pan Am check-in counter. He left the newspaper on the bar.

Don Ho's baritone voice faded away behind him: *Beyond the reef—*

Yankee Station

Valiant was quiet, tucked in for the night. The dawn patrol didn't launch until 0400, and that was hours away. The airplanes could rest. Even the paint chippers had called it a day.

Terry Anders hunched over the small writing desk built into the wall of metal drawers and closets welded to one side of his steel stateroom. The tiny bulb mounted above the desk provided barely enough light for the job at hand.

Jeb Wilson, Terry's roommate, lay stretched out on the upper bunk. Soft snores proved that the light didn't keep Jeb awake. Actually, nothing much ever did once the man closed his eyes.

Sighing, Terry opened his box of stationery from the Cubi Point Navy Exchange and pulled out a sheet of paper. It bore the Navy seal in the top, left-hand corner and little gold B/N wings in the other one. He paused to look at the wings, his wings. He always did.

The box was almost empty; *I should've bought two. I'll have to get some typewriter paper from the squadron admin office and rough it.*

Missing a day was not an option, not with Judy feeling the way she did. Even if several letters accumulated in the ship's mailroom before they made their way ashore and into the U.S. postal system, Judy expected a letter for every day.

Well, that was fair. After all, they had married only a month before he deployed to WESTPAC, and the poor girl knew very little of what he did—or why—especially why. So she worried a lot. Hell, most of the wives worried. But still, Judy seemed to dwell on it. If she'd moved near the base on Whidbey Island, she would at least have the other squadron wives around as a support group, but she wanted to stay with her folks until he got back, so there she was, still in Kansas.

How, Terry wondered, *does Judy's parents view the war, and me?* He picked up a ballpoint pen and stared at the blank paper for a long time before he started to write.

    Dear Judy,
        I had a bit of a scare today.

Terry looked at the words then tore them up. He pulled another blank sheet out of the stationery box and began again.

    Dear Judy,
        It's been just another day. They all are, but some more exciting than others. You asked a lot of questions in your last letter, so I'll try to give you some answers.
        My life aboard the ship centers on Ready Room Three, a steel-walled combination briefing and locker room under the carrier's hangar deck on the starboard (that's the right) side. There's a big wooden podium that dominates the front of the room. It faces five ranks of chairs, three chairs on each side of a center aisle. The chairs are artificial-leather recliners with little fold-down writing platforms and pullout storage drawers underneath. They remind me of high school.
        The podium and chairs are meant for flight briefings, but each chair has a fancy plastic headrest cover that advertises the name of a permanent occupant. Those preparing to fly use the forward ranks of chairs for the

briefing, but when the once-a-day movie rolls after flight ops, each man claims his own personalized chair. The chairs are located according to rank. The commanding officer and executive officer sit up front, junior officers in the rear. Mine's in the third row.

A steel desk for the SDO (that's short for squadron duty officer) sits behind the last row of chairs. It separates the seating area from a curtained-off collection of metal lockers that hold twenty-four sets of almost identical flight gear: our g-suits, torso harnesses, survival vests, hardhats, oxygen masks, and revolvers. Except for the weapons, the gear is state-of-the-art. The guns are war surplus, which war is debatable.

During flight ops, the ready room typically resembles a three-ring circus: flight crews briefing up front, others removing and stowing their flight gear in the back, and a harried duty officer situated in between. The SDO is usually on the phone to maintenance control, working on aircraft assignments.

But after the flying, and after the movie, the ready room becomes a real quiet place. Some nights, if Jeb invites a few of the guys into our little stateroom for poker or guitar picking, I go to the ready room to write you.

That's all for now, darling.

I love you. xxx Terry

Terry sealed the letter, kissed it and tucked it into his cap, thinking he would drop it into one of the mailboxes on his way to breakfast in the morning. He turned out the light, crawled into his bunk and stared into the darkness.

Kansas

Mrs. Swenson tossed the rest of the morning mail onto the kitchen table and held up a long, thin package wrapped in brown paper. "It's for you, Judy. From someplace called Subic Bay."

"That's from Terry," Judy said. "He wrote me about it. Something he bought in the Philippines ... a present for you and dad."

That brought Mr. Swenson in from the parlor. "A present? From Terry? Let's see it."

Judy pulled a kitchen knife out of its holder and sliced open the wrapping paper. The cardboard box inside yielded a fifteen-inch object wrapped in tissue paper. Judy tore off the tissue and held the gift up for her parents to see.

Mr. Swenson stared at it for moment, then said, "By golly, it's beautiful. Looks like polished teak."

"Oh dear God," Mrs. Swenson muttered, "It's a naked woman."

One leg was hinged and Judy moved it. "Look," she said, laughing, "it's a nut cracker."

Mrs. Swenson gasped.

"Let's see," Mr. Swenson said, reaching into a yellow ceramic jar on the kitchen counter and pulling out a walnut. "Give me that thing."

He placed the walnut between the figure's thighs, gripped the ankles in one hand, and squeezed the legs together. The walnut shell cracked open.

Her face flushed, Mrs. Swenson stared at the thing.

"It works," Mr. Swenson said, grinning. "Wait till the Robinsons see this."

"Over my dead body," Mrs. Swenson said. "Give me that."

She carried the statuesque nutcracker over to the kitchen hutch, pulled open the bottom drawer and buried the figure under a tablecloth they hadn't used in twenty years.

Judy sighed. "Terry meant well, Mom."

"You should've married the Haralson boy ... he's got a good farm."

Yankee Station

The squadron ready room was almost deserted when Mike came in a little before midnight.

Commander Jansen, slouched in his front-row seat, poring over a thick stack of naval messages, standard late-night duty for a squadron commanding officer, looked up and frowned. "Something wrong, Mike?"

"No, sir. Couldn't sleep ... and the peanut butter in the forward wardroom is stale again, so I came here. Did the film of my launch show anything?"

Jansen set the message board aside. "Went through the film twice. I expected to see ... well, I *hoped* to see what caused the fire. But everything looked normal until your starboard exhaust spit out flames. Could it have been a bird strike?"

"I didn't see a bird, Skipper, but that doesn't mean one wasn't there. I gather none showed up on the film."

"Nope. But a bird low on the water ahead of the plane might not show up; the fuselage could mask it. I've seen a few birds this far from land, and an albatross through the compressor blades would sure explain what happened."

Leaning over the podium, Mike looked around. The only other person in the ready room, the duty officer, seemed to be focused on some papers at his desk. He was a good twenty-five feet away.

With a low voice, Mike asked. "This won't go down as pilot error, will it?"

"You make a mistake?"

Mike almost came to attention. "No, sir."

"Then don't worry about it." Jansen reached into the drawer under his chair and pulled out a small box. "Here, have a cookie. Marion sent them for my birthday. They're just two weeks old ... chocolate chip."

Chapter 3
Day Two

Yankee Station

The converted S-2 Tracker's engine noise decreased a bit as the COD (carrier-onboard-delivery) aircraft started a straight-in approach to the aircraft carrier leaving a green wake five miles ahead.

Back in the plane's small passenger compartment, Navy Captain William (Spud) Franklin felt the *thump, thump, thump* as the landing gear snapped down into position, and he locked his shoulder harness. His mind processed the routine up in the cockpit as though he were the one about to land this lumbering utility aircraft aboard USS *Valiant*. Denied anything useful to do with his hands, Captain Franklin gripped the forward end of the armrests that flanked him.

Scanning the water below through the small porthole next to his shoulder, Spud Franklin tried in vain to assess the narrow view of sea and sky available.

A sailor sitting across the narrow aisle was reading a copy of *Stars and Stripes* that interfered with any view out the far side. Spud's brow wrinkled. *Reading a newspaper? On approach to an aircraft carrier? Jesus, doesn't the idiot realize how dangerous this is?*

Spud had almost seven hundred carrier landings as a jet fighter pilot, and some of them scared him, especially a few of those on black-ass nights. One had been disastrous. This one was merely uncomfortable; someone else was doing the flying. *Are the guys up front any good? Who knows? Maybe some reservists out for active-duty practice.*

"God," Spud whispered, "don't let some moron kill me today. Not today."

This was a big day for Spud—a huge day. After twenty-six years of Navy blue and sweaty green, he was about to fulfill a dream: command of an aircraft carrier—this carrier—the one a few miles ahead. Well, the dream would be his as soon as he could kick old Spanner out of the commanding officer's big leather chair on the port wing of the bridge.

The props went to max RPM, and Spud looked out the near porthole again. The bits of spray foaming off the wave crests looked close; they must be in the groove. The engine noise changed again as the throttles came up a bit and Spud's grip on the armrests tightened.

He could sense rather than feel the slight left-right rocking as the pilot tweaked first one throttle and then the other to make small corrections to the plane's rate of descent. A slice of the ship's wake, a frothy green, bubbled into view under the wing.

Unable to see it, Spud visualized the dashed white line running up the center of the angled deck and the bright orange *meatball* in the middle of the big mirror partway up the port side of the landing area. *Well, the ball damn well better be in the middle of the mirror. If this isn't an on-glide-path descent, they are—*

The pilot added power.

Spud held his breath. *We're too low.*

A piece of steel deck flashed into view out the porthole. Then in a half-second span of time, the COD slammed onto the carrier's deck, its engines roared to full power in case they failed to catch a wire, and Spud's body was thrown against his shoulder harness. A steel cable yanked the airplane to a stop. The engines went to idle power, and Spud exhaled.

The cable, known to purists as a cross-deck pendant, pulled the plane backwards a few feet. Spud pushed his face as close to the porthole as possible so he could see the ship—his ship. He saw the yellow-jersey controller give the hook-up signal followed by a two-finger twirl. The power came up again, and the controller pointed up the deck with both hands.

Taxiing forward, the COD came to a sudden stop abeam the ship's island. Spud could see Captain Grant Spanner waiting to greet him.

Twin engines spooled down and the deck became eerily quiet.

There was a cheerful tweet of a bosun's whistle followed by, "Captain, United States Navy, arriving."

An instant later, the plane's door swung open. Captain Spanner's smiling face appeared in the opening. "Welcome aboard, Spud."

Lance Corporal Del Jackson followed the two officers to the captain's in-port cabin then took up a position outside the door. He stood at parade rest, but there was nothing restful about his eyes.

Del and his fellow Marines aboard the aircraft carrier had two primary duties: running the brig and protecting the captain. A ship's captain meted out justice to the men under his command when required, and not everyone appreciated the discipline. Therefore, an armed Marine accompanied the captain as he moved about the ship, and one stood guard a short distance away whenever the captain was on the bridge or in one of his two on-board cabins.

Spud took in the details of the in-port cabin at a glance. It appeared to be a comfortable space, much like one of the better suites at a four-star motel. He smiled. It was undoubtedly luxurious compared to all the other compartments aboard save one: the admiral's cabin. The admiral's suite was vacant right now since Rear Admiral Frank Ruston, the task force commander, flew his flag from one of the other carriers now on Yankee Station. For this, Spud was grateful. He felt sure Captain Spanner thought the same.

Grant Spanner put a hand on his friend's shoulder. "You may as well get settled in here, Spud. I've packed up my stuff, and I'll stay in my at-sea cabin until the change of command."

"Looks comfy, Grant. Thanks for the hospitality. How soon is the ceremony?"

Grant laughed then said, "I suppose you're eager to take the wheel. We were going to do it next week in Hong Kong ... put on a little show for the Brits, but we got extended out here, so that fell through the cracks. Then we figured to do it as soon as you arrived, but the admiral wants to preside and—"

"Of course. Admiral Ruston wouldn't want to miss a chance to make one of his give-em-hell patriotic speeches."

"Ah, you know him."

"Yeah," Spud said. "I know him."

"At any rate, the admiral got called to a meeting with the Seventh Fleet staff in Yokosuka and found a reason to stay in Japan for a few days R&R."

"When's he get back?"

"Five days from now."

"Oh, great."

Grant laughed again.

A sturdy black seaman came through the doorway holding Spud's luggage, a green canvas *parachute bag* and a similar hanging bag. Both bags bore leather ID patches that displayed gold Navy wings and *Captain W. R. Franklin* in gold letters, the name set inside a wavy outline meant to represent a potato.

"Stow the captain's gear in the bedroom," Grant said. "Thank you."

"Yes, sir." The sailor disappeared into the bedroom and reappeared a moment later with a big grin. "That's a nice bed in there, Cap'n. Sure wish I had one like that."

"Tell you what, Turlock ... you apply for the Naval Academy. After twenty-some years of hard work and good luck you can get such a bed for yourself. But remember, it's a loaner. Before you know it, some new guy comes along and kicks you out of it."

"Well, sir, I think I'll just concentrate on making petty officer third class."

"You do that, Turlock. That'll be all."

"Aye aye, sir."

Turlock turned and almost bumped into the steward coming through the open doorway with a silver coffee service.

"Put the coffee there," Grant said, pointing at the plush furniture clustered around a coffee table in one corner. Moving around the table, he settled onto the couch parked against a paneled bulkhead.

Spud nodded to the steward and took one of the chairs across the table from his host. The steward set the coffee service on the table and poured two cups.

Grant leaned back, crossed his legs, and threw one arm across the back of the couch. "Manuel here has been my personal steward since I came aboard. He's good at his job, but watch him when you pull into Subic."

Manuel grinned and added cream to Grant's coffee. He looked at Spud, who waved the creamer away.

"He's got a wife and two girlfriends there," Grant continued, "and he'll try to bamboozle you into more shore leave than he's due."

"No, sir," Manuel said. "I visit my mother in Manila."

"Yeah, right. Manuel, this is Captain Franklin. He'll be replacing me in a few days. You better be on your good behavior or he may send you back to the galley."

The grin evaporated from Manuel's face, and he hurried out.

Spud said, "I can't tell you how sorry Alice and I were to hear about Vivian's cancer. Her death came as quite a shock."

"Yeah, Spud. To me too. I miss her every day. We spent a lot of time apart, as you well know, but she was always with me in some way. Now, she's just ... gone."

"How's Robin doing?"

Grant hesitated. "She was pretty distraught for a while but seems to be coping now. She's staying with my brother Henry in Long Beach and started as a freshman at USC a couple of months ago. What about your troop?"

"Well, now that Gail, the youngest, is going to school, Alice went back to work. She has a part time job as a receptionist at a law firm."

"Good for her. What about your son? Fred, isn't it?"

"Yep, a sophomore in high school."

"Interested in girls yet?"

"Only if they're holding a football."

Grant said, "Okay, Spud, what about your mother?"

"You had to ask. Feisty as ever. You'd think an eighty-one-year-old woman with bum knees would settle down. Not her. She's been out demonstrating against the war."

Grant whooped and spilled a few drops of coffee on the table. "You're kidding me. Elizabeth?"

"Yep. She has Fred help her make the peace signs."

"Good for her," Grant said, wiping up the spill with his fingers. "I hope she stays safe ... I hear some of those demonstrations are getting violent."

"Some are," Spud said. "Certain factions in the media egg them on, supporting propaganda such as the ridiculous North Vietnamese claim that all we're doing over here is killing Catholics and cows."

"I sure hope it's ridiculous," Grant said, licking a drop of coffee off one finger.

Spud leaned forward. "Tell me about the real war, Grant. I suspect what we get back in the Pentagon contains a fair amount of bullshit."

"What did you hear back at the puzzle palace?"

"The party line is the war's going pretty well. We're pounding the hell out of North Vietnam, and supply shortages will eventually make them give up and stay home."

"You're right, Spud."

"That's all true?"

"Hell no, it's true that you've been fed fertilizer. Look, we drop a bridge and it's repaired the next day. We blow up an ammo truck and another one takes its place that night. The Russians are bringing in weapons and other supplies faster than we can blow them up. Worse, we're losing airplanes and flight crews at a rate we cannot sustain."

"Jesus. How's morale?"

"Among the aircrews? Surprisingly good. They're professionals, and most of them feel they're doing the job they trained for. Their bottom line seems to be, if Joe can fly into that maelstrom every day, so can I. But all the restrictions are getting to them."

"I imagine. What's the current status?"

"We can't fly within four nautical miles of Haiphong or twenty-five miles of China. And targets within ten miles of Haiphong and thirty miles of Hanoi are restricted … you have to have permission from CINC-PAC-FLEET to hit them."

"And we're trying to win this war?"

"Good question," Grant said. "We've got three carriers out here now … and we could do one hell of a lot of damage if we were turned loose."

"How do you keep the strikes from interfering with each other?"

"One carrier operates midnight to noon … another flies noon to midnight, so there's no coordination problem between them. We're flying oh-four-hundred to sixteen-hundred right now, and Ruston's staff tries to make sure our strikes don't conflict with anyone else."

"What about meshing with the Air Force?"

"North Vietnam has been divvied up into seven chunks called *route packages*. The Army controls attacks into the package just north of the DMZ (Demilitarized Zone) … the Navy bombs in the other four contiguous to the gulf … the Air Force attacks targets in the two big western packages."

"Does it work?"

Grant laughed. "Most of the time. You'll get a thorough briefing on all this tomorrow."

"Good," Spud said. "How did the *Forrestal* fire in July affect your operations?"

"It meant more time on the line for the rest of us. God, what a disaster that was. I never did get the final tally. What was it?"

"A hundred thirty-four dead officers and men plus another hundred sixty-one injured. Worst aircraft carrier disaster since the big war. You hear about the bomb problem that exacerbated the fire?"

"What do you mean?"

"It's being kept pretty quiet, but word around the Pentagon is that because the new Composition H-six bombs are in short supply, the ammo ship gave *Forrestal* Composition B weapons left over from the Korean War. The older ones blow at lower temperatures."

"Was that a factor in the fire?"

"Oh, yeah. Once that Zuni rocket went off by accident it triggered the conflagration on deck, and things went to hell fast. The fire fighters thought they had three minutes to cool the munitions down, but those old thousand pounders didn't give 'em that much time. Nine cooked off in the first two minutes. Eight were the old Composition B bombs ... the one H-six explosion was triggered by a co-located Comp B."

"Jesus ... and McNamara swore to Congress last year that there's no bomb shortage."

"He still swears that. You have to parse everything they say in Washington very carefully."

The sound of jet engines starting up on the flight deck penetrated the steel bulkheads, preparation for the next launch.

Listening, the two men paused for a moment and sipped coffee.

Spud set his coffee cup down. "What about the sailors? Their morale as good as the aircrews?"

"Now that's a bit stickier. The old hands are fine. *Valiant* is a typical ship of the line. It's run by the warrants and the chiefs, and those old sea dogs are happy if they get saltwater in their face once a day. But a lot of the crew is teenagers doing dangerous jobs for damn little recognition, financial or otherwise. Some of them are here because they wanted to beat the draft and stay out of Nam. A surprising number enlisted because a judge told them to join up or go to jail. All in all, though, they do a hell of a job and don't complain any more than sailors in previous wars, maybe less."

"At least that sounds a bit encouraging."

"Glad you think so, Spud, because here's the hard part ... I'm afraid racial problems are coming."

"You mean race riots ... like Newark and Detroit?"

"Not that bad, I hope, but I'm concerned. It doesn't take much to convince some black sailors that they're being discriminated against."

"Your advice?"

"When you have to discipline a black sailor, and you will, make damn sure you explain to him ... and everyone else ... why it's not discrimination. And, you know, sometimes that can be pretty difficult."

"Oh, you're a font of good news, aren't you."

"Sorry, Spud. But there is good news ... *Valiant* is a proud ship with a great crew. You've got a strong air wing commander and a well-trained bunch of aviators. It's just a damn shame they have to fight such a shitty war."

Chapter 4
Day Two Continued

California

The bus smelled. Robin wasn't sure what the odor was—not quite feces—but it reminded her of Grandpa Walter's pig farm. The last bus hadn't been too awful bad, but this one stank to high heaven, and the odor came from the back end. She'd been careful to choose a seat near the front of the bus, away from the human trash in the rear, especially the one-eyed derelict who kept sucking on something in a paper sack.

Maybe he's the source. Maybe he went in his pants. God.

Robin cracked the long window next to her head—she was lucky to have the latch accessible from this row—and let the summer scents of a California afternoon flow through her long, red hair. The sweet air washed her face.

An old woman in the next seat smiled her approval.

Closing her eyes, Robin allowed memories of her last fight with Henry to march across her consciousness, ghost soldiers. There was a time when these thoughts would have troubled her, but not so much anymore. She willed the apparitions to retreat, then drifted into sleep.

A sudden swerve pushed Robin's head against the window. Her dream melted away and she woke up. She threw a dirty look in the driver's direction; it had been a good dream.

The bus driver beeped his horn at some errant vehicle, and the bus resumed its humdrum roll up Highway 101. The traffic was thick now. They were past the mud flats, and the open water of San Francisco Bay glittered off to the right.

Robin reached into the small knapsack at her feet, her only luggage, and pulled out a ragged copy of *The Grapes of Wrath*. It was Henry's book, but she had taken it. Borrowed it, she figured, on her way out the door. Henry loved that book. Robin smiled and thought, *Henry will miss it soon. He'll scratch his head and wander all over the house looking for it, and then know. He'll stop and scrunch up his nose, like he always does when he's upset, and he'll know. 'Son-of-a-bitch,' he'll say, 'that little vixen took it'.*

Robin flipped the book open to a random page and let her eyes skim across the printing. She wasn't much of a reader, but Henry said the book was dirty, and she wanted to find one of the sexy scenes.

"That's a good book," the old woman in the next seat said.

"What?"

For a hundred miles the woman hasn't said a word. Now, one glance at Henry's book and she wants to talk.

"I said, that's a good book. Lot of truth in it."

"Truth? What kind of truth?"

The lady shifted around in her seat, as if she needed to lift some heavy object. "It's about rich people takin' advantage of poor folk down on their luck. That's what it was like back then. Still is."

"What was like?"

"You really readin' that book, dearie? You're halfway through it, but you don't seem to know what it's about."

Robin laughed, an insincere sound, even to her own ears. "I borrowed it. I haven't actually read much of it."

"Ah, you're lookin' for the sex in it, aren't you, dearie? Shame on you."

"There's sex in it?"

"I hear tell."

"So, you haven't read it either?"

"Can't."

"You can't read?"

"Nope. Had to work in the fields down by Coalinga since I was nine. I forgot what little I ever knew in the few years I went to school."

"If you can't read, how do you know what's in this book?"

"Recognize the cover. Friend of mine has the book."

"So you know this book is about grapes."

"It ain't about grapes, dearie ... it's mostly about greed."

"I see."

"Maybe you do, maybe you don't. But you'll find out, dearie." The woman shifted back to her old position and closed her eyes.

Robin glanced at the book again, but she'd lost interest and put it back into the knapsack. Her knuckles brushed against the blue velvet purse stashed inside the pack. It held all she had in the world now: three hundred dollars. Henry would miss that too, but not as much as the book. Robin patted the purse to make sure it was still fat.

The bus turned off the highway and worked its way up Fremont Street a few short blocks to the bus station. The driver spun the steering wheel and jockeyed the big vehicle into the sole vacant slot next to a run-down building.

"San Francisco," the driver called out. "Everyone off."

Awakened, the old woman opened her eyes and fixed them on the back of the torn seat ahead. She showed no inclination to move as the other passengers filed past.

Blocked in, Robin said, "We all have to get off here."

"Why?"

"Driver said so."

"Ah. I'm in no hurry. You?"

"Guess not," Robin said. "We can wait."

A minute later there were just the three of them: Robin, the old woman, and the one-eyed derelict in the back. The old woman finally stirred. She grabbed the seat ahead of her and grunted as she pulled herself erect. The grunt failed to conceal the sound of a small fart, and the woman smiled in contrition as she wiggled her way into the aisle.

Robin glanced toward the rear of the bus; she didn't want that gross man to exit close behind her. *God knows what he'd do with his hands.* But the derelict in back hadn't moved, and the eye without a patch was closed. It occurred to Robin that the man might be dead. She picked up her backpack and followed the old woman off the bus.

The balding man behind the counter let his gaze roam over Robin's body, seeming to vacuum clean her bell-bottom jeans and paisley blouse. Finally, his eyes settled on her breasts. "You a hippie?"

"Not yet," Robin said. "Where is this Ashbury place?"

"It's Haight-Ashbury. Ain't a place so much as a freak show spread out over a whole bunch of city blocks."

"Sounds like it. How do I get there?"

"Well, you drive north—"

"I don't have a car."

"That figures. Okay, walk north to Market Street and hang a left. Stay on Market till you get to Fell; it angles off to the right. Go down Fell to Masonic and hang another left. After a few blocks you'll see it."

"How do I know when I'm there?"

"You'll know."

"Okay. Thanks. How far is it?"

"All told, about four miles. Think you can make it?"

"I'll make it." Robin turned away from the counter. The old woman who couldn't read was watching two men in uniform carry the one-eyed man from the bus. The derelict was limp. The two men Robin assumed were cops stretched the old man out on one of the benches.

"He looks dead," Robin said.

"Maybe," the old woman responded. "Maybe not."

The reposed man sat up, a startled look on his face. He shouted, "Hey, where in hell's my sack?"

The two uniformed men laughed.

"Good-bye," Robin said to the old woman.

"Good luck, dearie. I suspect you'll need it." The woman turned and moved up to the counter.

Robin swung her backpack up onto her shoulders, adjusted the straps and walked out the door. She paused and looked for the sun, low on the horizon, to orient herself.

"North," she whispered, "to Market." Then she laughed. "And this little piggy stayed home."

Yankee Station

The RA-5C Vigilante loafed around the ship in a circle at thirteen thousand feet, waiting for its fighter escort. Over seventy-six feet long, with a wingspan of fifty-three feet, the reconnaissance bird was big, yet graceful, a giant metal goose. It was also fast; two big General Electric J-79 jet engines could ram it through Mach 1 at low altitude and carry it to Mach 2 up high.

What was once a bomb bay in the plane's previous incarnation was now crammed with electronic and photographic gear, most of it state of the art. The RA-5C's mission in this war was simple: photograph whatever the brass wanted. Today the brass wanted photos of a lengthy strip of Laos that abutted the Vietnamese panhandle, a piece of what was known as the Ho Chi Minh trail.

The trail was actually a web of intertwining dirt roads, bicycle tracks, and footpaths that started in North Vietnam, then ran down the squiggly Laos/Vietnam border, mostly in Laos, into Cambodia. Men from North Vietnam moved Russian supplies south along this trail, one tired footstep after another. And all along the southern part of the route, the men and supplies turned east, flooding into South Vietnam.

The Navy's mission—stop the flow.

Lieutenant Wolfgang (Wolf) Schumann, call sign Reaper 203, tucked his F-4B Phantom in close under the Vigilante's starboard wing and gave its pilot a thumbs-up. The fighter escort was on board and ready to rumble.

The Vigi pilot nodded then rolled out on a southwesterly course. He set up a slow descent meant to lose altitude and build speed.

Wolf Schumann double-checked the position of the switches that controlled his missiles. Because the F-4 had been designed as a supersonic interceptor, it had no guns. This caused Wolf great distress since he wasn't all that satisfied with the missiles he carried.

Four AIM-7E Sparrows were tucked into fuselage recesses. These semi-active, radar-guided missiles meant the shooter had to keep the target painted on radar until the missile hit. The Sparrow was designed to intercept enemy bombers out to twenty nautical miles; it wasn't much good in a dogfight.

Four AIM-9D Sidewinders were slung under the F-4's wings on the two inboard stations, two missiles per station. These IR heat-seekers were better in a fight, but still had limitations. The plane had to be in a forty-five degree cone behind the target and at three thousand to nine thousand feet range when the missiles were fired, and even then, the Sidewinder could be drawn off target by reflected heat from clouds or the ground.

As the recon flight approached the coastline near Hue, fifty miles south of the DMZ that marked the formal border between Vietnams, the Vigi's twin afterburners kicked in, and the plane accelerated.

Wolf followed suit, holding his F-4 alongside. Since the fighter had the same twin jet engines as the RA-5C, keeping up did not pose a problem, but it would burn a lot of fuel. Because of that, Wolf's fighter carried more than a thousand gallons of extra gas in three drop tanks.

Lieutenant JG (junior grade) Joey Pritchett, Wolf's backseat RIO (radar-intercept-officer) came up on his hot mike. "The Vigilante sure is a pretty airplane."

"And big," Wolf said. "Must be a real bitch to bring aboard when the deck is pitching."

"Yeah, especially when it's dark."

Lieutenant Pritchett was duly impressed with night carrier landings.

Wolf glanced at his airspeed indicator as they crossed the beach. It read 550 knots, about 630 mph. He smiled. God, how he loved to fly fast, and since this trip up Uncle Ho's trail was at a mere four thousand feet, faster was better.

"Firecracker Seven-hundred is feet dry," came over the UHF.

The Vigilante pilot was letting everyone on strike frequency know his flight was now over land. The nominally South Vietnamese city of Hue passed under the Vigi's port wing as the plane started a gentle right turn to set up a northerly track across the border in Laotian airspace.

Wolf throttled back and banked inside the Vigi's turn in order to put his fighter in a *combat-cruise* position about half a mile on the leader's right. In that formation, called a *loose-deuce,* each crew could watch the other's six o'clock for MIGs, and if some lucky gunner smoked one of them, the other crew would know where it went down, and if a rescue attempt was warranted.

Sliding over to the west side of the Truong Son mountain range that ran along the border, the RA-5C settled into its photo run, filming controlled by the plane's backseat RAN (reconnaissance-attack navigator). The RAN would use an on-board movie camera to shoot running footage of the entire route; other cameras were set to take still shots every few seconds.

The Vigi pilot started a gentle weave to throw off any ambitious gunners who might be in range. The turns complicated the job, the pilot had to be wings level for the still photos, but no one ever complained about it.

Wolf stepped up a few thousand feet so he was higher than the photo bird and could watch both plane and ground. He was fascinated by the deep, glorious green of the foliage. The Ho Chi Minh trail was easy to see right here.

So was the sudden stream of orange balls, 37mm tracer rounds, rising toward the Vigilante from the west. Common wisdom—four or five unseen rounds for each visible tracer.

Wolf keyed the UHF and said, "Flak at nine, Firecracker."

"Copy that." The Vigi pilot held his course, and the antiaircraft rounds drifted behind, then ceased.

Joey said, "I don't think that gunner understands we're haulin' ass."

"Yeah," Wolf said, "we're moving a lot faster than the strike birds he's used to. But next time he'll know; he'll lead us more."

The F-4's surface-to-air missile warning light began a slow, almost lazy, blinking, and *dedul ... dedul ... dedul* sounded over the plane's intercom. Enemy radars were looking at them.

"Got *low-warble*," Joey said. "Some SAM site has taken an interest in us."

"They've likely been waiting," Wolf said. "That Russian trawler chasing the fleet all around Yankee Station probably gave Uncle Ho's boys a heads-up. It could get exciting in a few minutes, up near Vinh."

Slow blinking continued as the two aircraft raced north. Halfway through the photo run, a string of white puffs from a 57mm gun chased them without effect, guidance from the weapon's Fire Can radar apparently not working.

When Vinh was finally at three o'clock, the Vigi turned hard right and headed back for open water.

Wolf sailed his fighter over the top of the photo bird to keep from overrunning his leader in the turn, then settled in on the Vigilante's port side as they crossed the beach and turned for home.

"Firecracker Seven-hundred is back feet wet," came over the UHF, and the RA-5C's afterburners blinked out.

Wolf eased his own throttles back around the detents, out of burner. "Well," he said, "that makes forty-two missions without a MIG kill."

Joey laughed. "You want one real bad, don't you?"

"Hell yes. There've only been thirty-some Navy MIG kills since the air war started and that was two years ago. Think of the monumental bragging rights for us at any bar. Damn right I want one. I'd give my left nut for one. What about you?"

"Yeah," Joey said, "I'd give your left nut also."

The telephone next to the captain's chair on *Valiant*'s bridge emitted a soft buzz. Captain Spanner picked it up, but his eyes continued to scan the rain that blurred the horizon a few miles ahead of the ship. "This is the captain."

"Captain, this is Sparks down in main-comm. We have a message from COM-NAV-AIR-PAC with a personal for you."

"Read it."

"Urgent for Captain Grant Spanner, USS *Valiant*. Robin dropped out of class and disappeared. Have notified USC, Los Angeles, and Long Beach police. Will keep you advised. Henry."

The captain lowered the phone, leaned back in his chair, and said "Damn" to no one in particular.

After a few seconds he lifted the phone. "Sparks, draft a response saying I'll be there ASAP. Then gin up another one from me to the admiral. Say I have a personal emergency at home and request permission to proceed with the change of command before he returns. Bring them here when you're finished."

"Aye, aye, Captain."

Spanner put the phone down and stared the rain some more. After a moment he turned to the OOD. "Bring her left ten degrees. We should clear that shower by the time we turn into the wind."

Chapter 5
Day Three

California

The mid-morning sun was warm and most of the people in the park sought out bits of shade. One of them, a young woman, sat under a large oak tree, her back against the sturdy wood, strumming on a well-used Gibson guitar.

Twenty or more young men and women, boys and girls really, sprawled on nearby patches of grass, but none were close to the pretty woman with the guitar. The woman was alone and nobody appeared to be listening.

Robin stopped and listened. She was hot, and the shade under the oak tree looked comforting.

She strolled over to the woman with the guitar. "My name's Robin," she said. "Mind if I sit here?"

"It's a free country," the woman said. "Gettin' freer all the time."

The woman wore straight-leg jeans, a peasant blouse, and cheap Mexican sandals. A saucy gold-hoop earring dangled on each side of her face.

Robin sat down cross-legged and put her knapsack in her lap. "I like your playing," she said. "You're pretty good."

"I'm only fair, but thanks. My name's Raven."

"Raven? Like the bird? That your real name?"

"Robin? Like the bird? That *your* real name?" But then she smiled. "I'm sorry. Raven's my adopted name. I liked it, so I took it. Yours adopted?"

"No, my mother gave it to me."

"Ah, a gift. That's nice. Got a favorite song?"

"Know Michelle?"

"The song?"

"Yeah."

"Sure."

She strummed a few chords before picking up the lyrics in a soft, breathy voice. After a while Raven stopped and looked away, distracted by a black bird perched on a neighboring tree.

Robin waited, not wanting to interrupt the woman's thoughts.

Then Raven turned and smiled. "I like you," she said. "You're not pushy. Want to stay with me?"

"Stay? Where?"

"Several of us live with a guy named Charley in a little house he rents over by Buena Vista Park. You're welcome to join us."

"A guy, huh? Do I have to sleep with him?"

Raven laughed. "No. He gets all he wants. But humor him if he gets into a bad mood."

"I have some experience with that. Does he get into a bad mood often?"

"Just when he runs out of weed."

"I'll think on it," Robin said. "Thank you."

She looked around. A boy and girl under a similar tree thirty yards away lay together. They giggled. The boy's hand went under the girl's skirt, and she moaned loud enough for Robin to hear.

Robin turned away and asked, "What do you do for food? Everyone has to eat."

"No problem. Some people here, they call themselves The Diggers, get food and stuff from stores and give it away."

"Free food?"

"Yeah. A lot of it's out-of-date bread and stuff like that, but it helps. Then there are free pancake breakfasts at the church a couple times a week. Sometimes Charley steals stuff and sells it."

"And you all get by on that?"

"Pretty much. If things get real short, Mary Ann ... she's one of our little group ... goes downtown and screws salesmen for money. Says she enjoys it."

"I see. What about pot?"

"No problem around here, Robin. It's cheaper than food. Want a hit?"

"Sure."

Raven leaned the guitar against the tree and reached inside her loose blouse then pulled a small red-velvet sack from between her breasts.

Giggling, Robin looked around. No one looked back. The moaning girl and her boyfriend seemed too busy to care what anyone else did.

Raven tugged at the tiny drawstring that held the pouch closed then held it upside down over one palm. After a light shake, the stub of what had once been a hand-rolled cigarette fell out.

"It's all I got on me," Raven said. "But there's enough for a couple of hits."

"One should be enough for me," Robin said. "It'll be my first time."

"You're kidding."

"Nope. I come from a real square place."

"Where in the world is as square as that? Iowa?"

Robin laughed. She didn't answer the question.

Raven shook the little sack again, and a wooden match fell out. She caught it, struck it against the sole of her sandal, waited for the match to flare, then lit the last inch of her cigarette. She held the cigarette stub between her thumb and forefinger, fingers up, palm toward her chin.

Very European, Robin thought.

Raven inhaled, blinked her eyes and passed the stub to Robin.

Robin dropped it and said, "Damn."

She managed to pick up the cigarette and turned her hand to get the unlit end in her mouth. She winked at Raven and sucked.

She wheezed. The raspy cough that followed made the now almost nonexistent stub fall onto the grass once more.

Raven reached over and used a small rock to grind out the burning end. Then she put the remains back in her velvet sack and pulled the drawstring tight.

"Every little bit helps," she said. "We save the butts and roll a new ace once we have enough." She tilted her head in little girl fashion and looked at Robin. "You okay?"

"Yeah," Robin managed to say, her eyes teary. "That wasn't what I was expecting."

"You a smoker?"

"You mean regular cigarettes?"

"Yeah."

"No. My dad would've had a stroke."

Raven laughed. "No wonder you choked. It'll be better the second time, sort of like sex." She paused. "You aren't a virgin are you?"

Robin blushed and looked away.

"My God, you are," Raven said. "Oh man, this is going to be a real adventure for you, isn't it? How old are you? Eighteen?"

"Seventeen. How about you?"

"Twenty. God, you need a nursemaid. Guess I'm stuck with the job. Where you staying?"

"I flopped at a hostel up the street a ways last night."

"That can get expensive. Come on, let's go home."

"Home?"

"Charley's place."

"You sure I'll be welcome?"

"Hell yes, Charley calls us his family."

Yankee Station

Mike and Terry ate their lunch, corned beef hash and eggs, in silence. The meal choice at Wardroom One's buffet line had been undercooked chicken with wild rice or another breakfast, currently served all day. Neither man hesitated before asking the steward for eggs and then spooning large globs of hash onto their plates.

Both men wore short-sleeved khaki uniforms and felt oddly out of place. They'd lived mostly in their green Nomex flight suits ever since *Valiant*'s last port call in the Philippines fifty-four days ago.

Finished, Terry pushed away his plate and said, "I don't like this."

"The hash?"

"No, Mike, being ordered to see the captain on the bridge at thirteen hundred. You figure we're in trouble over losing the plane?"

"Don't see how. Hell, the ship loses almost as many aircraft to accidents as it does to combat. Besides, it wasn't our fault."

"Maybe they found something we don't know about yet."

"Like what?"

"A mistake."

"No way. We didn't make any."

A few moments later, Mike stopped on the catwalk leading to the navigation bridge, Terry right behind him. Having just finished landing twenty aircraft, the ship's flight deck below was alive with action as tow carts and taxi directors reshuffled the deck. Looking down on it, Mike was reminded of an anthill: ants coming, ants going, all in response to some unseen, mystical rhythm.

Mike checked his watch then stepped inside the hatch. "Request permission to enter the bridge."

"Permission granted," the OOD snapped.

Captain Spanner was lounging in his elevated chair on the port side of the ship's wide bridge. A blue baseball cap, its bill encrusted in gold *scrambled eggs*, was tilted low over his aviator sunglasses. He ignored the two newcomers as he pointed out some activity on the flight deck to a stranger, a young man in casual civilian attire beneath red hair, freckles and the bluest eyes Mike had ever seen.

Mike whispered to Terry, "The civilian looks like Howdy Doody."

"Didn't know you were a fan," Terry whispered back.

The civilian leaned close to the thick glass panel next to the captain's chair and peered down at the flight deck.

"Yeah," Spanner said, "the one with the big nose is an A-Six. We have a squadron of them. We also have two squadrons with F-Four-B Phantom fighters and two squadrons of A-Four-E Skyhawk attack aircraft."

The civilian pointed. "What's that plane with the flying saucer on its back?"

Spanner chuckled then said. "That's an E-Two Hawkeye, an airborne radar site. That saucer is a rotating radar dome. We also have some RA-Five-C photo birds, KA-Three-B refueling tankers, and a couple of UH-Two-A helicopters for rescue."

"How many total?"

"We started with sixty-seven, but we've lost a few."

The tall chair swung around, and Spanner gave Mike and Terry an appraising look. "You boys recovered from your little adventure?"

In unison, "Yes, sir."

"Good. How was the medicinal whiskey? I wanted to test it first but got busy up here. The doc didn't try some himself did he?"

"The doctor left it alone," Mike said. "Can't say I blame him much. It was a bit raw."

Spanner laughed. "Fellows, I want you to meet someone who came aboard in the COD this morning." He put a hand on the stranger's shoulder. "This is Roger Brackett, a reporter from Washington out here to write about the Navy's air war. He heard about the A-Six crew that ejected off the bow and wants to chat with you two."

Pointing toward the aviators, Spanner said, "The tall one is

Lieutenant Mike Roamer, the pilot ... the skinny one is Lieutenant Terry Anders, the B/N."

Brackett stuck out his hand, and Terry shook it.

Hesitating, Mike thought, *Another damn reporter,* then shook the proffered hand.

Spanner said, "Okay, guys, take Mr. Brackett to the wardroom and get him some good Navy coffee. And don't lie to him ... there's enough bullshit about this war already in print."

"Aye, aye," Terry said. "I'll keep Mike honest."

Mike snorted and said, "Follow me." He led the way out the hatch and onto the set of steep ladders that led down through the ship's island to the vast living and working area beneath the flight deck.

The three men traveled down numerous ladders and passageways to a large space situated amidships below the hangar deck. It was obviously a wardroom; several officers lingered after lunch, sharing coffee and cigarette smoke at one of the long tables.

Roger stopped inside the door and looked around. "Nice place," he said, nodding his head. "Green felt on the tables. Filipino stewards standing by the sideboard, ready to serve. First class."

"Yeah," Mike said. "This is Wardroom Two where the ship's company officers eat. It's got linen, silverware, and stewards serving meals at fixed times. Like being on a cruise ship."

"All the stewards Filipino?"

"No," Mike said. "Some are American Negroes." He turned and walked toward a sideboard where pyramids of upside-down coffee cups stood next to a large urn.

"Hmmm," Roger said. He looked around again, then hurried after Mike.

Trailing behind, Terry said, "We hardly ever eat here. Too formal."

"I see," Roger said. "Where should I eat?"

Terry responded, "Well, if you want to savor the atmosphere as well as the food, I'd say eat where we do, Wardroom One. It's the dirty-shirt buffet up in the bow under the flight deck. Pretty good chow and you can get breakfast almost around the clock. Even when no real food is available, the stewards put crackers and peanut butter on the tables with Kool-aid to wash it down."

"Sounds good."

Mike filled a cup with coffee and headed for a remote table.

Terry waited while Roger added cream and sugar to his coffee then they joined Mike.

Ignoring his coffee, Roger pulled a small notebook out of his hip pocket and went right to work. "Okay, Terry, I hear you ejected first. What did it feel like?"

"Like being kicked in the ass by the Jolly Green Giant."

"I see," Roger said. "You've had that done to you?"

Terry laughed. "I was once kicked in the ass by an offensive tackle on the Ohio State football team. I figure anything worse than that qualifies."

"Colorful," Roger said. "I can probably use it." He scribbled some notes on his pad. "Same for you Mike?"

"I wouldn't know. No one's had the balls to kick me in the ass." Mike sipped his coffee and looked bored.

"Okay," Roger said, "I'll try this another way. Was it like one of those thrill rides at the fair?"

"I got a kick out of it."

Roger put down his pen. "I see. This is going to be more difficult than I thought. You don't want to talk to me, do you?"

Mike glared at Roger. "Does it show?"

"Yeah, it does. Why?"

"You aren't the first press guy to pass through here," Mike said. "You all come with your dumb-ass questions—"

"Such as what does it feel like to eject?"

"Even worse. Then a few weeks later we see the clipping as it appeared in some New York or D.C. paper ... and it's garbage."

"Give me an example."

"Okay." Mike leaned forward, hands clasped, forearms on the table. "Couple of months ago we spent a day bombing mud flats and old bomb craters near Nam Dinh. One of our A-Sixes ate a missile, and flak took out an A-Four. We didn't—"

"What happened to the men?"

"They died." Mike said. He paused. "Two in the air and one on the ground."

"I see," Roger whispered. "Sorry, go ahead."

"Anyway, some Joe Reporter came out here and wanted to know how we were doing. I told him we were getting our bloody ass kicked ... sorry 'bout that ... bombing mud flats and old bomb craters. Then the article comes out in a New York paper and says we're doing God's work stopping the communist horde. It's pathetic."

Terry added, "The captain called it bullshit."

"Okay," Mike said. "Pathetic bullshit."

He leaned back, tipped his chair on its two rear legs and glared some more.

"I see," Roger said. "You're taking serious losses hitting a lot of worthless targets."

Mike faked a laugh. "Terry, I think he's got it. By Jove, he's got it."

Roger ignored the parody. "Are all the targets worthless?"

"No," Mike said. His chair slammed back down onto all fours. "But a lot of them are. And we aren't allowed to hit the juicy ones."

"Such as?"

"The port of Haiphong is a good example. We can see Russian ships offloading surface-to-air missiles onto the piers. Can't hit 'em."

"Jesus," Roger said. "You want to attack Russian ships?"

"Nah. I want to hit the piers. Last week I saw SAM crates stacked up twenty feet high and a hundred yards long on one of those piers. Couldn't touch 'em."

"But—"

"The crates are gone now. Hauled across the seven bridges that connect the port area to the mainland. Now those missiles are waiting for us at Kep, Hanoi, and lots of other places."

"Why not take out the bridges?"

"Ha," Mike said. "Johnson won't let us."

"You're kidding."

"I shit you not. Hell, we couldn't hit enemy airplanes sitting on their airfields until six months ago. Our fighters still aren't allowed to shoot at airborne aircraft until they have visual ID, so they can't use their long-range missiles even if they know the target has to be a damn MIG. It's stupid."

Roger finally took a sip of his coffee. "I almost hesitate to ask, but how do you two feel about the war?"

"It sucks," Mike said. "We should have sub-contracted it out to the Israelis. Hell, we could do North Vietnam in six days ourselves if Johnson would just turn us loose."

"What about you, Terry?"

"It's a travesty. When you write about the war, please don't glorify what we're doing. We don't belong here ... this is not a good war. Our country should be ashamed."

"I see," Roger said. "One of you wants to attack; the other one wants to get the hell out. The hawk and the dove ... flying together."

Leaning back again, Mike asked, "You going to write that?"

"Too glib. My readers would think I made it up. But you're a crew with a real split personality. You know, that's pretty much how I read our country as a whole."

"Divided on the war?"

"More so every day. Tell you what, I'll make a bargain with you guys. You'll see what I write before I send it; if you don't like it, I won't use it. Deal?"

Mike wiggled his jaw. "What say you, Terrance?"

"He looks honest," Terry said. "Besides, if he cheats on us, we can throw him overboard."

Chapter 6
Day Three Continued

Yankee Station

Twenty-two airplanes were chained to padeyes on *Valiant*'s broad flight deck, so it took Lieutenant JG Bowie Jones most of a minute to locate his assigned aircraft, a VA-64 Skyhawk with 411 painted on both sides. Parked forward of the ship's island, the plane's tapered tail jutted out over the deck-edge catwalk.

Saltwater corrosion was beginning to eat away at the squadron logo, a stallion's head, painted on the A-4E's vertical stabilizer, and Bowie wondered what the rust was doing to the metal under the paint. Corrosion control was part of his job as a member of the squadron's maintenance department.

Bowie handed his hardhat and oxygen mask to the smiling teenager in a brown jersey standing next to 411. "How's it going, Crowder?"

Airman Albert Crowder looked even younger than the other *plane captains*, average age nineteen. Bowie realized he wasn't much older himself, but thirty-six missions over North Vietnam had put some mature mileage on his face, plus maybe even a few gray hairs.

Crowder grinned at Bowie and said, "It's going good, Mister Jones," then he laughed.

"What's so funny?"

"It just struck me. I wonder what my pa in Tuscaloosa, Alabama would say if he heard me call a black man mister."

"Like Bob Dylan says, *the times they are a-changin'*."

"I guess so, sir."

Crowder scrambled up the red aluminum ladder attached to the side of the A-4 and set Bowie's hardhat and oxygen mask on the glare shield above the cockpit's instrument panel. Looking down, he asked, "Where you headed today?"

"Someplace easy," Bowie said. "We're doing a road recce down south of the DMZ. Since only a certified idiot would be out driving a Ho Chi Minh truck on a sunny day like this, we won't find anything."

Bowie ducked into 411's nose wheel well and started his preflight walk-around inspection.

When Bowie came out of the wheel well, Crowder asked, "What do you do with all these bombs if you don't find a truck?"

"We put a bunch of holes in a dirt road or some ox trail."

Crowder slid down the ladder and jumped to the deck.

"No shit ... in the dirt? Jesus, these bombs have to cost as much as my pa makes in a month of work. Can't you bring 'em back on board?"

"The plane would be too heavy for a carrier landing. And what do you think might happen if one of them went flying up the deck when the plane catches a wire?"

"I guess you're right, sir. This war must waste a lot of money."

"They all do," Bowie said.

Turning, Bowie started around the plane in a clockwise direction, making sure the free-floating slats along the wing's leading edges moved in and out without binding and all access panels were closed. He pushed on the centerline fuel drop tank to make sure it was secure. The faint sloshing sound was reassuring; it was full.

Moving under the plane, Bowie gave special attention to the ordnance hung below the plane's stubby wings. The A-4E had five external store positions: two pylons beneath each wing and one on the centerline under the belly. A single MK-81 250-pound bomb hung from stations one and five, the two outboard positions. TERs (triple ejector racks) were slung under stations two and four, with three 500-pound MK-82s attached to each.

The bombs were all painted a dull green with a yellow stripe around the nose. Someone had used a black grease pencil to scrawl a greeting on one of them: *Eat this, you commy bastard.*

Bowie pushed on each one to make sure the sway braces kept it in place, then he checked the fuse. Each bomb was rigged with an M904 mechanical nose fuse that featured a small arming vane, a stubby propeller. A wire came out of the wing pylon above, ran under the sway braces and then passed through a hole in the arming vane. The wire protruded about four inches in front of the vane, secured in place with three metal Fahnestock clips. When the bomb released, the wire pulled out, and the vane began to spin. After it made the requisite number of revolutions, the fuse armed. At least in theory, the system kept the weapon from exploding close to the airplane.

Bowie checked to make sure the fuses were set for zero delay, to detonate on impact, and had their arming wires secured. He liked these mechanical fuses because the electrical ones were known to have malfunctioned on occasion and blown the wings off some aircraft. That could sour your attitude.

Satisfied with the plane and its ordnance load, Bowie climbed up the ladder and slid into the airplane's tiny cockpit. The running joke was that you didn't get into an A-4, you strapped it on. It was no joke to Bowie. His shoulders rubbed against the cockpit's sides, and once the clamshell canopy came down, he couldn't turn his head more than a few degrees before his hardhat hit the Plexiglas.

Because the A-4 had a swept-back, delta wing, Bowie couldn't see any part of the plane he was flying except for the cockpit directly in front of him. It was a strange feeling, like being inside the tip of a spear. It was no place for a claustrophobic, but Bowie didn't suffer from that problem and he loved the agile little airplane. The pilots of other aircraft called the A-4 *tinker toy*, but those who flew them preferred the nickname Heinemann's Hot Rod, a tribute to the designer. Of course, the A-4 wasn't much of a hot rod with all this ordnance strapped on.

Airman Crowder didn't care about aerial performance; he just owned the airplane when it was on deck. He was proud of his job and his plane, and cared for the little A-4 as if it were his very own, something he could take back home to impress Pearly Mae. He even wrote his pa about his job and sent photos of himself with 411.

Crowder stood on the red ladder and helped Bowie strap in. Two Koch fittings hooked the pilot to a survival pack under his butt, and two more connected him to the parachute on his back. All four fittings also attached the pilot to the ejection seat and the airplane.

Finished, Crowder said, "Good luck, Mister Jones. Get a truck for me."

With a wink, Bowie gave his plane captain a thumbs-up. Crowder took the ladder away as Bowie started his cockpit preflight routine. Then both men waited.

The entire flight deck, crammed with armed warplanes and people, waited. The deck remained quiet, the crew mostly stationary. The ship's bow rose and fell in gentle passage through long, rolling swells.

Resting his arms on the cockpit's sun-warmed canopy rails, Bowie gazed across the deck at the sea he had come to love and admire. The deep blue stretched not quite forever, meeting up with the lighter shade of sky far, far away. He smiled behind the oxygen mask dangling from one side of his hard hat. Crowder's comment about calling him mister reminded him yet again how fortunate he was. In a big, bad world, he'd found a good place.

Yeah, I am one very lucky black man.

The air boss, an experienced naval aviator himself, ruled the Air Department and *Valiant*'s flight deck from Primary Flight Control, the tower perched several decks up on the side of the ship's island.

With a glance at the clock mounted overhead, he punched a button on the side of a microphone and said, "Start engines."

The order boomed out across the ship's broad deck and the waiting came to an end. Abruptly, the quiet space around Bowie's A-4 surged into life. Pneumatic starter units blasted air to spin waiting jet compressors, pilots moved throttles *around the horn* to send fuel and ignition into the jet's burner cans, and the sixteen aircraft comprising the next launch roared into readiness.

Once the plane's Pratt & Whitney J-52 engine spooled up to idle, Bowie ran through his instrument checks and looked up. He could see hot exhaust gas spewing from the tail of Lieutenant Tony Romano's A-4, side number 407, parked across the way on the angled deck. Good, his leader had an up bird. If either of them had been down, neither would have gone. A-4s didn't go over enemy territory alone.

Bowie liked flying on Romano's wing. The guy was on his second tour out here and a smooth leader who looked out for his wingman. It occurred to Bowie that 407 and 411 made 7-11, a good omen.

Maybe we'll find a truck.

A plane director positioned himself ahead of the port wing, held his arms over his head, and gave Bowie the clenched-fists signal to apply the brakes. Bowie nodded his head in response. Bowie's director lowered his hands below his waist, then with a hand-washing motion, signaled the crew huddled under the plane.

Aircraft handlers, identified by their blue jerseys, stripped off the chains holding the A-4 to the steel deck. They stuffed the chains into a large canvas sack that went down into the catwalk along the deck edge, off the flight deck. Any chains left on deck were apt to be flung into the sea by jet exhaust once planes began to move.

An ordnanceman in a red jersey popped out from under the port wing with five pins, red banners attached. Bowie gave the man a thumbs-up. Then Crowder appeared holding up the three landing-gear pins, and Bowie gave another thumbs-up. Both men stepped back under the port wing and vanished.

Bowie swung his attention back to the plane director, who sent frantic signals to get off the brakes and taxi. When 411 moved forward, the director turned and pointed at a colleague fifty feet farther up the deck, transferring authority. The new director took command with hurried come-ahead motions.

Half a minute later, Bowie taxied his A-4 onto the starboard bow catapult and hit the brakes on the director's signal. The plane nodded as it stopped.

At this point, other Navy carrier-based aircraft spread and locked their wings. The A-4 didn't have to; its wingspan was so small—a little over twenty-seven feet—it didn't need folding wings.

The plane hunkered down as it was tensioned between the shuttle and the holdback fitting. Bowie glanced at the port cat. Romano's A-4 was there; it would be a formation shot.

Bowie's director passed control to the catapult officer standing between the two aircraft, and the ship's deck tilted as the OOD began a turn to bring the aircraft carrier into the wind.

Twenty seconds before launch time, the cat officer, leaning against the growing gale across the deck, twirled two fingers at Tony Romano on the port catapult then two fingers at Bowie. Both pilots pushed their throttles to a hundred-percent power and scanned engine gauges. The two planes strained against the holdbacks. Satisfied, each pilot saluted the man in the middle.

Turning, the cat officer checked the deck forward and waited. Four seconds later, as the ship steadied up on the new course, he went to one knee and flung his right arm forward. The two bow catapults fired.

Bowie came off the starboard cat flying wing on his leader. Their landing gear came up in unison, then the flaps. Trailing thin, almost invisible, smoke trails, the two jets turned toward the beach and climbed.

Twenty minutes later, Romano called "Union four-zero-seven is feet dry," and Bowie pulled out to his combat cruise position.

They set up a gentle weave at four thousand feet, looking for anything of interest, especially things that moved.

The other squadron's A-4s had stumbled onto a moving North Vietnamese train about ten days ago, and the air wing had a grand old time picking it to pieces. Bowie was jealous as hell and hoped to get that lucky some day. This did not look like the day.

A stream of bright orange tracer rounds the size of tennis balls lashed across the front of Bowie's airplane.

WHAM.

A shell slammed into 411's port wing, and the A-4 whipped into a high-G spiral, spinning out of control. In a blurring world, Bowie fought to reach the ejection seat handle above his head.

The seat fired and tumbled, the drogue chute popped, and the main canopy blossomed.

By the time Bowie got his hands on the risers to guide his descent, he plunged into the forest. The parachute canopy draped itself over a rubber tree and slammed his head against the trunk. His hardhat took much of the blow, but Bowie blacked out.

He hung there, unconscious. His body swung in the on-shore breeze like a lazy pendulum.

South Carolina

Congressman Fox thundered out his standard question to the fifty-some members of the Midcap County Grange Association gathered in front of him. "If we don' stop those godless commies in Vietnam, then wheah in tarnation will we? In California? At the Mississippi?"

An elderly man in bib overalls stood and shouted, "Right on, congressman. God bless you, sir."

The woman seated next to the man grabbed his loose side pocket and tugged him back down onto his folding chair, but forty heads nodded agreement with her husband.

Jason Fox grinned down at them from the makeshift podium atop the makeshift stage in Roy's Barbeque Barn. This was the part he loved, when the crackers were eating out of his hand and the future looked sunshine bright for a freshman congressman named Jason Fox.

"You know," Jason said, "we call that the *domino theory*." He paused for a long count. "Countries topplin' to the communists, one aftah anothah, fallin' like dominoes. First Vietnam, then Laos, Cambodia, Thailand. Maybe more. South Korea, Burma, India. Total catastrophe."

He had them now. Mouths open. Eyes big, staring up at him.

"But we can stop that. You want proof? What did Indonesia do last year? Ah'll tell you. Their gov'ment took one look at America's commitment to South Vietnam then they kicked all the darn communists out of Indonesia. That was one domino that did *not* fall."

Cheers and clapping.

"But some people in Washington say we should let the communists have Vietnam. It's a civil war, they claim. None of our business. They don' believe in the domino—"

Boo's interrupted him.

"Well, ladies and gentlemen, we have some darn fools up in Washington who don't understand. And some folks round heah, too."

A middle-aged woman in the third row looked up from her knitting and belted out, "Who's that?"

"Won't mention any names, but ah heah one of them is gearin' up to oppose me in next year's election."

"Aw, that's just Jamie Traynor," the woman said. "He don't have no sense. Look who he married."

Jason laughed and waited for the smattering of applause mixed with catcalls to die out.

"Be that as it may," he said, "we're facin' a crisis in this country. We need to stop those commies right in their tracks, and ah'm the man to make sure it happens. If y'all agree, come on out next election and vote for me. Remember … Fox for freedom."

Annie Hill watched the faces in the audience. Who's nodding and smiling? Who's not? Who's important? There, the guy with the tan suit and green tie. Not a believer, not yet anyway, but probably useful. Real estate, if she remembered right. He'll talk to a lot of people.

She worked her way over to the man as the group straggled out of the building into the warm morning air.

"Hi, I'm Annie Hill, Congressman Fox's admin assistant."

The man stopped and tipped his hat, a snap-brim Chicago job, somewhat out of place here.

"Pleased to meet you," he said. "You need a real estate man?"

Annie laughed. "No, but I'll keep you in mind if I ever do."

"Then what can I do for you?"

"You could give me your mailing address. I have some literature back at the office I'd like to send you."

The man gave Annie a wary look, one eyebrow up. "What kind?"

"You're obviously one of the town's leaders, and we want people such as yourself to be familiar with what the congressman is doing in Washington."

With a smirk, he said, "I know what he's doing. I read the papers."

That damn tax vote, Annie thought, then forced a smile. "I'm sure you do. That's why I want to stay in touch with you. Send you one of the congressman's thought pieces and get your view and reaction."

"You mean my opinion."

"Exactly. The congressman values input from citizens such as yourself. Please. It would be very useful."

"Hmm, I guess."

He handed her a business card. The bold print stated he was Harold Askew, Askew Realty, Inc.

"Thank you, Mr. Askew. I ... we appreciate your help." *Big smile now*. "You'll be hearing from us."

And, *escape*.

Jason grinned at her. "You doin' that Dale Carnegie routine with the peddlah in the tan suit? Horrible necktie."

Congressman Fox slid behind the wheel of his gun-metal-blue 1966 Pontiac Grand Prix.

"He's in real estate," Annie said. She opened the passenger door and tossed her bulky purse onto the floorboards. She tested the temperature of the leather seat before settling onto it. "He must spend a lot of time talking to newcomers in his car. They might vote for you if he says nice things. I'll send him one of your bumper stickers. Who knows?"

"You're worth everythin' ah pay you, Annie."

"And much, much more. Roger thinks I should quit and get a good-paying job in publishing."

"Sounds dull. Wheah is your red-headed rabbit, anyway?"

"On some ship off the coast of Vietnam. Writing about dominoes, no doubt." She looked around then said, "I wish you'd ditch this car."

"Why? It's a great car. Like the famous Batmobile."

"Exactly. But these folks want to vote for somebody who drives a pickup truck."

"How about a flatbed Ford?"

"Perfect. You'll do it?"

"Hell no."

Chapter 7
Day Four

Vietnam

Bowie Jones returned to consciousness in tiny pieces. Shards of pain came first; slices of memory straggled in later. The ejection—the chute had opened—he was alive. *Where?* He hung upright from his chute? Everything was dark, unfocused—and quiet.

He tried to move, but couldn't. He struggled then gave up as reality dawned: he was lashed to a rubber tree, back pressed against smooth wood, wrists tied behind the trunk with wire. It cut into his flesh. He coughed and spit up a glistening wad of bloody phlegm. The gooey mess fell on his knees. He looked down and saw his ankles tied to a tree trunk. More wire.

Where are my boots? My survival gear?

Gentle flapping noises lured Bowie's eyes upward. His torn parachute canopy hung lodged overhead in the tree. *So, I'm a prisoner right where I landed.*

It was night and his vision blurry, but he made out an expanse of black water off to his right lit by a soft glow on the far horizon. *It has to be the eastern horizon. Sunrise? Was all that yesterday?*

Ever-present pain, but nothing he couldn't handle. Fear might be something else. *Stay cool, man. Badass cool.*

Bowie looked around through puffy eyes. The half-light showed him more rubber trees, a dozen or so, the remains of what looked to have been a working plantation before the war. *Which war? Against the Japanese in the forties, the French in the fifties, or this crock of—*

A cough snared Bowie's attention. Three men, all young, sat under a nearby tree, smoking. They wore olive-drab uniforms with V pockets and web belts. Pith helmets lay on the ground next to them. *Gotta be North Vietnamese Army. Ho Chi Minh's vaunted NVA.*

One of them, seeing Bowie awake, picked up a pebble and chucked it at the prisoner. This amused the other two, so all three soldiers took turns throwing pebbles. They all laughed when one struck Bowie in the face and he flinched.

Growing daylight allowed Bowie to take in more of his surroundings. There appeared to be a substantial force of NVA troops bivouacked here. The surviving trees served to hide them from marauding *Yankee Air Pirates* such as himself. And at the far end of the grove, hidden under camouflage netting spread over shattered tree trunks, stood their protection: a 37mm gun on wheels.

Probably the one that nailed me.

The sound of a distant jet seeped into the grove and the gun's crew manned their weapon. One man spun a wheel that drove the gun barrel's elevation; another man controlled azimuth with a similar wheel. The gunners sat on concave metal discs that reminded Bowie of tractor seats back on the farm—back home.

Understanding came to Bowie. He was going to die here. They were a hell of a long way from Hanoi, and these NVA types wouldn't go to the trouble of hauling his black ass all the way there to toss him in the Hanoi Hilton. Even if they did, that wasn't good news. The aircrews had all been briefed on what to expect if they became POWs. When the North Vietnamese paraded Commander Denton out for a dog and pony show last year, he'd blinked TORTURE in Morse code. Yeah, now they all knew.

But Bowie figured they would torture him right here and then slit his throat, or maybe shoot him if they didn't mind squandering precious ammo. Never a religious man, Bowie closed his eyes and mouthed a silent prayer, a faint memory from childhood. *Our father, who art in Heaven, hallowed be thy—*

A sudden noise brought Bowie's eyes open as far as they could manage. The three NVA soldiers were forming a tight arc about twenty feet in front of him. A man Bowie hadn't seen before stood nearby, a cigarette dangling from one side of his mouth. The pistol at the man's hip identified him as an officer. So did the fact he wore Bowie's flight boots. Bowie couldn't tell the man's rank and he soon quit trying.

The officer gave an order, and the three soldiers aimed their rifles at Bowie's chest. They waited for the next command.

Closing his eyes, Bowie repeated his prayer, out loud this time. "Our father, who art in heaven, hallowed be—"

"You Catholic?"

"Huh?"

Bowie opened his eyes. The rifles were still aimed at him, but the officer had stepped a bit closer, the cigarette no longer in his mouth.

"Baptist," Bowie said—a lie.

"Ah ... an honest man. What is your name?"

The man's English carried only a slight accent. *A Catholic school?*

"Bowie Jones."

"So, Bowie Jones, why do black men fight the white man's war?"

"It's our war too."

"Ah, you are a slave, I think. It is as we were taught ... the Americans built their country on the backs of slaves. What is your unit, slave?"

"I am Bowie Jones, lieutenant junior grade, seven-four-four-nine-zero-one."

The officer rattled off some instructions in Vietnamese and raised his arm.

Closing his eyes again, Bowie started over. "Our father—"

CRACK.

His stomach muscles tightened in a spasm. The wire cut deeper into his wrists as he jerked away from the tree. His eyes flared open.

Slivers of wood were flying in all directions as the officer laughed.

It took Bowie a full two seconds to realize the soldiers had aimed above his head. He sagged against the tree.

The officer stepped forward. "Well, slave, I have decided to keep you alive, at least for now. I will make you a present to my colonel when we join up with his victorious forces. He might enjoy having a slave. So, you now belong to the People's Republic of North Vietnam."

He grinned. "By the way, I do not need you to tell me your unit. That information is painted on the side of the airplane that crashed a kilometer from here. It tells me you are a pilot for squadron number sixty-four. We have some of your colleagues as guests in Hanoi. If you cooperate, you may live long enough to see them."

Bowie spit out another glob of phlegm. *Screw you, asshole.*

Yankee Station

Roughly a hundred fifty miles to the north, the rising sun at their back, two A-6s crossed the coastline southeast of Hanoi at a place in the Red River delta the aircrews called *the armpit* because of its shape.

Mike Roamer turned the lead aircraft southwest and the flight spread out. They were after targets of opportunity, which meant trucks whose drivers were dumb enough, or brave enough, to move on such a sunny, cloudless morning.

They found none. The North Vietnamese truckers appeared to have gone to ground at dawn, as expected.

Valiant came up on strike frequency as the A-6s reversed course and headed back up the panhandle. "Banner Five-zero-one, this is Wigwam. New tasking, over."

Terry Anders keyed his UHF button. "Wigwam, this is Banner Five-zero-one. Go ahead."

"Intel reports an ammo convoy moved into Tru Lac last night and is still there. The trucks will be dispersed and hidden in huts. See what you can take out. Copy?"

"Banner copies."

After a quick glance at the authentication card tucked into his kneeboard, Mike transmitted, "Authenticate Bravo Echo."

"Wait one."

Grinning at Terry around the oxygen mask that dangled on one side of his face, Mike said, "Bet they can't find their card."

A minute later, the ship came up. "Wigwam authenticates Romeo Zulu."

"Banner five-zero-one concurs. We'll be over Tru Lac in about four minutes."

"Roger that. There's a Catholic church in Tru Lac. It's the biggest building in town. Do not hit it. Repeat, do not hit it."

"Banner Five-zero-one, wilco."

The church was in the exact center of the village and five times larger than any of the twenty-some huts surrounding it. Mike gave the village a practiced look then issued instructions.

"I don't see any flak sites, Banner Two, so set up a racetrack. We'll dive east to west, two bombs per pass. Pick a building that looks big enough to hide a truck and hit it."

"Wilco."

Mike picked a house adjacent to the narrow road that ran through the middle of town and rolled in on it.

His wingman did a short weave to get some spacing from the lead aircraft and set up his own attack.

Mike's target hut disappeared in a small mushroom of smoke and dust; there was no secondary explosion. Same with the next hut—and the next.

"This sucks," Mike said.

Terry said, "Well, at least it's good practice for you."

Finally, Mike keyed the UHF. "Wigwam, this is Banner Five-zero-one. You sure Tru Lac is the right village. We're getting zero secondaries."

"Banner, this is Wigwam. Affirmative. Repeat, affirmative."

"Copy that." Mike looked over at Terry. "How many Mark-eighty-twos left?"

"Four. Two under each wing."

"Okay. Give me all four on this pass."

"You got it." Terry reached up and reset the switches on the armament panel. "Switches set for four bombs. Master Arm is on."

"Roger hot."

Mike rolled the A-6 into its attack run. Terry leaned forward and peered over the glare shield.

"Mike? Don't do it, Mike. It's a church. A Catholic church."

"I'm not Catholic."

"Don't do it, Mike!"

Four bombs made their slight *bump, bump, bump, bump* as they came off the racks.

The church disappeared in a raging fireball that chased them all the way up to four thousand feet. Mike did a tight turn to the left and looked over his shoulder at what had been the target. Smoke and dirt soon cleared away to expose a wasteland across what was recently a village. Two small huts on the far west side were all that remained of Tru Lac.

"Oops," Mike said. "I musta missed that hovel I was aiming at."

Terry grumbled, "You are a low-life son-of-a-bitch."

"Don't take it personal, Terrance. There's a war on, remember?"

"Yeah. I remember. A real shitty one. And you've just made it shittier."

As Mike pulled the aircraft into a climb, his wingman came up on UHF. "Banner Two has four bombs left. Where do you want them?"

Mike glanced at his fuel gage. It read 2400 pounds, not enough to support any more searching and destroying.

"There's a ferry crossing about four klicks north of here. Put everything on the grove of trees northeast of it. Looks like a possible truck park to me. I'll stay high, I'm *Winchester*. Say your state."

"Two copies. State twenty-one."

"Roger that. We'll do a running rendezvous on zero-niner-zero."

Mike watched as the other A-6 pounded the grove of trees into submission. There were no secondary explosions.

Banner Two sidled up as they crossed the beach, and Mike made his UHF call. "Banner Five-zero-one is feet wet."

Other flights appeared in the distance, all streaming for home. There was no chatter on the air; everyone knew the routine. The A-6s switched to *Valiant*'s landing frequency and settled into a lazy racetrack overhead the ship at twenty thousand feet.

The aircraft were stacked by fuel considerations. The fuel-hogs, six F-4s, were lowest; they'd be first aboard. Several A-4 flights waited their turn above the fighters. The two A-6s would follow them, with the RA-5C, an A-3 tanker, and the turboprop E-2A last.

Valiant's bow catapults slammed a pair of A-4s into the air and the ship radioed "Charlie six." The first F-4 scheduled to trap aboard was to be at the ramp, hook and gear down, in exactly six minutes. That should coincide with the last launch bird going off one of the bow cats.

With a quick glance at the clock mounted in the instrument panel, Mike added thirty seconds for each aircraft ahead of him. *Valiant* expected to trap an aircraft aboard every thirty seconds in good weather, one every minute at night or bad weather.

He timed their descent and brought the small flight up the starboard side of the ship at six hundred feet and three hundred knots. Mike dropped his tail hook, and the wingman followed suit. When the last A-4 was abeam on the downwind leg, providing the desired thirty-second interval, Mike blew a kiss to his wingman and broke left into a hard, level turn.

Mike put the plane's big wing-tip speed brakes out and brought both throttles back to idle. As airspeed bled off, he lowered the landing gear, then the flaps. He rolled out on a reciprocal course to the ship's *Fox Corpen*, brought the power back up, and ran through the landing checklist.

At the *one-eighty* position abeam the carrier, two A-4s were ahead of him: one at the carrier's ramp and one at the ninety. Mike reduced power on both throttles and started a descending 180-degree turn.

The A-6 crossed the ship's wake as the A-4 ahead trapped, and Mike settled the aircraft onto its final approach up the centerline of *Valiant*'s angled deck. He used the control stick to maintain angle-of-attack, which determined optimum speed, and used the throttles to keep them on the descent path.

When a yellow ball appeared in the center of the large mirror mounted on the port side of the ship's landing area, Terry keyed the UHF. "Banner Five-zero-one ... Intruder ball, twelve point zero."

The arresting gear would be set for an A-6 with twelve hundred pounds of fuel.

Tiny movements of stick and throttles kept the ball centered on the mirror as Mike brought them down the approach path. The ship loomed large; then the wheels slammed into the deck. Mike retracted the speed brakes and rammed the throttles to full power in case the hook skipped all four wires, but it caught number three.

Back on the LSO platform next to the mirror, the Landing Signal Officer wrote '501 OK 3' in his notebook. The OK grade was as good as it got; there were no superlatives in this business.

Lieutenant Commander Mark McAuliffe, the wing's AIO (air intelligence officer), made crisp notes on the ship's standard flight debrief form, and he wasn't smiling. "What were you aiming at when the church blew up?"

"The hut a few meters this side of it," Mike said.

"So blowing up the whole ammunition convoy was a mistake?"

"Guess so."

The AIO leaned back on the two rear feet of his chair and grinned. "Too bad. If you'd been aiming at the church you'd probably get an air medal. Hell, maybe even a DFC (Distinguished Flying Cross)."

Terry snapped, "It was a church ... a Catholic church. Doesn't anybody give a damn?"

The AIO's chair crashed back onto all four feet. "Easy Lieutenant, there's a war on."

"So I've heard ... sir."

"He's Catholic," Mike said. "Devout."

"Yeah," the AIO responded. "It shows. You blow up anything else today?"

"Huts and trees."

"Okay. Good job." He put down his pencil.

The bosun's whistle sounded over the ship's 1MC system, and almost everyone aboard USS *Valiant* stopped what they were doing to listen.

"This is the captain speaking. As many of you know, I've been called back to the five-sided puzzle palace to do critical paperwork."

Scattered boos filtered through the steel bulkheads.

"My replacement, Captain William Franklin, came aboard two days ago and we've been discussing the ship and our mission ever since. I've known Captain Franklin for many years. He's a fine man and will make a great commanding officer. There will be a brief change of command ceremony in hangar bay two at noon tomorrow. Then I'll COD off to Cubi Point and catch a MAC flight to the states. I'll have more to say to you before I leave. That is all."

Mike stepped out of the darkened hangar bay onto one of *Valiant*'s sponsons, a balcony of sorts, jutting out from the ship's side. The aircraft carrier was quiet now, resting as it sliced through the night. Sea and sky were both an inky black precluding a horizon. Little flecks of white appeared here and there—flying fish breaking the water's calm surface.

The night breeze ruffled Mike's hair and an occasional salty spray touched his cheek. He leaned against the railing and stared into the void. He wondered who'd been in that church. *Innocent Catholics? Maybe. Weapons and ammo bound for South Vietnam? Absolutely. But did the strike make any difference? Terry was right ... it is a shitty war.*

He stayed out on the sponson for a long time then turned and went through the open hatch back into the hangar bay.

Back at his stateroom, Mike closed the door, sat down on the metal chair by his desk and proceeded to remove his flight boots.

Cherokee Ridge sat at his own desk, laboring over a letter. Without looking up he said, "I hear you pissed off the Pope today."

"Jesus Christ, there's a war on," Mike said as he tossed one boot into the corner.

"Terry said you took out the church on purpose. The XO said it was an accident. Which was it?"

"I told the Intel doofus I missed a hut and hit the church by mistake."

Mike threw his second boot after the first one.

"Uh huh. White man speaks with forked tongue."

"Yeah, but the white man has firewater." Mike opened the small safe tucked inside his desk and pulled out a bottle of Jack Daniels. Holding it up, he asked, "Want a shot?"

"Can't. I'm running the Bac Giang thermal power plant before dawn."

"Lucky you."

Cherokee folded his letter and tucked it into an envelope. "I need a favor, Mike."

He handed over the envelope.

"What's up?"

Mike turned the envelope over. There was a round lump in it. One word was written on the front: Marie.

"Listen," Cherokee said, "If I get shot down, will you make sure Marie gets this?"

Mike laid the envelope down on his desk and stared at it. Then he glanced at Cherokee's left hand. The wedding ring was missing.

"Your good-bye letter?"

"Yeah. Will you do that for me?"

"I'll hold it for you until we sail for home. How's that?"

Mike placed the envelope in his safe.

"Just promise me you'll get that to Marie if I get smoked."

"Okay, Cherokee. I promise."

Chapter 8
Day Five

Yankee Station

Grover Cleveland Parker swung his chipping hammer against the peeling paint. Then he swung it again—and again. He was on his knees, on a gray steel deck five levels below *Valiant*'s hangar deck, almost in the bilges. Flakes of dull gray paint flew away from each impact, and some of them stuck to the sweat on Grover's black face.

It was still early, only 0740, but the temperature in the closed-off steel space was already well over a hundred degrees. It would get worse as the day went on.

A burly white sailor swinging his own chipping hammer a few feet away paused and said, "How you like bein' on the deck force so far, Gomer?"

"It's Grover. Grover Cleveland Parker."

Chip. Chip. Chip.

The sailor laughed. "Yeah, right. I thought all you darkies was named for Washington or Jefferson. You tryin' to be uppity?"

Except for a shake of his head, Grover ignored the man.

Chip. Chip. Chip.

"Hey, Gomer. I'm talkin' to you, dude. Answer me."

The chipping hammer stopped, and Grover said, "Get to work. I ain't going to chip all this paint by myself," then went back to his task.

Chip. Chip. Chip.

"Whoa, Gomer. I don't take orders from no black boy."

The sailor stood up, towering over Grover.

Head down, Grover continued his work.

Chip. Chip. Chip.

"You listen to me ... niggah."

Grover swung his chipping hammer at the sailor's shin and heard bone break. He recognized the sound.

The sailor screamed in agony and fell to the deck. He clutched his leg in both hands and rolled back and forth, shouting obscenities at Grover.

Smiling, Grover went back to chipping paint.

Chip. Chip. Chip.

The petty officer who stuck his head into the small space to determine why all the screaming, didn't smile a bit.

Mike bent over the stateroom's tiny sink and brushed his teeth. He timed himself: thirty seconds for the uppers, thirty more for the bottom ones. Finished, he rinsed his mouth out with tap water that tasted of JP-5 then stowed the toothbrush in the built-in cabinet above the sink. He pulled out his comb and—

BANG.

The stateroom door swung open and hit the bulkhead. Cherokee stood in the opening, hollow-eyed, red marks from an oxygen mask still imprinted on his cheeks, marks he liked to refer to as war paint. The armpits of his flight suit were moist, the edges white-tinged with dried salt, the products of prolonged sweat. He slammed the door, then pulled the metal chair away from his desk and slumped into it, silent.

"And a cheerful good morning to you," Mike said, running a comb through his hair while admiring the result in the cabinet's built-in mirror. "How was Bac Giang? You get the power plant?"

Cherokee tilted his head back until he was staring at the overhead. "I never, ever want to do that again. Jesus. We got two SAMs down the throat at ten miles, solid thirty-seven and fifty-seven fire the rest of the way in, then another SAM on the way out. Only thing that saved our ass was we were too low for the radars to track us, and most of the gunners were shooting over our head."

"What about the power plant?"

"Oh yeah, we got it. There weren't many lights on in that part of the country before our run ... none after. I guess it's always good to do something useful."

"Congratulations," Mike said. "I hereby award you the fond fungool with cat crap cluster." He pulled on his Nomex flight suit. "Now, if you'll excuse me, I have a flight to catch."

"Who's leading?"

"CAG."

Commander Bud Stennis strode into Ready Three with all the leadership presence required of an air wing commander, a CAG. The term was a holdover from earlier days when a carrier air wing was called a carrier air group. Many aviators waited to see if the wing commanders would accept being called a CAW. They didn't.

A naval academy graduate, class of '48, Commander Stennis was well on his way to flag rank. The two hundred fliers of Air Wing Sixty respected his flying ability, feared his wrath, and wondered if he was any relation to Senator Stennis of Mississippi, Chairman of the Armed Services Committee. Any one of those factors could explain the CAG's success.

Stennis banged his kneepad down on the podium, kicked the heavy wooden dais a foot forward, and glanced around the room at the men assembled there: fifteen pilots, four F-4 backseat RIOs, and four A-6 B/Ns. "We're going to Kep today."

Groans rolled through the room.

A RIO raised his hand. "The paper-maché airplane again, CAG?"

"No. I think the PAC-FLEET targeting bozos have figured that one out by now. We're supposed to crater the runway, keep the MIGs off it for a few days."

"More like a few hours," someone muttered in the back.

CAG ignored the comment. "Mike, I want your four A-Sixes in the lead today, so you're pathfinder. Standard alpha strike rendezvous overhead at angels fourteen. We'll have four A-Fours from VA-Sixty-Three to the left and four from VA-Sixty-Four to the right. Maintenance willing, we'll have two F-Fours on each flank."

He paused to make a note on his kneeboard. "Mike, as soon as we're all together, head northwest and start a slow climb."

"How high?"

"Eighteen thousand. We'll coast-in over the mountains north of Haiphong; make it about two miles north of Cam Pha. Follow that limestone karst ridge there until we get close to Kep. Once we're pretty well lined up with the runway, bring us down off the ridge and head for the target. Remember, when the party starts, it's every man for himself. Dodge what you have to … get to your roll-in point, and go for it. Any questions?"

Mike raised a hand. "Where will you be, CAG?"

"I'll be in the lead F-Four on your right, Rawhide One."

"You going to call *Buster*?"

"Yes, about twenty miles from the target. The F-Fours will go into burner and accelerate out ahead. We'll hit the flak sites strung along the north side of the airfield about the time the rest of you get to your roll-in points. I want the A-Fours to hook right and hit the runway fifteen to twenty degrees left of runway heading. VA-Sixty-Three hits the first half, and VA-Sixty-Four goes for the second half."

Mike raised a hand again. "What about the A-Sixes?"

"Put two straight up the runway. I want the other two to arc around to the south and go in left to right. Everyone pull off to the southwest, away from the flak sites."

"CAG," Mike said, "those two A-Sixes hooking around to the south are going to come off target belly up to the flak sites, and they'll be tail-end Charley's."

"Your point?"

"I sure hope those gunners are still down in their hidey holes."

"We'll put 'em there, Mike. Who are you going to send on the arc?"

"My section."

"Good. Any other questions or concerns?" He looked around the room, his eyes daring someone to respond. No one did. "All right, gentlemen. See you in the air."

CAG gave the podium an affectionate slap and departed.

Terry jabbed Mike with an elbow and said, "This is not good."

As Mike swung the writing desk aside and stood, he muttered, "No guts, no glory. This'll give you something to write home about."

"Thanks a lot."

The E-2A Hawkeye launched first, twin turboprops *thrumming* as it hoisted its rooftop radar antennae into the air. Its mission—set up an orbit over the Tonkin Gulf and, along with a picket destroyer, call sign Red Crown, monitor all air traffic over North Vietnam and adjacent waters.

While the E-2 focused on friendly forces, Red Crown's primary job was to call the position of unknown and enemy aircraft in relation to Hanoi, known as Bullseye. Unknown aircraft were *bogeys*. Those known to be enemy were *bandits*. If any came toward the gulf, the E-2 or Red Crown would vector CAP (combat air patrol) fighters to intercept them.

The A-6s, A-4s, and F-4s followed the E-2A into the air, their order dictated by position on the deck and fuel considerations; aircraft with *long legs* launched first. The A-3 tanker went last and would position itself to intercept any plane returning from the strike with a low fuel state.

Leading the rendezvous, Mike set up a port orbit around the carrier at fourteen thousand feet. One by one, two more A-6s drifted up from below and settled in on Mike's outboard wing. They checked in on the squadron's dedicated frequency. "Three's up ... Four's up."

"One copies," Mike answered. He gave a hand signal that switched all three to strike frequency.

Terry said, "Don't see our wingman."

"They must have downed their plane."

"That's one smart crew," Terry said. "Smarter than we are."

Aircraft from the other three squadrons rendezvoused at their own altitudes—eleven, twelve, and thirteen thousand—then moved up to form on Mike. By his third trip around the circle, all the strike birds except the missing wingman were in position, so Mike rolled out on a northwest heading and eased the throttles forward to establish a slow climb.

Terry punched a key on the computer. "I've got the cursors parked just north of Cam Pha, steering's good. It's a hundred ten miles to the coast-in point."

"Roger that."

Mike turned to center up the steering bug on his HSI (horizontal situation indicator). Then he gazed at the horizon far ahead.

The bright blue of the sky and the softer hue of the sea were separated there by little fluffs of white clouds, a scattered layer at about three thousand feet. The scene was both beautiful and reassuring; the clouds would not interfere with the strike.

Mike looked over his shoulder at the six aircraft off his port wing. He loosened his shoulder harness, leaned over to the right, into Terry's space and looked at the eight planes stacked off his starboard wing. The strike formed a large V in the sky—geese on the wing.

Terry said, "You enjoy this, don't you? Being out front, leading."

"I love it. If we had contrails, it'd be *Twelve O'clock High*."

"And I suppose you want background music too."

"Yeah. With a heavy beat, building and building ... something like 'Bolero.'"

They crossed the beach at eighteen thousand feet, and Mike turned left to take the flight down the ridge line toward Kep.

Terry cycled the computer, and HSI steering jumped to a point eighty-two miles ahead on a heading of two-seven-five degrees.

"Steering's to the target."

CAG called on strike frequency. "Rawhide One, feet dry."

"Red Crown copies."

Leaving the power as it was, Mike eased the aircraft's nose down to put the loose formation into a gentle descent. They would accelerate all the way to their roll-in points, around thirteen thousand feet above the target.

A lush green ridgeline lay below them, a jeweled arrowhead with its tip far ahead, just north of their target. Off to the left lay the harbor of Haiphong and the immense Red River delta. Hanoi lay a hundred miles inland, at the delta's center. Forty miles to the right were the rugged mountains that marked the Chinese border.

Mike led the strike force in a series of random, gentle turns, one way then the other, so they wouldn't present any eager Vietnamese gunners with a predictable flight path. The 85mm antiaircraft guns could reach this altitude.

The A-6 cockpit's red SAM warning light blinked a slow beat, and the *dedul... dedul... dedul* aural tone occupied the crew's headsets; Fan Song radars were tracking them. The light would flash bright red, and the warning tone would jump to *high-warble*, once the radar went into missile-control mode. *That,* Mike figured, *should happen in about three minutes.*

"This might get wild," Mike said. "Lock your shoulder harness." He checked his own then made sure the bombsight mounted above the instrument panel's glare shield was illuminated. He set the sight for a thirty-degree dive and tweaked the brightness up to compensate for the sunlight reflecting throughout the cockpit.

As details of the target airfield became visible, CAG's voice came up on strike frequency again. "Buster. Buster."

F-4 tailpipes gleamed white hot as their afterburners kicked in, and the fighters accelerated away from the rest of the flight.

Deduldeduldedul.

A missile alert tone screamed over the ICS and the warning light in front of Mike's face flashed bright red.

Terry said, "SAM rising at one o'clock ... another at ten."

"Got 'em."

Racing upward, the missile on their left arced to intercept them. Its exhaust formed a bright halo around the dull nose cone.

"Donut at ten," Terry said. "It's after us."

"Banner One breaking left," Mike called over the UHF.

He horsed the big airplane into a tight, descending turn toward the missile. The strike force behind him scattered, every man for himself.

The missile's nose came down.

"It's tracking," Terry said.

"Yeah."

Mike pulled the A-6 up into a tight barrel roll back to the right. He played with the G-force: too much and they'd stall out, too little and the missile would have them for lunch. Unable to get its own nose back up in time, the missile detonated below them. There was no clatter of metal on metal; the missile's lethal fragments missed.

"Missed us," Mike said. He steadied the airplane and turned toward the airfield. Several A-4s appeared off to the right, seeming to materialize out of nowhere.

"Two SAMs at twelve," Terry said. "They're after the F-Fours."

Mike started his left hook around Kep airfield. A string of winking lights, muzzle flashes, marked the dense array of antiaircraft guns that occupied a mile-long arc along the north side of the runway.

"Check the Master Arm on," Mike said.

Terry reached up to the armament panel and threw the switch. "Master Arm is on."

The weapon release button, the *pickle*, on Mike's control stick was now hot.

Off to Mike's right, the fighters pulled out of their flak-suppression runs. Their CBU cluster munitions exploded above ground, scattering hundreds of antipersonnel bomblets—hand grenades, really—across the flak sites. Small, bright flashes danced among the enemy guns as the bomblets exploded.

Antiaircraft fire diminished.

The attack birds rolled in on their designated pieces of runway from multiple directions. Someone shouted "Big sky" over the radio, a reminder—or perhaps a hope—that running into another aircraft, or one of the falling bombs, was actually a low-probability event.

The flak flared up again.

Heavy, black puffs of smoke from North Vietnamese 85s popped up across the area at the strike's roll-in altitude; smaller white puffs from 57mm weapons rippled across the target area at mid-dive altitudes; strings of orange tracers streamed up from dozens of 37mm rapid-fire guns.

The air above Kep airfield became a spider's web of aircraft, bombs, and flak, all weaving their own path through the melee.

When his angle off the runway was about fifteen degrees, Mike rolled the A-6 almost inverted and pulled it hard down and right, into a steep dive. As the aircraft's nose crossed an imaginary line to the target, he rolled upright and steadied the plane in its dive.

They accelerated to 380 knots—400—430. The bombsight's crosshairs, the *pipper*, marched across the ground toward the runway.

Flak rippled around the aircraft, but Mike focused on three things: airspeed, altitude, and the pipper. All three had to come together at a single point in space in order to achieve a good hit or else the pilot had to make an eyeball correction: too fast—pickle early, too slow—pickle late. And pipper placement had to account for the wind that would affect the weapons on their flight to the target.

"Reaper Two is hit ... good chute, good chute."

The call penetrated Mike's busy mind, but he ignored it. The pipper touched the runway, airspeed and altitude looked good, and his right thumb squashed down on the pickle. The A-6 lurched as twenty-two bombs rippled off in less than two seconds, the center of the *string* destined for the middle of the runway.

Mike looked up and calibrated the scene.

Black smoke from the downed airplane rose from its crash site beyond the runway. The three surviving F-4s were south of him, back at altitude, out of the fray. The last of the A-4s was in a climbing left turn to the southwest, chased by 57mm bursts and 37mm tracers.

All the gunners were obviously back on the job. Mike's A-6 was about to be low, belly up to them and the only target still in range.

Screw this.

Mike pushed the A-6's black nose down into a zero-G dive and aimed right at the flak sites that lay dead ahead.

Terry screamed, "Holy shit!"

He gripped the glare shield in front of him with both hands.

Diving at zero-G, aerodynamic drag was reduced and the now-clean A-6 ripped past five hundred knots before Mike hauled back on the stick and pulled the plane into a hard right, still-descending turn. They leveled off less than fifty feet above the surprised Vietnamese gunners and roared east along the string of flak sites.

All along the line, the gunners spun their little control wheels, but they couldn't swing the gun barrels fast enough to catch up with the fleeing A-6 just a few feet away.

At the end of flak-site row, Mike yanked the nose up and the A-6 streaked skyward, jinking. A few black puffs from a frustrated 85mm gun crew chased them eastward without success.

CAG's voice came up on UHF. "How many chutes did you see?"

Someone answered, "Only one, Rawhide. Only one."

Mike and Terry clomped into the Intel debriefing room, sweaty and tired. They'd been one of the last crews to trap aboard, and most of the strike's crew members were already clustered in front of the long table where the intelligence officers debriefed everyone after a mission.

"I said that everyone was to pull off target to the southwest," CAG roared. "What in hell were you doing, Roamer?"

"Saving my ass, CAG."

"So you think your ass has been saved?"

"Yes, sir."

"So do I, you got good hits across the runway. Where's Anders?"

Terry stepped out from behind Mike. "Right here, CAG."

"I have a question for you ... what is the current color of your underwear?"

The room erupted with laughter, and Terry blushed. "White as snow, CAG. My sphincter is still so tight you could pop the caps off beer bottles with it."

"Well," CAG said, "I guess from now on you'll be known as Tight-ass Terry." Then his eyes went bleak. "Anyone see what took out Reaper Two?"

An F-4 RIO in the back said, "I think a thirty-seven nailed them. I saw a white puff real close as they pulled out and the pilot ejected a couple seconds later."

"That was Cal Carson," CAG said. "Anyone see him land?"

No response.

CAG checked his kneeboard notes. "Dave Emerson was the RIO. Anybody see him get out?"

The room was silent.

"Okay," CAG said, "at least we know Carson had a good chute. I better go topside and brief the captain. Hell, I better brief both of them."

Chapter 9
Day Five Continued

Yankee Station

Commander Jansen leaned back in his chair, pushed the stack of papers away, and rubbed his eyes. He'd spent the last two hours poring over the squadron's maintenance records, a painful exercise for several reasons. Now his eyes hurt, his blood pressure was up, and one of his rare headaches came to life.

The knock on his stateroom door was welcome.

"Come."

The door opened a crack and Lieutenant Commander Don Rundle, the squadron maintenance officer, peeked in. "Is it safe?"

"Yeah, it's safe. Get in here."

Lieutenant Commander Rundle swung the door open. "I brought Master Chief Gronski with me."

"Good." Jansen pushed his lone guest chair toward the pair. "One of you can sit on the bunk."

Rundle took the bunk and Master Chief Gronski settled onto the metal-and-plastic chair. Both men looked at Jansen, silent questions on their faces.

"I'll get to the point," Jansen said. "I've been going over our aircraft availability records, and the trend line is depressing. We've got eight A-Sixes left, counting that sorry replacement bird, but just half of them are flyable at any given time, and not all of those are full-system."

"It's all about spare parts," Rundle said. "The longer we're at sea, the worse it gets."

"I understand. So it'll get worse before it gets better. But it's clear to me that the air war is heating up, and that means an increasing demand for our night capability. How many full-system birds can you field for the oh-four hundred launch tomorrow?"

Rundle looked at Gronski. "Will five-zero-six be ready?"

"No, sir. We're short a computer board and a radar horn."

"Then the answer's three," Rundle said. "Unless we cannibalize. Another two will be available for day alpha strikes, but there's no radar in one and no computer in the other."

"Damn," Jansen said.

Rundle said, "Well, sir, we can cannibalize. Strip one of those day-only birds. Make a hangar queen."

Gronski snapped, "I don't want to do that. It'll bite us in the ass a day or so later. It increases the amount of work required to do the repair job, and every time we move a part, we risk damaging the thing. Don't want to do that. No, sir."

Jansen leaned toward the man. "Got a better idea, Master Chief?"

"Get those CINC-PAC-FLEET supply pukes off their dead asses. Parts have to be out there ... somewhere."

Jansen laughed then paused. "That's a thought, Master Chief." He turned to Rundle. "Hold off on the cannibalization. Maybe later, but let's wait. You got a sneaky thief in your department?"

A pained expression came over Rundle's face. "What?"

"I want you to put somebody with kleptomaniac tendencies prowling the bowels of this ship."

"Stealing parts? Hardly anybody else's stuff will work in A-Sixes."

"I know that; I want you to steal from the supply system."

"Huh?"

"Look, we requisition a part then a supply weenie looks at their records and tells us they don't have that item on board. So they send the request back to CONUS and several weeks later the part arrives ... maybe. In the meantime, we're screwed."

Rundle shook his head. "But Skipper, we—"

"Wait. The Master Chief's right; parts have to be somewhere. Why not here? A-Sixes have been on this ship for two cruises before this one, and supply folks have been storing boxes of parts throughout the belly of this beast for all that time. I bet there's stuff in this ship the records don't show anymore and no one who's still on board remembers. Send somebody down below who knows A-Six parts when they see 'em ... someone who can hide what we're doing from the pork chops."

"You mean grab it?"

"Grab it and run. You know the supply types ... they'll go ape if they find out we're bypassing their hallowed system."

Master Chief Gronski broke out a long-lost grin. "Wanted to do that myself, Skipper, but figured I'd be court-martialed if I tried it."

"There's a war on," Jansen said. "The rules change. You tell whoever you send ... I'll stand behind them ... and both of you. Now go and ferret me out some damn parts."

"Yes, sir," Rundle said as he stood up and got in line behind the slower-moving Master Chief.

Gronski opened the stateroom door then looked back. "You know, Skipper, you'd have made a damn good chief," then he stepped out and disappeared down the passageway.

Rundle grinned at his boss and followed his maintenance chief into the passageway, closing the door behind him.

Jansen looked at the picture of his wife propped up in the far corner of his desk. "How about that, Marion ... I think I just got a pretty rare compliment."

Washington State

Junior Jansen could sulk with the best of them, Marion figured. Her son was slumped on the living-room couch taking exaggerated pains to ignore the TV show—and her. Marion went about her business in the kitchen, putting together a casserole for tomorrow's luncheon with the other squadron wives.

Junior said, "Dad would let me go."

Marion glanced at him and saw the boy's face was trying to register sincerity. "I doubt that very much," she said. "It's a long way to Seattle, and you've only been driving for three months."

"I'm a good driver."

"Yes, you are. But you aren't very experienced."

"How about if you let Burt Jenkins drive? He's had his license for almost a year now."

"I don't think so."

"Okay, what if we can talk Burt's mother into letting him drive their car?"

"No. You're not going to Seattle tonight ... I don't care who is driving or who is playing football there."

"If Dad was here, he'd take me."

"I suspect he might, but he's not. And it should be 'if dad *were* here.' It's the subjunctive case."

"*Arghhhhh.*"

Junior leapt off the couch and ran from the room. He slammed the door behind him.

Marion looked over at Harold's photo taped to the refrigerator door, the official Navy one taken the day before he took command of VA-66. He looked so damn competent.

"Oh, Harold," she whispered, "I wish you were here. I really do."

Yankee Station

The hangar-deck crew had rigged a low platform against the port bulkhead and pushed the nearby aircraft into a line facing the dais. Some of the planes looked wounded, pieces missing—lifeless.

Two hundred enlisted men selected to represent each of the ship's departments stood at ease in ten ranks of twenty sandwiched between the airplanes and the platform. Another rank, positioned in front of the ten, consisted entirely of chief petty officers.

CAG and the ship's other department heads flanked the platform on one side; the squadron COs and XOs formed two ranks on the other. All were in summer white uniforms that looked out of place in the maintenance area, especially with the sound of aircraft movement continuing on the flight deck above.

"Attention on deck."

The 224 men present snapped to attention. Several dungaree-clad sailors working well away from the ceremonial area also came to attention, a reflex action.

Captain Spanner stepped through a nearby hatch and headed straight for the platform with long strides; Captain Franklin followed a step behind. Each man carried a single sheet of paper.

Spanner stepped onto the raised platform, slapped his piece of paper down on the podium, and looked out at the assembled men. Franklin stood at attention a few feet away.

"At ease," Spanner said.

Officers and enlisted relaxed in place, feet apart, hands clasped behind their backs. No one spoke. All eyes were on the captain.

Spanner let his gaze wander past the men and aircraft to the patch of rolling sea visible through the open elevator bay across the deck. Flecks of white foam curled off greenish waves. For several seconds, Spanner savored what might be his last moments as a seafaring man; then he focused on the men arrayed in front of him.

"It has been the honor of my life to command this ship and the brave men of the United States Navy who man her. I will forever be grateful for the opportunity."

Then he paused and pulled a plastic case from his hip pocket. He extracted a pair of glasses, grinned his embarrassment away, then used them to peer at the paper in front of him.

"I will now read my orders ...

> From: Chief of Naval Personnel.
> To: Captain Grant K. Spanner, USN
> Commanding Officer, USS *Valiant*.
> When relieved in October 1967 as commanding officer, proceed and report to the Deputy Chief of Naval Operations for Air Warfare, Washington, D.C., for further assignment. Thirty days leave en route is authorized."

Looking up, Captain Spanner blinked several times then stepped to one side. The glasses went back into their case.

"Captain Franklin?"

Captain Franklin stepped up and set his own piece of paper down. He also took a few seconds to look over the men and airplanes in front of him. A smile that could not be suppressed snuck across his face and many of the men smiled with him, perhaps understanding what he must be feeling. The smile went away as he turned to his friend.

"Captain Spanner, I know the men of this fine ship will miss you. You've done a magnificent job here under difficult and dangerous circumstances. I hope and trust that I will be able to follow in your footsteps."

He faced forward again and picked up his piece of paper.

"I will now read my orders ...

> From: Chief of Naval Personnel.
> To: Captain William R. Franklin, USN
> Office of the Chief of Naval Operations, Washington, D.C.

When detached in October 1967, proceed by whatever means necessary to USS *Valiant* operating in the Tonkin Gulf and assume command."

Captain Franklin turned to face Captain Spanner, and the ship's XO called out, "Attention on deck."

The sound of shoes clicking together echoed through the hangar bay.

Franklin saluted Spanner and said, "I relieve you, sir."

Spanner returned the salute and said, "I stand relieved."

The two friends shook hands; then the new commanding officer turned to his XO and said, "Dismiss the men. We have a war to fight."

USS *Valiant*'s new commanding officer escorted his friend to the COD aircraft waiting by the ship's island. The flight deck was quiet in the brief lull before "Start Engines" would trigger the cacophony of the next launch.

Grant Spanner turned and stuck out his hand. "Good luck, Spud. Fair winds and a following sea. You know the rest."

Spud shook the proffered hand. "Thanks, Grant. And I appreciate you getting the admiral to let our change of command proceed without him."

"I didn't do it for you, Spud. I didn't say anything because, well, I didn't want to dampen your moment. I have a family emergency back stateside." Spanner's eyes turned grim. "Robin's run away, and I've got to find her and bring her home."

Concern spread across Spud's face. "Where do you start? Got any idea where she went? Or why?"

"Not a clue. My brother has the local law looking for her, but I've got a hunch Robin's put some distance behind her. I'll have to get lucky."

"Hell, Grant. Maybe she'll be home by the time you get to Los Angeles. Kids do that you know. They run away then come home when the money dries up."

"Did yours ever run away, Spud?"

"No."

"Start engines," blared over the loudspeakers.

Grant Spanner snapped to attention and saluted his friend. Spud Franklin returned the salute and they separated. One strode into the island and his future; the other crawled into the COD, on his way to the past.

"Captain, United States Navy, departing," came over the 1MC as the COD roared down the cat track and clawed its way into the sky.

Terry slugged down a shot of the orange Kool-Aid he often referred to as panther piss and glared at his pilot. "Mike, I thought you'd gone nuts and were going to *kamikaze* the bastards."

The two men sat across from one another at the end of one of the long tables in Wardroom One. An open jar of Skippy peanut butter and a tray of stale crackers sat on the green felt tablecloth between them. Dinner was an hour away.

Mike smiled and said, "O ye of little faith … don't I always bring you home?"

"Always is a very small database right now."

Roger Brackett pulled out a chair next to Terry, sat down and picked up a cracker. He stared at it as he said, "You guys do lead exciting lives. I heard about your little excursion today … and the lost F-Four. You see the paper-maché airplane?"

"Didn't notice it," Mike said.

"I did," Terry said. "It was sitting at the east end of the runway, off to one side."

Looking up, Roger asked, "Did it get hit?"

"Don't know," Terry said. "I was busy praying about that time. Why?"

Roger dropped the cracker into an empty ashtray. "Guess I'm not that hungry." He leaned forward, fingers drumming on the table. "I'm writing a piece about the paper-maché airplane. The Intel guys told me they know of at least three bombing raids against it. Can we possibly be that stupid?"

"Apparently so," Terry said.

Mike snapped, "Today's raid was against the runway, not that stupid paper airplane."

"Yeah, I know," Roger said. "But the paper-maché airplane is a good hook for readers. Hitting an airfield makes sense, so it isn't all that interesting."

"Ride along with Mike," Terry said. "I think you'll find it quite interesting."

Mike said, "Here's a story for you. Go back and talk to the Intel guys tomorrow morning. Ask them how long the raid today kept that airfield closed down."

"But you just struck it a few hours ago."

"Yeah, and a photo bird is scheduled across that part of Vietnam just before sundown. They'll have the photos done by breakfast. Intel will be able to tell how many craters we put in the runway today, and how many were already repaired."

"That fast?"

"Look," Mike said, "the gomers can fill the crater from a Mark-eighty-two and lay a steel mat over it in about forty minutes, and they have enough equipment, men, and materials set aside to fix several craters at the same time. We lost an F-Four and its crew closing that airstrip down this morning … and I bet the little yellow bastards have it up and running before dark."

Roger looked puzzled. "What about the airplanes there? You guys hit any?"

Mike snorted. "What airplanes? You see any planes, Terry?"

"Just the paper one."

"You mean you did all that to close a runway for a few hours … a runway that wasn't being used anyway?"

"Welcome to our war, Roger."

Chapter 10
Day Six

Vietnam

Bowie's feet began bleeding again. The narrow jungle trail was dark except for an occasional slice of dim moonlight, and every so often some unseen piece of jungle detritus tore at the soles of his bare feet. New pain developed, but it registered only at the margins; after two nights of this, his receptors were already conditioned by old pain.

Wire bound Bowie's hands behind his back, and a wire noose around his neck led back a few feet to his current guard, one of the three young NVA soldiers who took turns watching him. Whenever Bowie stumbled the wire tore into his neck. If he slowed, the sharp point of a makeshift bamboo spear jabbed into his rump.

He fell once, sprawling face down on the path, then lay there flat on his stomach, unable to rise. The guard reached down, grabbed the wires binding his hands behind his back, and yanked him to his feet. Bowie thought his arms might come out of their sockets, so he tried hard not to fall again.

A strange thing happened as the night went on. Although exhausted and miserable, Bowie replaced his fear with anger—a controlled anger. A cool anger. *Badass anger.*

He almost smiled.

They crossed an open space near dawn, and Bowie had a chance to better assess the unit that captured him. From what he could see and hear, he deduced about forty men in the column, the right size for a rifle company. Probably untested reinforcements headed for the combat zone, but they appeared to be well trained and a disciplined force.

The fact they were NVA was undoubtedly the reason he was still alive; Vietcong on the move wouldn't have bothered with a prisoner. But he figured the reprieve was temporary, and once this jackass company commander turned the slave over to his colonel, the value of Bowie's life would depreciate. Colonels up to their armpits in firefights didn't need a slave. Then would come the bullet or the knife.

Daylight brought the column to a halt in yet another thick grove of trees. The officer wearing Bowie's flight boots issued quiet orders, dispersing his men into cover and giving them permission for a light meal of what appeared to be precooked rice and tepid water.

Bowie's guard force increased to three again before they sat him against a tree trunk and wired him to it. They bound his hands in front of him with more wire and one of the guards used hand motions to indicate he could eat. *Eat what? Did I eat yesterday? Think. No.*

Eat? Bowie didn't care if he ate now, but he was desperate for water and asked for some, first with words then with hand gestures.

The soldiers ignored him.

Finished with the prisoner, the guards settled down a few yards away and broke out their rations. They ate from little tin plates held close under bobbing chins, shoveling sticky rice into eager mouths with chopsticks. They paused every so often to drink from canteens.

One of them made a point of teasing Bowie by grinning at him every time he finished drinking. He added insult by smacking his lips.

After about twenty minutes, the officer appeared carrying two bowls of rice and a metal canteen. He sat down cross-legged a few feet away, set one bowl aside, and ate from the other one.

Done, he took a long drink from the canteen then looked at Bowie and asked, "Want some food, slave?"

"Water."

"Oh, you want water?"

"Yeah."

"Not so cocky now, are you, slave? Say please."

"Kiss my black ass."

The Vietnamese officer rose and stood over Bowie, glaring down at him. With sudden speed, he grabbed Bowie by the hair and yanked his head back.

Bowie yelled, "You son of a—"

The man jammed the canteen's metal opening into Bowie's mouth and laughed while his prisoner choked on the warm water.

California

Robin was sprawled on the steps leading up to the front porch of what had once been one of San Francisco's better working-class homes.

But that was then. Now, the house bore all the marks of neglected old age. Faded yellow paint peeled away from an even older white coat underneath, especially near the sagging downspouts where water damage was prevalent. One pair of dirt-colored shutters hung akimbo, the frames broken. The wooden steps under Robin were still functional, but termite trails were visible if you knew where to look.

The screen door creaked open and Raven stepped out onto the porch, a pack of matches and an unlit cigarette in one hand.

She shielded her eyes from the eastern sun and smiled down at Robin. "Good morning. You look happy."

"I feel lucky," Robin said. "Bumping into you the way I did. Finding a place to stay."

"Karma," Raven said. She sat down on the top step. "Fate meant you to come here. It's your destiny."

"Destiny?" Robin waved her hand at the decrepit building looming above her. "You mean this?"

"No, silly. Us. Raven and Robin, birds of a feather—"

"All flock together," Robin said. "Could be."

Raven lit the cigarette and offered it to Robin. "What do you think of Charley?"

Robin waved the cigarette away. "Oh God," she said. "Those eyes. You know, he's just a real skinny guy with long hair until he looks at you. Then it's kind of—"

"Yeah," Raven said. "He sort of mesmerizes you. Like a hypnotist."

"But it's scary, too. You know, he could make you do things."

"I know. Sometimes he makes me shiver. Of course sometimes he makes me tingle too."

"You mean you ... and him?"

"Me? No way. I'd catch some disease. I know some of the girls he's been with."

"You mean VD?"

"Jesus, Robin, you really are square. Trust me on this one and keep your legs together. You sure you don't want a cigarette?"

"Well, I—"

"Here," Raven said. "Help me finish mine. You need to go slow until you're used to the smoke. Inhale a little then blow it out."

Holding the cigarette at an awkward angle, Robin took a tiny puff. Her eyes began to tear up, but she managed to exhale without coughing.

"Good," Raven said, applauding. "You'll be a smoker in no time. Then you can do *ganja* with the rest of us."

Robin held the cigarette away from her face so the smoke avoided her eyes. "Look, Raven, I don't mean to pry, but why are you here? I mean—"

"What's a nice girl like me doing in a place like this?"

Raven reached out and took back the cigarette. "Running away." She took a long drag on the cigarette. "Like you. What did you leave behind?"

"A cranky old uncle. We fought all the time."

"What about your folks?"

"Mom died last year and my dad went to sea on a ship. He left me with the uncle."

She took the now-short cigarette away from Raven and tried another shallow puff, more successful this time.

"My folks got a divorce," Raven said. "A couple years ago. Then last June my mother married a guy she'd met in a bar. Some guy. A week after their honeymoon he was letching after me."

"Letching?"

"Giving me the eye. Then he started coming into my room when he figured I was undressed. He'd knock once and open the door."

"Jesus, that's a lot worse than my uncle."

"One day he caught me naked. Stood there staring, licking his lips. I marched up to him, slapped him silly and chased him out of my room."

"Still naked?"

Raven laughed. "Yeah. Mom came upstairs, saw us and had a fit. Accused me of trying to screw her husband. I left."

"Just like that?"

"Packed some clothes, raided my piggy bank and stormed out."

Robin stared. "Didn't they try to stop you?"

"No way. They stood on the porch and watched me walk away. I raised one arm and gave them the finger before I turned the corner."

"Why'd you come here?"

"To Haight-Ashbury? Hell, everyone comes here. You did."

Yankee Station

Terry said, "Wrote another letter to Judy." He tapped the breast pocket of his flight suit as if to prove the point. "I suggested she move to Whidbey Island soon and get us a place before she gets too big."

Mike finished chewing the bacon strip in his mouth then washed it down with orange juice. "All on her own?"

"Sure. We don't have much to move right now and her folks can help with the packing up. The Navy will pay for it."

Leaning back, Mike asked, "I ever tell you my plan to save the Navy money on moves?"

"Don't think so. What is it?"

"Suppose you have a typical Navy family. When you get orders to move, a van shows up, crams all your stuff into boxes, loads them up and disappears. Then you pile your cranky wife, crying kids, barking dog, and screeching cat into your car and drive across the country. If you're lucky, all of you get together with your sanity and belongings at some future date."

"Okay, what's your plan?"

"Soon as you get orders, you go down to the supply office and turn in one house, one wife, several kids, one dog and one cat. Then you get in the car and drive across country by yourself, via Las Vegas. At your new duty station, you go down to the supply office and requisition new stuff ... one house, one wife, several kids, one dog and one cat."

"I don't think Judy would ever go for that."

Roger Brackett slid onto an empty chair across the table. "Take a look at this," he said, pulling a single sheet of paper from a folder and handing it to Mike.

Leaning over, Terry peered at the typed paragraphs. "What is it?"

"I told you guys I'd show you what I wrote before I send it out. If you don't want it to go, I'll kill it. Here's my first column."

"The paper airplane one?"

"Sort of."

Mike pushed his plate aside, laid the paper on the green cloth, and read it.

Terry read over his shoulder.

Aboard USS *Valiant* in the Tonkin Gulf
by Roger Brackett

    Aircrews of Air Wing Sixty struck North Vietnam's Kep airfield yesterday morning. The paper-maché airplane was there, intended to lure the United States into wasting munitions and American lives as it has done before. But this strike wasn't after the paper-maché airplane. No, their mission yesterday was to close the airstrip so that North Vietnamese fighter planes couldn't use it, nor could the MIGs flown by visiting Russians.

    And close Kep they did. The strike force put twenty-one 500-pound Mark-82 bombs into the Kep runway. Each of them left a crater about six feet deep and twenty feet across.

    A reconnaissance flight took photos of the Kep airstrip thirty minutes before sunset, only hours after the strike. All but two of the twenty-one craters had been filled in and covered with steel mesh. One picture showed a MIG aircraft about to land.

    An F-4 fighter plane was lost, shot down at Kep. Its pilot is presumably a POW; the fate of the backseat flyer is unknown. And Kep is back in business.

    One of the strike's pilots summed it up for me: "Welcome to our war."

Mike leaned back. "It's not Hemingway, but I guess it works. What about you, Terrance?"

Terry nodded and went back to his corn fritters.

"Well," Roger said, "that was easy." He picked up the paper and slipped it back into the folder. "Now, want the hot scoop on your new captain?"

"Yeah," Mike said. "You got the skinny on him?"

"Some of it. Before I left Washington, I talked to a colleague who's been on the Pentagon beat for the last six months. He promised to do some snooping around. Just got a letter from him; there's some good stuff in it about your Captain Spud Franklin."

"Spud?"

"Flew a straight-wing Banshee into a carrier's *spud locker*. That's how he got his nickname."

Mike blinked. "Hit the stern? In a jet? And lived?"

"Yeah. Here, I'll read you that part." Roger tugged a piece of paper from the folder and scanned the text then said, "Here it is. Your Captain Franklin crashed a couple of trainers but still managed to get his wings in late forty-five, apparently because he was the best tenor in the training command's choir. The captain earned his nickname during the Korean War when he was bringing a crippled Banshee aboard after a mission. The engine coughed on final and he hit the ramp. The airplane broke in half forward of the wings. The cockpit slid up the deck into a barricade, but the rest of the airplane wound up in the ship's open fantail, the so-called spud locker. He's been known as Spud Franklin ever since."

"Wow," Mike said. "Three crashes … and now he's on his way to glory and maybe even admiral. Makes you wonder, doesn't it?"

"Not anymore," Roger said," grinning as he tucked the letter back into the folder.

The telephone at the end of the wardroom rang. The officers ignored it, waiting for a steward to answer the thing. After the fifth ring, Terry rose and trudged over to the phone.

He listened for a moment then spun around and yelled, "Mike, it's the SDO. Cherokee's down on the beach."

Mike stood up. "Where?"

"Don't know. The XO called the ready room from CIC … said to notify you and the skipper."

"They get to Jansen yet?"

Terry spoke into the phone then shouted, "No. He's not in his stateroom … they're trying the other wardroom."

Roger asked, "Who's Cherokee?"

"My roommate," Mike said. He pushed his chair out of the way and headed for the wardroom door. "Tell the duty officer I'll be in CIC."

Roger jumped up to follow him.

Mike and Roger stood a few feet inside the ship's dimly lit CIC (Combat-Information Center) listening to the action unfold on UHF radio. The rescue operation was underway. Multiple radar presentations glowed in the background; digital read-outs showed range and bearing to the event.

The radio receiver mounted on a bulkhead became quiet for several seconds then chattered again.

"Red Crown, this is Sandy Lead. We'll be over the crash site in one minute."

"Red Crown copies. Banner Five-zero-eight is anchored there."

"Banner Five-zero-eight, this is Sandy Lead, how many chutes did you see?"

"One. He landed in the trees about a hundred meters from the beach. The plane crashed about two klicks north of here."

"We have you in sight, Five-zero-eight. You orbiting over the chute?"

"That's affirmative. And, Sandy, we got a column of trucks up by the crashed plane. They're headed this way along the beach."

"I got 'em, Banner. Sandy Two, take 'em out."

"Wilco."

Roger leaned over and whispered in Mike's ear, "What's a Sandy?"

"A Spad ... an A-One. It's a single-engine prop job used for rescues like this. They carry more shit than a World War Two bomber and can stay on station for hours."

"Nice shooting, Two. Hit 'em again."

"Sandy, this is Banner Five-zero-eight, you got the chute?"

"Affirmative."

"Okay. I'm bingo. Take care of my wingy."

"That's our job, Banner."

"Banner Five-zero-eight, this is Red Crown. Your steer to Wigwam is one-zero-three, ninety-two miles."

"Copy that. Banner Five-zero-eight is switching."

"Sandy Lead, this is Angel Niner. I'll be feet dry in one minute. I have you in sight. Is the area hot?"

"Not yet, Angel, but you never know."

Mike leaned close to Roger. "Angel Niner is one of our UH-Two choppers."

Roger nodded.

"This is Sandy Two. I see people moving in. They're about three hundred meters west of the target."

"Hit 'em, Two. I'll stay high."

"Wilco."

"Angel Niner sees a chute in the trees. That the only one?"

"Affirmative, Angel Niner. One chute."

"Copy that."

"Sandy Lead, this is Sandy Two. More movers southwest. Four hundred meters."

"Got 'em, Two. I'm rolling in. You follow."

"Two Wilco."

"One's off."

"Two's off."

"Angel Niner has orange smoke. Dropping a penetrator ... taking fire from the south."

"Sandy Lead copies. Two, put some napalm about fifty meters south of the orange smoke."

"Wilco that."

"This is Angel Niner. The target is on the penetrator. Extracting now."

"Two's off."

"Good burn, Sandy Two. Love that stuff."

"Angel Niner has the target aboard. Hauling ass."

"Sandy One copies, we're on your tail."

"Angel Niner, this is Red Crown, your steer to Wigwam is one-zero-four, eighty-nine."

"Angel Niner copies."

"Angel Niner, this is Sandy Lead. Good job. We're out of here. Adios."

"Thanks for the help, Sandy. Break. Wigwam, be advised we have the B/N onboard. He states flak killed the pilot in the cockpit."

Roger glanced at Mike.

The pilot's face bore no expression.

Chapter 11
Day Six Continued

Yankee Station

Lieutenant Tony Romano kept his eyes roaming over the terrain below. They weren't far from the spot where Bowie was shot down three days prior, and losing a wingman weighed on Romano's conscience. A radio call interrupted his thoughts.

"Union Four-zero-six, this is Wigwam. We have a new mission for you."

"This is Four-zero-six," Romano answered. "Go ahead."

"A special forces unit is about to be overrun and has requested close air support. Steer two-three-zero degrees, sixty-five miles. Switch two eighteen point five and contact Sweetness."

"Sweetness?"

"Affirmative. He's an Air Force FAC (forward air controller) pulling duty with the snake eaters."

"Wilco. Authenticate sierra echo."

"Stand by ... Wigwam authenticates bravo uniform."

"Concur, Wigwam. Switching," Romano said. He turned to his new heading and added power.

The wingman slid in close enough to give a thumbs-up then drifted off to one side again. Romano switched radio frequency.

"Two's up."

"One copies."

Romano looked at the chart clipped to his kneeboard and penciled in a rough line along the new course. Using his fingers as calipers, he used the distance separating two lines of latitude as sixty nautical miles then swung his spread fingers over to the course line.

An eyebrow went up. If this was accurate, the grunts being rescued were over the line—in Laos. *Was this legal? Oh well.* He marked an X on the chart.

Eight minutes later, Romano keyed the UHF. "Sweetness, this is Union Four-zero-six, over."

A moment of garble and static ensued. Then, "Union Four-zero-six, this is Sweetness. *Hola.* Glad to hear from you; we're down to the short hairs. What's your status and position?"

"We're two A-Fours about seven miles northeast of you. Can you give me smoke?"

"Affirmative, Four-zero-six. Popping yellow smoke."

"Tally ho." Romano turned his A-4 toward the colored plume visible against the green background.

"Okay," Sweetness said. "We have you in sight. You see that big clearing to our north?"

"Affirmative."

Romano set up a port orbit around the clearing at ten thousand feet.

"The bad guys are all over that clearing. We're on the small hump at the south end. Put some hurt on the center of the open space."

"Wilco. Break. Okay, Four-ten. Serve up four bombs this pass. Lead's in." Romano rolled into his dive, let the pipper walk up to the center of the clearing and pickled. "Lead's off."

"Two's in ... two's off."

Romano looked over his shoulder as he turned into his high orbit again. Smoke pretty well covered the middle of the clearing.

"Yahoo," Sweetness yelled into his mike. "That was great. Can you do it again?"

"No problem."

"Thank you, Jesus. Put 'em a little closer to us this time. Popping red to mark us again."

"Got it. One's in." Romano pickled and pulled. "One's off."

"Two's in ... two's off."

Eight explosions marched across the open space, missing the red plume by no more than fifty yards."

"Got 'em," Sweetness shouted. "The survivors are high-tailing out of here. If you have anything left, put it in the woods at the other end of the clearing."

"Sorry, Sweetness, we're Winchester. Heading home."

"Copy that, Four-zero-six. Thanks, you guys saved our bacon. Wait one."

Romano pointed the nose of his A-4 into a climb in the direction of home as his wingman slid back into cruise position.

"Union Four-zero-six, this is Sweetness. We estimate two hundred bodies in the clearing. Good job. Cleared to switch."

Romano paused. Bodies were not what they dealt with. Trucks, bridges, yes—bodies not so much.

"Good luck, Sweetness. Union Four-zero-six is switching."

Washington, D.C.

Annie Hill's high heels clicked a staccato rhythm down the marble hall of the Joseph Gurney Cannon building, oldest of the three edifices housing congressional offices. She smiled at everyone she met along the way and took time to add a "Congratulations, Bob" when she passed a just-promoted special assistant to a congressman she despised.

Bob responded with a grin and a thumbs-up.

She turned into the open doorway next to a blue metal sign that read, *Representative Jason Fox.*

The large black woman at the reception desk ignored Annie and continued her assault on an IBM Selectric keyboard. The nameplate identified her as Naomi. A fake hand grenade mounted on a wooden plaque dominated the near corner of her desk. The grenade's metal pin sported a large red numeral one and a plaque that read, *Complaint Department – Take a Number.* People who knew Naomi wondered if it might be a real grenade.

Pausing in front of Naomi's desk, Annie asked, "Where is he?"

"In the henhouse," Naomi replied, nodding toward the door labeled *Private.*

Annie rapped twice on the door then opened it.

Representative Jason Fox had his shoes off, stocking feet propped up on the desk. The rest of him hid behind a copy of the *Washington Post.*

She shut the door behind her. "Jason, we—"

Jason peered around the edge of the paper and interrupted her by saying, "Have you read this heah garbage?"

"What garbage?"

"There are more allegations in heah about a bomb shortage. Hell, McNamara already took care of that charge. We have plenty of bombs, they just get tied up in transit sometimes."

"Doesn't that mean our pilots don't have them to drop? *They* might consider that a shortage."

Jason let the newspaper sag onto his legs. "Then ah imagine they get a day off."

"Somehow, I don't think so," Annie said. "At any rate, we have our own problem."

"Oh yeah?" Jason folded the paper and tossed it aside. "What kind of problem?"

"I'm ... pregnant."

"Who's the—"

"None of your business."

"Okay, ah'll grant you that. Got to be that red-headed guy, anyway. He goin' to marry you?"

"Guess not. I was nervous about telling him, so I tucked a letter into his bag when he was packing. That was over a week ago. He had to see it when he stopped off in L.A., but there's been no phone call ... no telegram ... nothing. So, I need to take care of this and—"

"Not an abortion."

"Why not? Two of my friends have had them. It's no big deal."

"No big deal? No big deal?" The stocking feet disappeared and Jason's chair banged the carpet under his desk with a convincing thud. "It's against God's will. Jesus."

"Well, God's will or no, I'm going to have one and I need an advance on my salary to pay for it."

"You have got to be kiddin'. If word got out that ah'd paid for an abortion, mah ass would be grass. Ah'd nevah get anothah vote in mah district. You'll have to get that money someplace else."

"Okay, Jason. I'll ask your wife."

"Ha. She'll nevah give it to you."

"She will when I tell her you're the father."

"Sweet Jesus. You'd lie about that?"

"Damn straight, Jason. Do I get the advance?"

"How much do you need?"

Yankee Station

Grover Cleveland Parker stood behind the bars of his cell, both hands gripping the steel rods that imprisoned him. The other prisoners lay asleep on their bunks, but not Grover. He didn't say anything, just stood there, watching the Marine.

Fifteen feet away, Lance Corporal Del Jackson manned a steel desk, in absolute control of the six unhappy inhabitants of *Valiant*'s brig. His attention appeared to be focused on some kind of manual; the Marine globe-and-anchor emblem dominated its cover.

Grover suspected the manual hid a *Playboy* magazine. Not even a gung-ho Marine could spend that much time focused on some document the Government put out.

After a while the Marine looked up and Grover spoke. "You're a black man, Corporal. Why you do this for the man? Keep a brother locked up like this?"

"It's my duty."

"Duty? Duty to what? To who?"

"The Corps."

"Where you from, brother."

"Long Beach."

"No kiddin'? I'm from Oceanside. We're neighbors."

The Marine went back to his reading.

"Hey," Grover said. "What's gonna happen to me?"

"The XO did his investigation. You're going to captain's mast."

"What's the charge?"

"Assault."

"Assault? Man, all I did was defend myself."

"Against what?"

"That honky was threatening me. Stood tall over me. Called me nigger."

"Tell it to the captain."

Grover was thoughtful for a moment. "What in hell is this captain's mast? One of those kangaroo courts I heard about?"

The Marine sighed and set his manual aside. "It's an inquiry into the facts of your case under Article Fifteen of the Uniform Code of Military Justice."

"Military justice. I bet that's a joke."

"Shut up and listen," the Marine snapped. "After the captain hears all sides, he can dismiss the charges, award non-judicial punishment or refer you to a court-martial. You satisfied now?"

"What you figure the captain's gonna do to me?"

"New captain has to make a name for himself. I figure he'll give you brig time rather than send you off to a court-martial."

"What's the max?"

"Thirty days."

"Damn."

"That's if you're lucky. If not, he'll have you court-martialed."

"Oh yeah. What's that like?"

"It's a trial. You ever been to one?"

"Yeah, my uncle's. The white jury said he was guilty and the honky judge gave him ten years."

"Put uniforms on everybody in that scene and you have a court-martial, except likely a hell of a lot fairer."

"Fairer? Who's gonna be on that jury?"

"Officers."

"White officers?"

"Probably. In case you haven't noticed, there aren't too many black officers around here."

"What can this here court-martial do to me?"

"About whatever it wants to. Sometimes it can have you executed."

"No shit?"

"No shit. You better hope the captain handles this himself."

"You think a white captain gonna be fair to a black man?"

"Yeah. Seen it with my own eyes. But that was Captain Spanner. Like I said, this new captain might want to make a name for himself."

Chapter 12
Day Seven

Yankee Station

Mike stepped into Ready Room Three and paused.

Commander Jansen stood leaning over the squawk box mounted on the bulkhead next to the squadron duty officer's desk; the CAG's voice boomed through the squawk box living up to its name.

The box said, "Get that bird into Cubi Point today."

"Yes, sir. I'll send Mike and Terry. They could use a break."

"Good idea. And tell them I want that bird back ASAP."

The squawk box made a strangling noise and went silent.

Mike said, "I heard my name. What's up, Skipper?"

"Our Five-zero-three took a hit early this morning over by Nam Dinh and has a couple of holes in the port wing. Nothing too major, but it's more than our metal benders can handle here. We need to get her patched up at the repair facility in Cubi."

Terry came to Mike's shoulder. "And you want us to fly her in?"

Jansen said, "Yeah, another good deal in the service of your country. You two get your liberty togs together and get back here. Master Chief Gronski wants a few words with you before you go."

"Yes, sir," Terry said, a broad smile on his face. "I can call my wife from Cubi Point."

He hurried out of the room.

Mike didn't move. "I'd rather stay here, Skipper, if it's all the same to you. I hear we've been moved north. I think CINC-PAC-FLEET is finally going to let us at Haiphong."

"And you don't want to miss that, I suppose?"

"No, sir. I crave a piece of that action."

"Sorry, Mike, you're going to Cubi. The NARF should be able to get Five-zero-three back in shape by tomorrow morning, so if there is any action at Haiphong, which I doubt, it'll still be happening when you get back. Did you pack up Cherokee's gear?"

"Yes, sir. Last night. It's all in a wood crate the maintenance guys made. I figure we can ship it from our next port."

"Good idea. I don't think it's wise to put his letter to Marie in the mail, not with that ring so obvious. I'll put it in a package with my letter and get that in the mail from here."

Mike pulled an envelope from his flight suit. "Can you include this one, Skipper. It's from me."

"Sure, Mike." He took the letter. "Now get cracking. You've got a plane to catch."

Master Chief Gronski stood waiting for them when Mike and Terry returned to the ready room. He had Fidel Ramos, 503's plane captain, with him.

Gronski pointed at the two green hanging bags Mike and Terry brought with them and said, "Ramos, put those bags in the cargo blivet we stuck on Five-zero-three's centerline. And make damn sure you get the dzus buttons tight."

"Sure thing, Chief," Ramos said.

"Sure thing, Master Chief," Gronski corrected.

Reaching for the bags, Ramos grinned and said, "As you wish, Master Chief."

Ramos winked at the two officers then hustled the bags out of the ready room while Gronski glared at him.

Mike watched his bag bang against the steel door frame before he turned back to the squadron's maintenance chief.

"Okay, Master Chief Gronski, what are your orders?"

The Master Chief handed Mike a sealed manila envelope. "Give this to whichever sand crab is gonna be in charge of fixing Five-zero-threes. He'll need the info."

"Sure thing, Chief ... ah, Master Chief."

Gronski raised an eyebrow. "And Lieutenant, make damn sure you keep that bird below three hundred knots going in today. If any skin peels off my airplane, I'll patch it with some of yours."

"You got it ... Master Chief."

"Have a nice vacation, Lieutenant. You too, Mister Anders."

The Master Chief swiveled his ample bulk around and stomped out.

Mike leveled 503 off at twenty-one thousand feet and made sure the airspeed still indicated less than three hundred knots. He checked the cockpit cabin pressure then turned off the oxygen and let his mask dangle free on one side.

Terry glanced at Mike and did the same with his own mask. He tapped some data into the keyboard between his knees, and the computer slewed their steering bugs to a southerly course.

"Aha," Mike said, looking at the new steering. "You notice we have to do a dog-leg around Hainan?"

He stabbed his thumb at the huge Chinese island drifting past the port wing tip.

"So?"

"That's because the ship has moved north," Mike said. "Close to Haiphong. That tell you something?"

Terry peered into his radar screen. "You pushing that rumor again?"

"This time it's for real. I can smell it."

"What you smell," Terry said, "is my rancid flight suit."

"We'll see, amigo. What are your plans for tonight?"

"First a long, slow shower. I am damn tired of one-minute Navy showers. God, I wish we were landing in Japan; a *hotsi bath* would be perfect. Small women trekking up and down my spine with little bare feet has appealed to me ever since the ejection."

"Yeah, but we're headed for the Philippines."

"Now we are," Terry said as he tapped his keyboard and computer steering swung to a more easterly heading.

Mike banked the airplane to follow and said, "Well, after your shower at the BOQ, want to hit the Kalayaan Club for dinner and some gambling?"

"Not me. I'm going to get twenty dollars worth of quarters, find a nice quiet pay phone, and call Judy. Her last letter was a downer ... she doesn't seem happy. Maybe it's part of being pregnant. I'll try to cheer her up."

"Don't say anything about Cherokee. I don't know how long it'll take for the Navy to notify Marie."

"Don't worry. That bit of news would really turn on the tears."

"You write Judy about our little swim?"

"Hell no."

"Well, you'll tell her if you call. You'd be better off getting shit-faced at the club."

Spud Franklin grinned as he read the CINCPACFLT message. So the rumor was true: *this* was why they'd been moved north. Three rapid taps on the door of his at-sea cabin interrupted him.

Spud called out "Come," but he continued to read for another moment.

Finished reading, he raised his head.

The Air Wing Commander stood in the doorway, his flight suit sweaty, oxygen mask indentations on his face. The Marine guard held the door open for him.

"Have a seat, CAG." Spud pointed at the chair across the coffee table, then looked to make sure the Marine closed the door. Once CAG was seated, Spud handed him the message. "Enjoy."

Five seconds into his read, CAG looked up. "It's about damn time we hit the Haiphong bridges."

"Yeah, but you better read the rest of the message; there are some caveats you won't like."

CAG read then re-read the long message and finally laid it down on the coffee table. "Says we're prohibited from flying over Haiphong itself, but we're still allowed a lot more freedom to attack than the last two times they let American aircraft anywhere near the place."

"Okay," Spud said, "how do you want to hit the bridges?"

After taking a moment to think, CAG tapped the message with a forefinger. "Says here open season starts at midnight tonight. Our present oh-four hundred to sixteen hundred op schedule will give us one strike before dawn and then seven cycles during daylight."

"You want to hit the bridges every cycle?"

"Can't. We'll have to use alpha strikes during the day to get a lot of aircraft over the target area at a time, and the alphas take too much ordnance. If you agree, I'll send A-Sixes in at night then schedule three daylight alphas. We'll go heavy on *Iron Hand* to suppress the fire control radars clustered around the port."

"Okay," Spud said. "How will you divvy up the targets?"

"Day strikes against the northernmost bridges. The alphas can hook around Haiphong and attack to the southwest. That avoids flying over Haiphong and gives them a relatively short egress to the sea."

"What about the night strikes? Low level?"

"Yes, sir. Against the two southernmost bridges. To keep from overflying Haiphong, the A-Sixes will have to run their targets at a pretty hefty angle. We'll give them Mark-eighty-three thousand-pounders, but there's a high probability the weapons will straddle the bridge or go through it without a direct hit."

"You better explain that, CAG. I'm an old fighter pilot."

CAG laughed. "You don't drop a steel-truss bridge with anything but a direct hit on a critical piece. They're pretty much a skeleton structure. You can put a bomb dead center on the bridge, and there's a good chance it'll pass right through the thing and explode on the ground or water below."

"Are you telling me it's going to take some time to drop those bridges?"

"Yes, sir. A lot of strikes ... and some losses."

"You think we'll be able to surprise them?"

"Hell no. Some stripe-pants clown from State has undoubtedly talked too much to another diplomat who's tipped off a foreign friend. And that Russian trawler that's been harassing us will alert Ho Chi Minh whenever another raid is on the way. The gomers will know everything about our strikes before we go feet dry."

California

"I have to pee," Robin said. She pulled away from Charley's sweaty hands and slipped out of the dark, smoke-filled living room.

At the arched portal that led to the hallway, she paused long enough to look back over her shoulder. Charley was fixated on the incense burner that sat on the stone fireplace mantle, not caring that she'd left him. *Good. Let his glazed eyes stare at something else besides my bare breasts. Those eyes aren't so damn compelling now, are they?*

She turned away from the bathroom and fled down the hall. At the far end, she pulled her bra back where it belonged, adjusted her blouse and crawled out the open window.

"Hey, Robin," Charley yelled. "Get your ass back in here."

The voice was thin ... husky. Robin guessed it was the end result of a pack of cigarettes, an unknown number of reefers, and some quality time with a bong.

She ran barefoot across the darkened street and hid in the shadows of a huge oak on the neighbor's lawn. After a moment she peeked around the tree trunk at the little house she had fled.

A gaunt figure appeared in the doorway and leaned against the jam. "I see you, little bird. Come back here."

Robin whispered, "You can't see me. Hell, you can't see to the edge of the porch with those bloodshot eyes." She eased back farther into the shadows.

"Dammit, little bird. Come here. I want you."

Again she whispered, "Oh no."

She was a fool to stay with Charley—alone with Charley—while Raven went off with some boy she met at the park. But he was never this way before, at least not with her. *Had to be the drugs*. She had one spiff, that's all, not enough to get too high. Not enough to want to screw Charley at any rate. She smiled to herself.

Charley shouted, "Screw you." He turned, stumbled and caught the door to steady himself then staggered into the gloom behind the doorway, saying, "Verrrry mucho."

When she felt certain Charley wasn't watching anymore, Robin rose and hurried toward the park. She wanted to be with people, and even this close to midnight, the park would have plenty of them. Maybe she would find Raven there. She did, under the old tree where they met, on her knees, throwing up into a shallow depression between two exposed roots.

A suntanned surfer dude—blonde hair, pale blue eyes, spotty chin stubble—sat nearby, looking confused.

"My God," Robin said, dropping to her knees by Raven. "What's wrong?"

"Bad shit," the boy said. "Man, we got some bad shit."

Robin saw the white flakes on his nostrils. *Cocaine*. She pulled Raven to her and hugged the girl, rocking back and forth.

The boy started to get up and said, "I got to go."

"You aren't going anywhere, studly. You sit your ass back down. God knows what human trash is going to come by here tonight, and you're going to stay right here and protect us. Savvy?"

The boy blinked several times, but he eased back down onto the grass. "Protect you? With what?"

"Your fists, moron."

"Oh."

Raven twisted away from Robin and threw up again. "I'm sorry," she whispered. "So sorry." She closed her eyes and seemed to go to sleep.

Yankee Station

The ship's executive officer snapped out, "Attention on deck," and turned everyone rigid as the words bounced off four steel bulkheads.

Captain Franklin strode into the room and took up his position behind a large podium. He glanced at the two dozen officers, chiefs, and sailors gathered before him, all at attention; then he nodded to the executive officer.

The XO said, "At ease," then pulled a file from the stack before him and handed it to the captain. "First case is Seaman Grover Parker, sir. Charged with assault." He turned to the assembled men and said, "Seaman Parker, front and center."

Grover Cleveland Parker stepped up to the podium and came to attention. The ship's first lieutenant, the young officer in charge of the deck force, briefed him on what to do. The chief bosun's mate gave Grover more pertinent advice on what not to do. The officer and the chief both stepped forward and stood beside Grover, one on each side.

The captain scanned the file's brief contents, starting with the XO's report. Written statements from the first lieutenant, the chief bosun's mate, Seaman Parker and the injured sailor, Seaman Frost, followed. Finished, the captain gave Grover a baleful look then read from the file.

"You are suspected of committing the following violation of the Uniform Code of Military Justice ... assault. You do not have to make any statement regarding the offense of which you are accused or suspected, and any statement made by you may be used as evidence against you."

Grover fidgeted.

Pausing, the captain gave Grover another hard look, then went back to the standard text.

"You are advised that a captain's mast is not a trial and that a determination of misconduct on your part is not a conviction by a court. Further, you are advised that the formal rules of evidence used in trial by court-martial do not apply at captain's mast." Holding up a sheet of paper the captain went on. "I have here a statement signed by you acknowledging that you were advised of your legal rights pertaining to this hearing. Do you understand this statement and do you understand the legal rights explained therein?"

"Yes, sir."

"You struck Seaman Frost with a chipping hammer and broke his leg. Why?"

"He called me a nigger ... sir."

"And you consider that sufficient justification to injure the man?"

"Yes, sir."

The captain turned to the chief bosun's mate standing next to Grover and addressed him. "Boats, what's your opinion of Seaman Parker?"

"Good worker, sir. No trouble before this incident."

"And your read on Seaman Frost?"

"A bigmouth, sir, but not a troublemaker."

"Ever heard him use the word nigger?"

"Yes, sir."

"What have you done to stop him from using that word?"

The chief blinked. "Why ... nothing, sir. He's from Mississippi; those people talk that way all the time."

The captain snapped, "Not in my Navy." He turned to the first lieutenant. "Mister Hanrahan, there's a problem in your unit. Fix it."

"Yes, sir."

Eyes boring a hole in Grover's forehead, the captain said, "Thirty days in the brig—"

Grover flashed a smile.

"... and forfeiture of base pay for two months."

Grover's smile evaporated.

"Next case."

Chapter 13
Day Seven Continued

Yankee Station

The VA-64 line shack, a metal-encased cube under the flight deck forward of the island, was stifling hot despite the autumn weather outside. The space's single opening was a hatch leading to the starboard catwalk, and the heat from the nearby steam catapult penetrated even the steel bulkheads. The deafening bang of the catapult firing every minute or so made the space even more uncomfortable.

Airman Albert Crowder worked alone in the line shack, sorting tie-down chains, one of several menial tasks he'd acquired since his beloved 411 was shot down over Vietnam. He scratched his head, a nervous habit his mother hated, as he held up a maverick tie-down chain and puzzled over its ownership; it wasn't marked with the squadron's international-orange paint color. Giving up, he tossed the chain into the corner.

The line chief stuck his head in the opening and asked, "You done yet?"

"About. You heard anything new, Chief?"

Crowder posed this question at least once a day.

"Look, Crowder, forget about it. Mr. Jones is either dead meat or in a prison camp, and you'll be an old married man before you get any more word. The lieutenant was nailed by flak and nothing you did or didn't do to Four-eleven is responsible. Now get your ass up to Four-zero-two and spell McNeil. Tell him I want to see him here right away."

"Okay, Chief, but I don't believe what you said about Mr. Jones."

Crowder pulled on his brown skull cap with the built in *Mickey Mouse ears*, then he hustled past the chief onto the catwalk. He crouched on the short ladder leading up to the flight deck until he got a read on what was going on. The last strike of the day was about to land, so there was no preceding launch.

A flight of F-4s broke overhead and "Stand by to recover aircraft" boomed over the flight-deck speaker system.

The forward part of the flight deck would be relatively free of action for a few seconds, so Crowder made his way across the deck to A-4E 402 parked on top of the port bow catapult, a few feet from the dashed *foul line* that separated the angled landing area from the rest of the flight deck. He found Airman Jackson McNeil wiping down the plane with a semi-clean rag.

Crowder moved close, pulled one of McNeil's earmuffs away from his face and shouted, "Chief says to get down to the line shack ASAP!"

The first F-4 slammed down on the angle deck and the pilot shoved his throttles to the stops in case they didn't trap. The plane caught the four wire and came to a halt just twenty yards away from Crowder and McNeil. The engine's roar was overpowering until the pilot pulled his throttles back to idle.

When the noise subsided a bit, McNeil asked, "What's he want?"

"Beats me. Gimme that rag."

McNeil handed the rag to Crowder. "Crap. The chief's got another crap detail lined up for me."

He waited as the F-4 trundled off the landing area and taxied past on its way to a parking space farther up the bow. When the airplane cleared, McNeil trotted through the fading jet exhaust and disappeared down the ladder to the line shack.

Crowder moved around 402's nose wiping the salt spray from the aluminum. He heard the unique shriek of F-4 engines as the next Phantom came aboard, but his back was turned, so he didn't see the actual landing. He didn't see one of the plane's two nose wheels shear off and fly up the deck at a hundred twenty miles an hour.

He didn't see what slammed into his back and killed him.

Philippines

The Subic Bay Officers' Club, situated on the beach, was usually sedate, with or without a carrier present, as befitted a black shoe, ship-drivers hangout. It only became rowdy if some special event such as an all-girl Japanese band dragged in carrier aviators.

The Cubi Point Officers' Club, high on a bluff overlooking the air base across the bay, was different. If a carrier moored at the long pier flanking the airstrip, no one but aviators and courageous women ventured into what almost always constituted a wild-ass frat party with older kids and better booze. No carrier, no party.

The Kalayaan Club, on the other hand, was a taxi ride up into the hills where the families of Navy personnel assigned to Subic Bay lived peaceful lives. It offered cheap drinks, good food, and fair slot machines in a quiet atmosphere. But the main draw for the few carrier aviators who knew of them, was a handful of female American school teachers who lived in a two-story building nearby.

The wisest of dependents and teachers stayed home when a carrier was in, but the bay was empty now, so a few locals emerged to play the Kalayaan Club's slots and imbibe a little.

Mike stopped at the bar to change paper money into coins and, looking around, tallied as present four families plus three probable school teachers. He settled on a likely-looking slot machine, then proceeded to plug in quarters and pull its handle. He was up a couple of dollars when—

A feminine voice, "Damn."

Mike hadn't heard one of those in some time. He let the next quarter drop into the slot before he turned to look at the woman two machines away. *Nice. Thirtyish. Attractive in a brown-haired, girl-next-door sort of way. No ring.*

"Damn. Damn. Damn."

This time she pounded a tiny fist against the silvery machine. It didn't seem to care; no coins fell into the slot's catch basin.

Picking up his scotch-on-ice, Mike moved closer to the woman, wishing he had worn something more GQ than tan slacks and a green aloha shirt. "What's the matter?"

"Oh, nothing," she said, turning to smile at him. "I lost my dinner money in these contraptions, that's all. I'll survive."

"I'm a good Samaritan," Mike said. "I'll spring for dinner … it doesn't cost much here."

The woman gave Mike a calculating look. "You're a pilot, aren't you?"

"What makes you think so?"

"Your aspiration seems to exceed your abilities."

"What?"

"Sorry about that. Your pick-up line isn't all that original."

"I see. Well, I'm Navy, and we don't get out much."

"A naval aviator? Good, I've never had a date with one ... I hear it can be quite exhilarating. I'm Diane. Let's go eat."

Being a gentleman, by act of Congress no less, Mike let the lady precede him into the club's cozy dining room. But being a Navy man, he allowed his eyes to appraise her keel and stern.

Vietnam

Like his captors, Bowie slept most of the day despite being hog-tied and wired to a tall stump. The position was painful, but exhaustion prevailed and he soon dozed off. He was almost used to the routine now: walk all night, hide all day. *Tote dat barge, lift dat bale.*

He saw a flight of A-4s come over right after dawn, but the troops he was with were well camouflaged, and the planes flew on. It occurred to him that, if they had been spotted, the bombs would have wiped him out right along with the NVA soldiers. *Yeah ... and that jive-ass officer. Bring it on.*

As the sun eased down behind a nearby bank of abused rubber trees, the camp stirred into action, and small groups of soldiers clustered around their rice bowls. Bowie's trio of guards released some of the wires that bound him and, as before, tied his wrists in front of him so he could eat.

Bowie finished his meager bowl of boiled rice while he watched the sun set and tried to formulate an escape plan. Soon as it was dark, they would be moving again, heading south. Sporadic firing from that direction woke him sometime in the afternoon, so friendly forces had to be nearby. But so was the NVA colonel his captors hoped to please with the gift of one slightly used American naval officer trussed up like a Christmas turkey. *Christmas? Odds are I'll be dead long before Santa flies again.*

His guard for this shift, who seemed the youngest of the trio, poured a little water into the empty rice bowl and let Bowie drink before he took the bowl away and stuffed it into his pack.

The officer remained absent. *Busy spit-shining his new boots? Or merely bored with tormenting his prisoner? Poor bored asshole.*

Ignored by his companions, the young guard removed the wires around Bowie's ankles and then freed his prisoner from the stump.

Stepping back, he jerked on the chain around Bowie's neck and pointed his makeshift spear at the column of soldiers now moving down a dark trail.

Bowie set off down the path using the shuffling gait he'd adopted. It seemed to minimize the pain of movement yet satisfied the guard with the pointed stick. Just fast enough.

A few yards down the trail, Bowie realized his hands were still wired together ... in front of him. *This is new.* They were always secured behind his back except when eating his daily ration of rice. *An oversight? An invitation to run? This guard is, after all, a kid. Maybe he feels sorry for me.*

No matter, Bowie started to work his hands and wrists. Turn them, stretch, turn them again.

Two hours later, one of his forefingers reached the twist holding the wire handcuffs in place. The sharp end dug into Bowie's fingertip as he pushed at the tightly wound strand, and fresh blood dripped onto his wrist, lubricating it, helping. Finally, the wire gave a little and another finger could reach the knot.

An hour farther down the trail, the twist came undone. The wire almost fell, but Bowie caught it. He lost a step in the process and received a jab in the rear from the pointed stick. Bowie grinned. His hands and feet were loose.

The slave is free.

Concentrate. The soldiers were well trained and kept about twenty yards separation as they moved single file along the trail; an ambush would catch only a few before the others could react. So, if the man ahead of them was merely a dim shadow, the soldier behind his guard must be similarly distant.

All he needed was a few seconds. Bowie waited his chance.

It came an hour later: a sharp bend in the trail, thick brush on either side. As they rounded the turn, Bowie slowed a step. The tip of the spear prodded him. He whirled, grabbed the stick with his left hand, and swung a right cross to the kid's chin with all the strength adrenalin could give him.

The boy dropped without a sound.

Bowie jerked the spear away and ducked into the brush. He was ten yards away when the first cry sounded and another fifty yards before he heard the sounds of pursuit.

Kansas

Mrs. Swenson stuck her head in the stairwell and called out, "Come down to breakfast, Judy. You're eggs are getting cold."

"Coming."

Judy put the telephone back onto its cradle. The line had emitted a dull buzz for almost a minute now, but she didn't want to let go. Terry had been on the other end of that line, at least for a while. Until, that is, the overseas operator asked for yet more quarters—and Terry was out. A passionate "I love you" before the line went dead, then the buzz.

Plucking a tissue from the box on her dresser, Judy dabbed away the few tears remaining on her face. She peered into the mirror. *Eyes look a bit red, but not enough to tip off Mom.* Her mother had been mothering her ever since Judy's announcement that she was pregnant. Judy tested a bright smile in the reflection, then went downstairs for breakfast.

"Oh my," Mrs. Swenson said. "You've been crying."

"I hated to say good-bye, that's all."

Judy pulled out a chair and sat in her usual place at the kitchen table.

Frowning, Mrs. Swenson set a plate of eggs, bacon, and buttered toast in front of her daughter. "You were on the phone long enough. Why in the world did Terry call here so early in the morning?"

"It's late at night in the Philippines, Mom. He waited until he was sure we'd be awake here."

"So he's in the Philippines again. I hope he doesn't buy another of those gawd-awful nutcrackers. How is he?"

"He had to eject the other day."

"Eject?"

"They pull a lever or something, and their seat rockets up into the air. Then a parachute opens and floats them down."

"Oh my. Sounds very dangerous. Why did he do that?"

"His airplane caught on fire. He—"

The tears came again.

Mrs. Swenson rushed over, stood behind Judy, and hugged her. "I'm sure he'll be all right, honey. That ejection thing is probably the most danger he'll ever face, and he came through that, didn't he?"

Sniffling, Judy said, "Yes."

"See." Mrs. Swenson handed Judy a tissue, then patted her on the shoulder. "He'll be fine."

Judy clenched her fist around the tissue. "I'm going to fly up to Whidbey Island, Mom."

Mrs. Swenson returned to her stove. "That place somewhere in Washington?"

"Northwest of Seattle. Terry's squadron is based at Whidbey when they aren't at sea."

"That's a long way from here, honey. Why go?"

"I want to talk to the other wives. See how they feel about their husbands being in this war. Look at the housing situation."

"Housing? Why?"

"I may move there."

The frying pan crashed onto the stove's grill. "Move? Why in God's name would you want to do that?"

"That's where Terry will be after the cruise, so that's where I belong."

"I thought Terry was getting out of the Navy."

Mrs. Swenson sat down across from Judy, concern on her face.

"I suggested it, Mom, and he said he'd think about it. But I know him, he's not going to quit. Especially not while there's a war on."

"But you'll have the baby here, Judy. Things will be a lot different after that."

"I don't know, Mom." Judy sat up straight. "I may have the baby at Whidbey Island. I want to be there when Terry comes home."

"Oh my ... I better talk to your father."

Washington State

Marion Jansen had her hands in the sink, scrubbing the burnt-on remains of last-night's pork chops off the frying pan, when the telephone rang.

She paused, looking at the clock on the wall. *Eight o'clock in the morning? This early?* Bad thoughts crept into her mind.

The phone rang again.

Wiping her hands on the dishtowel, she walked across the kitchen to the black phone hanging on its wall mount.

"Hello?"

"Marion, this is Chaplain Hirsch."

"Oh no."

Marion's fingers trembled. She had to grab the phone with both hands to keep it from falling.

"It's not for you, Marion. It's not for you."

"Thank God." She took a deep breath. "Oh, what a terrible thing to say." Then after another breath. "Who is it?"

"Lieutenant Mathew Ridge."

"Cherokee? Oh, poor Marie. Missing in action?"

"The message says he was killed in action over North Vietnam. The casualty assistance officer just called me. They always call me before they notify the dependents."

"I know. How soon?"

"Right now, Marion. I'm heading over to Mrs. Ridge's house as soon as I hang up the phone. I know you skipper's wives want a heads-up whenever these things happen."

"Thank you, Chaplain. I'm on my way."

The click on the other end of the line sounded so very final. Marion used the dishtowel to wipe away some tears as she hung up the phone.

Marion stifled a cry as she brought the Chevy to a sliding stop behind the chaplain's sedan. Marie Ridge had met the chaplain halfway to the street. She was on her knees in the middle of a tiny lawn, pulling at her hair, a look of utter devastation on her face. The chaplain knelt beside her.

Sobbing, Marion threw open the car door and rushed across the grass. Falling on her own knees, Marion threw her arms around the grieving woman; their tears mingled.

Chapter 14
Day Eight

Philippines

A ruby-red fingernail traced a path though the small forest of Mike's chest hair, and with lips pressed against Mike's shoulder, Diane asked, "What time is it?"

Mike twisted his head and torso enough to see the luminous glow of his wristwatch on Diane's nightstand. "One minute past midnight." He moved back to his prior position so that the woman's bare breast nestled once more against his side. "You got an early class?"

Diane shifted onto one elbow and nuzzled Mike's near ear. "Not important. You got an early flight?"

"Not till I'm ready. It's good to be the king."

She laughed, which jiggled her breasts. "You going back to the ship? Back to the war?"

"That's what they pay me for."

He stretched, working one ankle until it made a small popping sound.

Suddenly serious, Diane asked, "What does your wife think of your job?"

He stopped stretching. "What makes you think I'm married?"

"The way you made love ... considerate, gentle."

"As opposed to?"

Laughing again, she said, "A young stud trying to prove himself."

"She hates it. Gave me a choice ... her or the flying. I guess you know how that turned out."

"Where is she?"

"Her mother's home ... Dallas. What about you? Ever married?"

"Still am, I guess."

Mike rolled onto an elbow himself so they were face-to-face. "You guess? What in hell does that mean?"

"He's over there," she said, pointing west over her shoulder with a thumb.

"Saigon?"

"Hanoi."

"Oh shit." Mike lay back down. "POW?"

"That's what the Air Force thinks. They don't know for sure."

"What happened?"

"He was a Wild Weasel. He—"

"The Air Force SAM hunters?"

"He flew F-One-Oh-Fives with special radar detection gear, looking for North Vietnamese missile sites. When they'd shoot a missile at him, he'd duck, and his wingman would attack the launch pad."

"Brass balls."

"Yes." She was silent for a moment. "He flew over here to Clark Air Base for R&R just before last Christmas. I was teaching up at Clark then, and we had three days together. I asked him one night ... we were lying like this ... how long do you have to be a Weasel, what's the normal tour length? He laughed before he answered. That was the last time I ever heard him laugh."

"What did he say?"

"'Don't know,' he said. 'No one's ever made it that far'."

"Jesus. When did he get smoked?"

"Christmas Day. His wingman said two sites opened up on him at the same time. He dodged the first SAM, but the second one blew a wing off."

"The wingman see a chute?"

"No."

"Then why—"

"Someone from Air Force Intel came to see me one night in February. He said they had reason to believe my husband might be alive in one of the POW camps near Hanoi. I tried to get him to tell me how they could possibly know that, but he wouldn't say. He told me to keep the faith; then he left."

"So you're here ... waiting."

"I couldn't handle all the sympathy from the other women at Clark, so I took a teaching position down here with the Navy."

"And I guess tonight was—"

"Needed."

"So you didn't really gamble away your dinner money."

"I have fifty bucks in my purse. Want to look?"

"Why me?"

"You reminded me of him, and all of a sudden I wanted this. Oh, that sounds so cold. Look, Mike, there's no future in this for either of us, but I'm glad you came along tonight."

"I don't know what to say, Diane."

"I didn't lure you here to talk, sailor."

She kissed Mike's chest.

Vietnam

The moon was gone, predawn darkness reigned. Bowie lay tight against a large, rotten log and tried to control his heavy breathing. His lungs ached from the long run.

He tried to move in unpredictable ways as he scuttled through black, unfamiliar terrain. Human nature is to seek high ground, so he'd stayed in the lowlands. Movement would be easier over more open terrain, so he avoided the temptation. The beach some distance off to his left called to him, but that way had to mean certain death on the open sand.

His pursuers seemed spread out in a line as beaters, hunting him as if he were some wild animal, pushing him straight ahead. *To what?* To the main force and the colonel, that's what. And their tactic was working; if he moved right or left too much, the searchers on that side grew closer.

They caught a glimpse of him twice, but their rifle shots missed, and he managed to evade them again both times. Now the inevitable dawn was near. *Maybe, if I hide well enough, they'll pass me by.*

So he went to ground.

Bowie pressed against the log as the soft sounds of bodies moving through lush growth betrayed the imminent arrival of his hunters. He willed his body to use slow, shallow breathing. *Inhale ... wait ... exhale. With any luck, they'll move past the log and by me.*

The nearest hunter was close now, no more than three or four yards away, the other side of the log. Bowie's hand tightened on the makeshift spear lying alongside his right leg.

A twig snapped, within a few feet.

He held his breath.

A dark shadow leaned across the log above Bowie's bloody feet.

The figure gasped.

That was the trigger Bowie needed. He jabbed the spear tip up and drove it into the center of the shadow. Pushing hard on the spear's shaft, Bowie rose and clamped his left hand around the soldier's throat, strangling a cry. When the hand gripping the spear encountered the man's stomach, Bowie released the wooden shaft and wrapped his right arm around the struggling body, hugging it close.

The man clawed at Bowie; then the two clung to each other for the few seconds it took the North Vietnamese soldier to die.

Heart pumping, Bowie lay the body on the mossy ground and pushed it against the dead log. *Ashes to ashes, dust to dust.* He tried to extract the spear, but the man's stomach muscles had contracted around it, and Bowie was too weakened to pull the stick out.

The sound of another searcher moving nearer got Bowie's attention. He gave up on the spear, grabbed the corpse's canteen, and ran into the darkest part of the shadows.

A shout. They were onto him again.

He ran, ducking and weaving, always returning to his base course: south.

Sometime later, Bowie couldn't tell how long, he had to slow and move crab-like through a jumble of fallen palm trees and shredded brush that marked a prior battle scene or possibly an attack by one of his fellow aviators. He couldn't tell which, and didn't much care. He stepped on something sharp, and a stab of pain raced up his left leg, but he moved on.

Bowie emerged into more open territory as the first caress of dawn filtered through the patch of surviving trees that now separated him from the beach. He could hear the sound of waves lapping at the sand, and he ached to lie in the surf and wash the blood away. *If I could rig a raft*—but it would be light soon and he had no choice: *I must hide.*

Doubling back to the battle scene, Bowie found a pile of broken palm branches and crawled under it. A viper of some unrecognized species slithered out of his way, and he considered killing it for food. Gagging at even the thought, he gave it up and settled for the last bit of warm water from the canteen.

Using the now-empty canteen for a pillow of sorts, Bowie lay down and tried to form a plan for the coming night. The surf lulled him to sleep within minutes.

Yankee Station

Roger Brackett hesitated at the open hatch leading onto the ship's bridge. The captain, leaning forward in the tall chair, had his back to the hatch, intent on whatever was off the port bow. The OOD and the rest of the bridge watch were also focused on it. No one noticed the stranger at the hatch.

There was a certain protocol to go through. People didn't wander onto the bridge of a warship without permission, but Rogers's mind failed to bring forth the necessary words.

Finally, he rapped on the hatch coaming as though visiting someone's home and said, "Can I come in?"

The OOD turned toward him and laughed. "Permission granted. State your business."

"I need to speak to the captain."

Captain Franklin turned his chair around and peered at Roger as if he were an alien creature.

"A civilian," he finally said. "You're too young to be a tech rep so you must be that reporter from Washington. It's Brackett, isn't it? What do you need?"

He swiveled forward again, his attention drawn away once more.

"Yes, sir." Roger stepped forward, nearer the captain's chair. "Sir, there's a COD flight to Cubi this afternoon and I—"

"The air boss handles COD flights."

"He turned me down, not enough priority. But I have a personal emergency, sir, and I need to get back to Washington ASAP. I need—"

"What kind of personal emergency?"

The captain's attention remained elsewhere.

Roger moved even closer and lowered his voice. "My girlfriend's pregnant."

The captain leaned back in his chair and laughed. Then, in a booming voice, "Your girlfriend's pregnant?" He turned to stare at Roger. "That's your emergency?"

Roger heard several chuckles behind his back. "Yes, sir. I just discovered a letter she wrote me before I left Washington. It was stuffed under ... she wanted to know my intentions. And I haven't answered. She'll be frantic by now. She might ... I need to get back there."

Captain Franklin leaned over Roger, a towering figure even sitting in his chair. "Son, every time the men on this ship put out to sea, they leave behind a whole passel of pregnant girlfriends, wives and total strangers. They leave the women behind because these men have a job to do and so do you. You're here to write about the Navy's air war, and right now we happen to have a doozie. The President has allowed us to hit some targets of importance, and hunting season won't last long. You're Johnny-on-the-spot to write about it, and there's no way I'm going to let you fly away to coddle your girlfriend."

"But sir—"

"Tell you what. You draft up a nice message to her, and I'll send it to somebody official who can deliver it. Where is she?"

"She's in D.C., sir. She works for Congressman Jason Fox."

"A congressman? Good, I'll send the message to the Navy's Congressional Liaison Office. I'm sure they'll be happy to deliver it to the congressman's office."

"But—"

"Carry on, Mr. Brackett. Bring your message here when you're done."

The captain spun his chair forward and picked up his binoculars.

Roger looked around at what seemed to be several smirks, then slunk off the bridge and down the first steep ladder he encountered.

Franklin glared past *Valiant*'s bow at the little ship now moving left to right no more than two hundred yards ahead. "That damn Russkie is beginning to piss me off," he said. "A fishing vessel with eleven antennas? Bullshit."

He turned toward the OOD. "How long has that vessel been out here harassing us?"

"Ever since we arrived on Yankee Station," the OOD said. "Captain Spanner threatened to ram him once, but we never did."

"How close has it come?"

"Two weeks ago we had to turn hard starboard to miss the sucker. We cleared his stern by about thirty yards. It's in the log."

"Close."

"Yes, sir. We were in the middle of a launch and the captain held off as long as he could. Personally, I wish we'd run—" The OOD leaned forward. "The Russian's stopping! We're going to hit him."

Franklin leapt from his chair. "I have the conn. Quartermaster, left full rudder. All engines stop. Sound the collision alarm."

The bridge crew rushed to follow Franklin's orders. The alarm rang throughout the carrier. *Valiant*'s bow inched to port, past the trawler's beam, toward its stern.

Separation between the two ships shrank: thirty yards … twenty.

"It's gonna be close," the OOD said.

"That son-of-a-bitch," Franklin muttered. "That Russian low-life son-of-a-bitch."

The trawler's engines kicked up a frothy wake, and the little vessel pulled away to starboard. As the space between the two ships widened, a sailor on the trawler's fantail looked up at *Valiant*'s bridge and gave an enthusiastic thumbs-up.

"Look at that," the OOD said, "he's giving us an atta-boy."

Franklin eased back onto his chair. "That's no atta-boy, Mr. Phillips. In Russia that gesture means *up yours*."

"That asshole."

"Concur. You have the conn, Mr. Phillips. Cancel the alarm then put us back on course and speed. I'll make the log entry."

California

The sun dipped into the Pacific as Pan Am Flight 607 from Hawaii came to a stop in its appointed slot at Los Angeles International Airport. Captain Grant Spanner, dressed in civvies, blended in with the well-tanned passengers who crowded the exits and then boiled out into the cavernous terminal. Spanner looked around until he spotted his brother leaning against one of the columns, away from the stampede.

"Hello, Henry," Spanner said. "Thanks for coming."

"No problem, Grant. Look, I feel terrible about Robin. I tried to make her happy here, I really did."

Henry scrunched up his nose.

The scrunching annoyed the hell out of Spanner, it always had, but he suppressed the urge to criticize and instead, Spanner put a hand on his brother's shoulder. "I know you did your best, Henry. Any idea why she left?"

"Not a clue. Not a damn clue. Oh, we had some arguments, but none I thought were real serious. And she seemed happy at USC."

"Apparently not. Any idea where she went?"

"I talked to several kids on campus, one of whom knew Robin at least a little bit. They tell me that almost all runaways these days go to a place called Haight-Ashbury in San Francisco. A hippie hangout. Ever hear of it?"

"Nope. You know the place?"

"I found it on a map I bought."

"Show me."

"The map's in my car. Let's get your luggage and go to my place; we can drive up to San Francisco tomorrow if you want. You eat on the plane?"

"No. Pick a restaurant on the way to your house. You still have my old sea chest in your garage?"

"Of course. What do you need out of it?"

"My revolver."

"Jesus. You think you need that?"

"I might," Spanner said. "I hear military people aren't exactly welcome in San Francisco."

He walked off in the direction of the luggage claim area.

Chapter 15
Day Eight Continued

Yankee Station

Three A-6s went in before dawn, and a recce flight at daybreak reported two spans down on the southernmost bridge. Two hours later, CAG led the first alpha strike and subsequently claimed it dropped three spans on two of the northern bridges. The aircrews returning to *Valiant* from the second attack at noon reported a total of seven spans down. That meant a dozen were still up, honest work left for the day's third alpha strike.

Wolf Schumann's F-4B, on the far right flank of that force, was on the outside of the turn as it arced left around Haiphong en route to the roll-in point. That was fine with Wolf, the extra speed was nice to have. The poor guys on the inside of the turn must be slow, near to stalling out.

The F-4s each carried a centerline drop tank, six 750-pound M-117 bombs outboard on two TERs, four Sparrow radar-guided missiles in fuselage recesses, and four heat-seeking Sidewinders on the two inboard wing stations. Loaded for bear and ready for anything, they would hit the bridges then *yo-yo* high to take on any MIGs trying to hit the escaping strike force. If MIGs came early, the F-4s would jettison tanks and bombs, then start the dance. Enemy fighters had made feints at the two previous gaggles, so dogfights were a possibility.

"Pretty down there," Wolf said.

The afternoon sun glinted off the harbor. Little, puffy clouds pranced along the shoreline.

Joey said, "I forgot my camera. We'll have to go back for it."

"No problem, amigo. We'll be coming here again tomorrow."

Dark puffs of 85mm flak erupted below the strike force's altitude; then a second string rippled through the flight.

A voice called, "Uptown Three-zero-three is hit. Turning back."

An A-4 on the leader's left dropped down and banked hard toward the sea.

"Roger, Three-zero-three."

The strike leader's voice sounded flat, unemotional, as his A-4 dipped a wing and rolled into its dive. That awakened a beehive. Dozens of white 57mm flak puffs appeared, and the sky became laced with streams of tracers.

The SAM warning light flashed, but Wolf was too busy to worry about it. That was Joey's job now. He picked his target, the far span on the second bridge, and rolled in on it. Planes, tracers, and flak puffs filled the sky in front of him.

"Two SAMs at nine," Joey said. "Not on us."

An unfamiliar voice called, "Frank, you got a SAM ... SAM at five. Break right. Break right."

Wolf's bombsight pipper kissed the bridge, and he pickled. The six bombs rippled off in less than a second, and Wolf horsed back on the stick.

Another voice. "The north span is down. It's down."

"Uptowns are feet wet."

"This is Red Crown, bandits Bullseye zero-four-five, fifty. Repeat, multiple bandits, northeast of Bullseye."

"Rawhide One is down. Two good chutes. Two good chutes."

"Where ... over the water?"

"Negative ... negative. They're drifting into Haiphong."

The nose of Wolf's F-4 swept above the horizon, and he picked up his leader a quarter mile ahead in a hard right turn to meet the MIG threat. Wolf pickled off his empty drop tank and the two TERs.

"I'm set up for Sparrows, Joey. If they come out, we'll be closing head on."

"Got 'em on radar, ace."

"Don't get premature, smartass."

Wolf slid into combat cruise position on Reaper Lead as the black trail behind that aircraft, common to F-4s at hundred percent (military) power, disappeared; Reaper Lead had gone into afterburner. Wolf pushed his throttles around their detents, and his own twin burners kicked in. The two fighters raced west, climbing.

"This is Red Crown. The bandits have turned northwest. Repeat, the bandits have turned northwest."

"Damn it," Wolf said. "The chicken-shit, yellow bastards are running away."

Joey laughed. "You're surprised? Hell, if they can't do a sneak hit-and-run, they don't want to play anymore."

Reaper Lead turned back toward the water and Wolf followed.

Off to his right Wolf spotted a lone F-4 also heading home. The three fighters joined in a loose formation as they crossed the beach a few miles south of Haiphong.

A tall column of smoke rose from a strip of beach between two bridges. Wolf had good eyes and could tell it was the burning carcass of a Navy F-4, Rawhide One. He wondered who the crew was.

They were cruising west at twenty-six thousand feet above the South China Sea in 503, now returned to fighting form, when Terry asked, "What did you do last night?"

"Won ten bucks at the slots and had a good dinner," Mike said. He grinned behind his dangling oxygen mask.

"That's it?"

"Pretty much. You get through to your wife?"

"Eventually."

"Tell her about our swim?"

"Yeah. She cried. Judy worries about me, wants me out of the war."

"Let me guess ... then you sat down and wrote her a long letter explaining how you had to do your duty, but you'd be real careful."

"Kiss my grits, Mike."

Mike changed the TACAN (tactical-air-navigation) channel and the needle swung forty degrees right. "I've got Wigwam." He paused while the mileage indicator settled down. "It's three-four-zero at one-ninety-two miles."

Terry swung his radar cursor, paused then said, "Concur, and we're clear of Hainan Island, take steering." The computer-guided steering bug slewed around to agree with the TACAN needle.

With a tiny movement of the control stick, Mike turned 503 northwest. "I'm switching to strike control," he said. "Let's see if anything's going on."

He re-set the UHF frequency and got a few seconds of hiss then—

"Frank, you got a SAM ... SAM at five. Break right. Break right."

"The north span is down. It's down."

"Uptowns are feet wet."

"Jesus," Mike said. "They're hitting the bridges. Listen."

More hissing then, "This is Red Crown, bandits Bullseye zero-four-five, fifty. Repeat, multiple bandits, northeast of Bullseye."

"They've got MIGs up," Terry said. "Must be big."

"It is," Mike whooped. "Remember, I told you this was coming. We've been turned loose on the Haiphong bridges."

Hissing again then, "Rawhide One is down. Two good chutes."

"Where ... over the water?"

"Negative ... negative. They're drifting into Haiphong."

Mike glanced at the clock. "If they haven't changed the cycle times, we have a recovery in twenty minutes. I'm switching to approach." He selected a new radio channel. "Wigwam, Wigwam, this is Banner Five-zero-three for Charlie."

After a few seconds the radio responded. "Banner Five-zero-three, can you hold until the strike is aboard?"

"Roger. We're fat."

They orbited the carrier at fifteen thousand feet and watched as the returning strike circled to land, fighters first, then the attack aircraft. The Russian trawler maneuvered close to the carrier.

"That Russkie is mucking up the works again," Mike said. "Look, the carrier did a ziggy by the bastard and two planes had to go around."

"A ziggy?"

"Half an octoflugeron."

"I see."

The radio cut in. "Banner Five-zero-three, your signal is Charlie following the whale."

"Wilco," Mike said. "You got the A-Three in sight, Terry?"

"Yeah, he's low off to the right. You going to dump some fuel? We're heavy."

Mike asked, "Can you see that Russian trawler?"

"Yeah, I see him. He's about to pass down the carrier's port side. He shouldn't interfere with our landing."

"Wigwam, this is Banner Five-zero-three. Request a low pass down the port side to get rid of some fuel."

"Stand by, Banner."

Terry laughed. "You going to do what I think you are?"

"I don't know what you mean."

"Banner, you are cleared for a low pass."

"Roger that."

The A-6 leveled out at three hundred knots, flight deck level and close aboard the carrier's port side. As the Russian trawler disappeared under the aircraft's nose, Mike hit the fuel dump switch and two hundred gallons of jet fuel sprayed across the length and breadth of the little spy ship below.

Spud Franklin broke into great guffaws of laughter. Jet fuel stained every inch of the trawler standing off the port beam, and liquid fuel sloshed in its bilges. Every Russian on board scrambled about the deck, trying to clean off the fuel before some electrical charge ignited it.

"Mr. Phillips, you have to see this. Come over here."

"Yes, sir." The OOD moved over behind the captain's chair to look out the port side of the bridge. "Damn," he said. "That is sweet."

Franklin nodded in agreement. Then it occurred to him: he was going to have to write up a good explanation of the *accident* to send over to the admiral. The Russians would undoubtedly file some sort of protest with the state department.

Tony Romano took it all in: the city of Haiphong nestled on the northeast corner of the Red River delta amid a maze of rivers and water channels, Cat Bi airfield to the south, and Halong Bay to the north. The bridges that tied the port to the mainland were easy to see, though it was hard to tell at this distance which spans were up and which were down. The strike force, still twenty miles away, began a sweeping turn to the west taking them to the far side of the port.

Romano's A-4 was one of two Iron Hand aircraft on the sixteen-plane strike. He and his wingman both carried a centerline drop tank and four AGM-45 Shrike missiles, one on each wing station. Their job: suppress the Fan Song and Fire Can radars in order to protect the strike birds from radar-guided missiles and antiaircraft fire. Actually killing an enemy radar site would be a bonus.

The strike leader, Uptown One, called, "Buster." The attack began.

Four F-4s went into afterburner. Two of them pointed their noses up, headed for twenty thousand feet, ready to take on any enemy aircraft heading for the target area. The other two F-4s raced ahead of the main force to throw cluster bombs at two SAM sites that fired on the previous alpha strike.

All ten attack planes continued to arc around Haiphong, heading for a roll-in point northwest of the port. Sporadic puffs of 85mm flak escorted them.

Arming his missiles, Romano went to max power and climbed above the strike force. His wingman followed.

The A-4's radar warning system went to full alert without the usual search-mode preliminaries. The plastic rectangle mounted on the instrument panel flashed bright red, and *deduldeduldedul* shrieked in his headset. The North Vietnamese knew where they were and what was coming; they'd gone straight into launch mode.

Romano pulled the nose of his A-4E thirty degrees above the horizon and fired the first Shrike. The missile, an AIM-7E Sparrow rocket body melded with a 66.5 kg blast-fragmentation warhead, roared ahead of the plane in an arc leading to the target area. Once the missile's nose fell through the horizon, its seeker head would home in on the first radar emitter it found and send guidance signals to tiny wings on the rocket body. The missile was designed to aim itself at transmitting radar sites.

He fired another Shrike then lowered the A-4's nose to regain airspeed. His radar warning system went silent; the local radars shut down to evade the Shrikes.

Both missiles, now with no radar signal to home on, would go ballistic and detonate in some farmer's field. But the bombers rolling in on their targets were not molested by SAMs, and that was the point.

Nothing suppressed the flak. Dozens of guns opened up on the dive bombers. Tracers and white puffs filled the sky over the bridges.

Several Vietnamese radars came back up as the strike force pulled off target, so Romano lofted his two remaining Shrikes into the fray.

Despite the on-going Shrike threat, the North Vietnamese launched two SAMs against the retreating pack of airplanes. One missile went ballistic, possibly because its guidance radar was shut down or struck; the second SAM plucked an A-4 from the sky.

Romano watched as the crippled plane rolled over and plunged into the water a short distance from the beach. There was no parachute.

Uptown One called the flight feet wet.

Chapter 16
Day Nine

Vietnam

The moon snuck behind a low-hanging cloud and left Bowie feeling his way through darkness again, everything blurred shades of black and gray. He tripped over a dirt hummock and staggered. His left leg cramped and dropped him to the marshy ground. He lay still, sucking air through clenched teeth until the spasm passed. Exhausted, he felt no hurry to get back up.

Struggling erect, Bowie listened for the dull roar of distant surf. Putting the sound on his left, he moved forward, south. Somewhere down there were friendly troops.

At least he didn't have to run any more. Sometime between sunset and midnight the hunters passed him by. He heard them coming and stayed curled up in a hidey-hole until they were well past. Now he was behind the hunters, following them.

Bowie paused every so often to listen. He had never been aware of so many sounds. The flutter of wings in a distant tree, the rustle of some rodent maneuvering away from him through thick brush, and the far-off cry of some lonesome sea bird all registered. So did gunshots.

A firefight erupted, up ahead, inland a bit. Bowie paused to listen.

Independent rounds, perhaps exploratory, were soon joined by the frantic chatter of machine guns and the dull thud of grenades. Over the course of a minute, the sounds ratcheted up to a blurred crescendo before tapering off to the occasional crack of an individual rifle.

Then—silence.

It has to be a mile ahead, Bowie figured, *maybe more*. He didn't have a good sense for how the sounds of gunfire could be translated into distance; the only shots he'd ever heard were on a television set.

But the battle sounded like a clash between patrols, and one of the patrols must be on his side of the war. South Vietnamese or American, it didn't matter. Salvation was near—if he could reach it.

First he needed water. He searched out a flowering Nipa palm at dusk, as he'd learned to do at survival school, and broke off the stem. Chewing on it produced a bit of sweet liquid that soothed his tongue and throat, but it didn't satisfy his body's urgent demand for the real thing. He had to find water, and not the sludge that lurked in the mushy bottom land around him. He needed running water, on higher land, so he turned west and headed for the karst ridges a couple of miles inland.

Washington, D.C.

The latch on Jason Fox's office door clicked, followed by the soft swish of wood against thick carpet. Jason waited for the next swish and click ... it told him the door was closed again.

He stood in front of his office window for several minutes and didn't turn away now, preferring to keep his eyes focused on the slice of Washington, D.C. that lay outstretched before him on this autumn afternoon. The leaves were turning, a beautiful time of year.

Jason waited a moment then said, "Well, Annie, how'd it go?"

No answer. Just the crinkle of leather. She'd sat in one of the guest chairs in front of his desk. *Weak? Fainting? Sweet Jesus, the quack had botched the abortion.*

He spun around.

Annie was slumped in one of the chairs. *She looks*, Jason thought, *like she's a melting ice-cream cone, sagging and about to puddle.*

"Mah God, Annie."

Jason went around the desk and knelt on one knee next to the chair. Annie's near hand dangled next to him, and Jason took it. It felt cold.

"Want me to call a doctor, Annie? Somethin' to drink? Ah'll get you a glass of watah."

He rose and moved toward the door.

In a tiny voice, Annie said, "I couldn't do it."

"What?"

Her voice stronger now, she said, "I couldn't go through with it."

Retreating behind his desk, Jason eased into his high-backed chair, and stared at her. "You didn't have the abortion?"

Annie shook her head.

"Why not? Ah mean—"

"I want to have the baby, Jason. I want to keep it, with or without that damn redheaded goofball."

Jason leaned back in his chair, grinning. "That's great news. Ah knew you couldn't do that terrible thing. God wouldn't let you."

"I don't think God was anywhere near that place, Jason. I was on my own."

Two quick taps on the office door drew their attention.

The door opened far enough to admit Naomi's head, and her eyes flicked from Jason to Annie then back. "Sorry to interrupt."

Frowning, Jason snapped, "What is it?"

"There's a Navy officer out here says he has a message for Annie. You want me to have him wait?"

Annie sucked in an audible breath and, hand to mouth, sat up straight. She shook her head.

Jason said, "Send him in."

Naomi's head disappeared, the door swung open, and a tall man in the Navy's short-sleeve, white uniform entered the office. A manila folder in his left hand bore the word *SECRET* in red letters.

The door clicked shut behind him.

"Sorry to intrude," the officer said. "I'm Commander Breckenridge from the Congressional Liaison Office. We received a naval message from USS *Valiant* that includes a personal note for Miss Annie Hill. That you, ma'am?"

"Yes." Annie rose and stared at the commander. "What does it say? Is it about Roger? Is he okay?"

The commander smiled and pulled a sheet of paper from the folder. "Seems to be, ma'am. I'll read it to you. Being a naval message, it's pretty cryptic."

He moved a finger down the sheet until he came to the right place. "Here it is, 'Found your letter today. I love you both. Please marry me. Roger'."

Annie collapsed into the chair and began to cry.

Jason went around his desk again, pulled a silk handkerchief from the breast pocket of his suit coat, and handed it to Annie. Then he took the commander's elbow and steered him toward the door.

"Thank you, Commander. We appreciate your courtesy, but ah think the lady wants to be alone for a few minutes."

"I understand," the commander said, his voice hushed. But he paused by the door. "Tell me," he whispered, "any chance that hand grenade on the black lady's desk out there is a live one?"

Jason whispered back, "We don' know. Been afraid to ask."

He opened the door and walked the commander out into the anteroom. The door swished and clicked shut behind them.

Annie was alone.

Yankee Station

Terry slumped down into the ready-room chair next to Mike. "Why is the dawn patrol always so damn early?"

His attempt to stifle a yawn failed.

"Cheer up," Mike said. "The night raids yesterday caught the gomers with their pants down. Maybe we'll do the same."

"I doubt it." Terry looked around the empty ready room. "Why are we alone?"

"There's just one full-system bird up this morning."

"And of course you volunteered."

"Didn't have to, the skipper knew I wanted a piece of this action."

"Oh great. Who's doing the briefing?"

Lieutenant Commander McAuliffe answered the question by opening the door and strolling to the podium. "Top of the morning, troops."

"And the rest of the day to yourself," Mike said. "Why are we honored with the presence of the air wing AIO himself?"

"You're special ... the early-bird special."

"Wonderful," Mike said. "The other squadrons sending anyone?"

"VF-Sixty-One is sending up a couple of Phantoms in case the MIGs come out, and we'll have a whale on the cat if you need gas, but you shouldn't ... this'll be a quick in-and-out."

"Yeah, right," Terry said. "What's the target?"

"I'll show you." McAuliffe unrolled a chart of Haiphong harbor and tacked it to the cork board attached to the steel bulkhead behind the podium. He pointed at the second bridge from the south end of the complex. "This is your target. It's a steel-truss job, all girders, which explains why it's still a virgin."

"Oh good," Mike said. "I always wanted a virgin."

"You are a sick man," Terry said. "What are the coordinates?"

McAuliffe read them off then added, "Remember, these charts were made by Frenchies before the big war, and we already know they're a bit off."

"No problem," Terry said. "All I need are numbers to get the computer in the area. I'll take it from there with radar. That bridge should stand out like a turd in the punch bowl."

Mike snorted. "And you call me sick." He peered at the photo for a few seconds. "Okay, we'll run it going northwest, low all the way. That'll give us about thirty degrees off angle on the bridge. What's our load?"

"Nine Mark-eighty-threes," McAuliffe said. "Thousand pounders, retarded."

"Jesus," Mike said. "Somebody's thinking."

"Thank you," McAuliffe said. "But remember, minimum release altitude is five hundred feet. How you plan to come out?"

"High-g turn to the left. That'll keep us away from the city that everyone is so loathe to damage and put us back feet wet in about a minute."

"A very long minute," Terry said, busy writing numbers on his knee board.

"Could be," McAuliffe said. He tapped the chart again. "You'll be in range of about six missile sites we know of and twenty to thirty guns … mostly thirty-seven millimeters. Any questions?"

"Yeah," Terry said, looking up from his work, "you want to take my place on this one? Give you some good experience."

"You know, I'd love to," McAuliffe said, "but I failed the damn flight physical … no guts."

He turned and walked out of the room.

Haiphong loomed ahead and a bit right, lit only by floodlights on the oh-so-sacrosanct piers. The big lights exposed two ships offloading long crates. The rest of the immediate world was blacked out.

"Ten miles," Terry said. "Got a lock on the bridge. Steering's good."

The computer-driven bug on Mike's HSI quivered a couple of degrees to the right, and Mike eased the airplane over to center up his steering. He focused on the flight instruments in front of him; they were doing better than four hundred knots, fifty feet above the water. Black water in a black world.

"Nine miles," Terry said. "Master Arm is on," then he moved the arming switch.

"Roger hot."

The SAM warning light blinked, and the search-mode alert tone sounded its slow beat in their headsets. At this altitude the enemy radars would have a tough time locking them up. Even so, Mike eased the A-6 down until the radar altimeter registered forty feet.

"Seven miles," Terry said. "Fifty seconds to go."

The missile warning tone went to high warble. The red light on the instrument panel flashed through the black grease pencil markings Mike had smeared over it to keep the light from blinding him.

A bright white tail rose into the night sky ahead.

Mike said, "SAM up at one o'clock."

A ragged row of flashing lights appeared ahead and off to the right; then a dozen strings of 37mm tracer rounds sailed toward them in flat arcs. The orange balls fell short.

"Flaks up too," Mike said.

"Oh joy." Terry's head was buried under the hood shielding the radar scope, fingers tweaking the radar cursor to keep it centered on the bridge. "Four miles," he said. "Stepping into attack."

"Roger that."

The computer now calculated a new weapon release every few feet; when the new solution was worse than the last one, the computer would release the bombs.

Muzzle flashes filled an arc from ten o'clock to two; tracers flashed by both sides of the cockpit; white flashes from 57mm rounds rippled around them.

Terry raised his head. "Jesus." After a moment he said, "Remember to climb."

"Wait," Mike snapped. He glanced up. The missile arced over and came down at them. Mike's focus went back to the instruments in front of him.

"Call the SAM."

"It's tracking," Terry said. "Wait ... wait ... *pull!*"

Mike yanked the A-6 into a climb, then rolled inverted and pulled the plane back toward earth.

Trailing a fiery tail, the missile passed beneath them and detonated.

When the nose came down to the horizon, Mike rolled the plane right side up and corrected his heading. Steering centered, the radar altimeter read six hundred feet—enough.

Deduldeduldedul. The missile guidance warning tone continued to scream.

"SAM arcing at twelve," Terry called. "Another rising at two."

The airplane shuddered as the nine heavy bombs rippled off at millisecond intervals. Mike rolled the plane into a steep left bank and hauled back on the stick, pulling the A-6 into a high g, descending turn to the south.

A bright flash of light lit up their belly and the airplane shuddered.

They headed back at the water and Mike rolled out of the turn. He leveled off at two hundred feet on the altimeter and eased the plane downward.

"That last missile went ballistic," Terry said. "But I think we took a hit from the one before."

Flak chased them until they were well away from land. Then the night turned still and black again.

Mike keyed the UHF. "Red Crown, Red Crown, Banner Five-zero-five is feet wet, but I think we took a hit. We're checking."

"Roger that, Banner Five-zero-five. Your steer to Wigwam is one-two-two degrees, seventy-three miles."

A new voice popped up on UHF. "Banner Five-zero-five this is Rawhide One. I've got you on radar. Put your lights on. I'll join up, and give you a once over."

"Wilco," Mike said. He put the exterior lights on bright and steady as he started a gradual climb toward the ship.

A minute later two F-4s emerged out of the darkness and joined up on the port wing. After a few seconds, the fighters slid underneath and moved over to the starboard side.

"Well, Banner, you got some shrapnel damage to your belly and the underside of your port wing. You're losing a lot of fuel."

"Yeah," Mike said. "I can see the fuel gauge dropping."

"We'll stay with you."

"Copy that. Break. Wigwam, Wigwam, Banner Five-zero-five is declaring an emergency. We're going to need gas ... in a hurry."

"Wigwam copies, Banner. Launching Texaco."

Valiant's flight deck leaned as the big ship turned, seeking the wind.

"Stand by to launch the whale," blared out of the loudspeakers positioned high on the island and along the deck edge.

A frenzy of activity started around the A-3 tanker strapped to the number two catapult. The JBD rose from the deck as the first traces of exhaust fumes sailed backwards from the A-3's twin jets.

Aboard the tanker, Rick Rendell brought the two Pratt & Whitney J-57 engines up to idle, checked his instruments, and gave a thumbs-up to the cat officer standing near the starboard wingtip. In response to the immediate two-finger turn-up signal, Rendell rammed both throttles to full power, checked the gauges once more, and flicked on the exterior lights. Two seconds later the catapult fired Texaco 301 airborne.

CIC came up on strike frequency with, "Texaco, your target is Banner Five-zero-five, three-zero-zero degrees, fifty-two miles. He's leaking fuel."

"Copy that. Break. Banner Five-zero-five, what's your situation?"

"I figure we've got no more than ten minutes worth of gas. I'm losing more than I'm burning."

"Okay, Banner, soon as I see your lights I'll do a one eighty in front of you and stream the drogue."

"Roger that. You're going to have to pump me all the way home."

"Wilco. Stand by."

Mike spotted the tanker three minutes later. "I have you in sight, Texaco. I'm at your one o'clock high."

"Concur Five-zero-five, turning now. I'll be at five thousand feet, three hundred knots."

"Roger that," Mike said. He glanced at the fuel gauge again, then sat up straight and flexed his fingers. He keyed the ICS. "I'll have to nail the drogue first try. You got your prayer beads on you, Terry?"

"I have faith."

"Use the beads."

Playing with the throttles, Mike eased 505 up behind the tanker.

The refueling drogue, looking much like an oversized badminton bird, danced at the end of a thirty-foot black hose.

"Call my fuel state, Terry. I can't look right now."

"Four hundred pounds."

"Damn." Mike inched the throttles forward, pushed a tiny bit of right rudder and jammed the refueling probe mounted above the A-6's nose into the drogue.

"Contact," Rendell called from the tanker. "You're taking on fuel."

"Roger that," Mike answered. Then on the ICS, "What's it look like, Terry?"

"The fuel gauge is still sitting at four hundred pounds. It isn't moving."

"Wonderful."

"Could be worse."

Mike went back on UHF. "Okay, Texaco, we're losing as much as we're getting from you. You'll have to take us all the way."

"Wilco. The Fox Corpen is south. I'll set you up with a straight-in and take it down to half a mile. What speed you want on final?"

"Make it two hundred. I'll unplug, dirty up, and trap ... hopefully."

"You got it. Turning south now and starting my descent. Switching to Approach Control."

"Switching," Terry answered, changing the radio frequency.

Aboard *Valiant*, the flight deck crew raced to re-spot the six aircraft still fouling the landing area.

"Let's hustle, gang," the air boss said into his mike. "The low state A-Six is at ten miles. This will be a straight in. Set the arresting gear for state zero point four."

Approach Control came up two minutes later. "Texaco, you're at two miles, slightly above glide path."

"Roger. I'll drop the A-Six at half a mile."

"Copy that ... You're down and on glide path, Texaco. One mile."

On ICS, Mike asked, "What's the needle say, Terry?"

"Still four hundred."

"Wonderful."

"On glide path, Texaco. One-half mile."

"Drogue coming in," Rendell reported. "You're on your own, Five-zero-five."

The drogue popped off the refueling probe and snaked up into the airplane's belly as the tanker turned away.

Mike extended the speed brakes, slammed the gear handle down, set the flaps, and concentrated on his approach. The airplane bucked a bit as it changed configuration.

"You're below glide path, Banner. Quarter mile, call the ball."

"Intruder ball," Terry called. "Three hundred pounds." On the ICS he said, "Three down and locked, Mike. We're good."

"Wonderful."

They caught the second wire. The engines flamed out before they could taxi clear of the landing area.

Chapter 17
Day Nine Continued

Vietnam

Dawn light splashed against the karst ridge in front of Bowie and revealed a trickle of water cascading down a steep rock slab, coming from higher ground—cleaner places. Bowie grinned as he positioned the mouth of the empty canteen under a tiny waterfall. No need to search further, this was as good as it was going to get.

Bowie didn't wait for the canteen to fill up. At half full, Bowie tipped the canteen to his lips and drank. When he brought the empty canteen down to refill it, he found himself staring at a shabbily dressed man, a Vietnamese peasant—holding a machete.

The man stared at Bowie as if he were some alien creature dropped from the sky or belched up from the earth. The tip of his machete, held waist high, made tiny figure eights between the two men.

A farmer, Bowie judged, now scared by the first green-clad black man he had ever seen. *Yeah, but a farmer with a machete.* Moving with care, Bowie raised both arms high above his head and spread them apart, growing larger. Then, with a sharp intake of breath, he roared like a bear.

The farmer turned and ran.

Exhausted, Bowie sat down on a piece of karst. He watched the farmer until the man disappeared into a patch of trees.

Yankee Station

Commander Ralph Spencer, VF-62's CO, call sign Reaper One, led his flight of two F-4Bs along the North Vietnamese coast, staying over water, out of SAM range. Loitering at twenty thousand feet, their mission was BARCAP (barrier combat air patrol). MIGs had made several feints toward Haiphong recently and Reaper flight's job was to take on any enemy aircraft that ventured close to the Tonkin Gulf.

The F-4s were both armed with four AIM-7E Sparrows and four AIM-9D Sidewinders. Each plane carried three drop tanks.

Wolf Schumann, Reaper Two, maintained a combat cruise position a mile off Commander Spencer's starboard wing. Wolf's head swiveled as he looked for motion in the sky and checked his leader's six o'clock blind spot.

In the back seat, Joey Pritchett used the F-4's pulse-doppler radar to scan the airspace far ahead of them. The winner in air-to-air combat was usually the one who saw the enemy first, and as Joey often claimed, the sighting these days most likely occurred on a radar scope.

At the turnaround point, Spencer started a hard right turn into his wingman, so Wolf banked hard left. The two planes crossed and wound up heading south in the same relative position, Wolf once again on his leader's right.

Joey said, "Ten minutes before we start home. Didn't pick up any blips on radar during the turn. Looks like another dry run. No chance of a MIG kill this trip."

"Keep the faith," Wolf said. "I got a funny feeling today's the day. The weather's good ... the gomers will fly."

"Yeah, sure. You and your—"

"This is Red Crown! Bandits. Bandits. We hold multiple bandits, twenty miles east of Bullseye. Course one-two-zero."

Wolf yelled, "They're coming out to play."

Spencer responded over the UHF. "Roger, Red Crown, Reaper flight is on it," then he turned his fighter to meet the threat.

Wolf accelerated, turned hard right and climbed in order to stay inside his leader's turn. When Spencer leveled his wings, heading west, Wolf slid back down into cruise position and brought his power up to a hundred percent. Spencer's drop tanks tumbled seaward, and Wolf pickled off his own.

Crossing the beach, Spencer called "Reapers are feet dry," and the thin, black trail of smoke behind his F-4 disappeared.

Wolf pushed his own twin J-79s into burner.

The two fighters raced westward.

The hunt was on.

Fan Song radars picked them up and the radar-warning unit played its low-warble tune in the crew's headsets.

Wolf asked, "You see anything on the scope?"

"Stand by," Joey said. "Okay, I got two targets thirty miles dead ahead and another two well north of them."

"Which way the near ones moving?"

"Right at us. We'll meet head-to-head in about ninety seconds."

"Good. It'll be Sparrows in thirty seconds, Joey my boy."

"Remember we're supposed to visually ID the bastards before we shoot."

"Yeah, I know. But Spencer has great eyes. If he shoots, we'll fire a—"

Deduldeduldedul.

"Damn," Wolf said, his head swiveling. "SAM launch."

Joey's head popped up from the radar scope. "I see it. Seven o'clock low. Going for the skipper."

"Reaper One," Wolf shouted on UHF. "Break left. Break left. You got a SAM at seven."

Spencer's F-4 slammed into a hard left turn then reversed as the telephone-pole-size missile soared past and detonated a hundred feet too high, its lethal fragments flying up and harmlessly away. Spencer steadied up on a westerly course, Wolf still wide abeam.

Thirty seconds later Spencer spotted the MIGs. "Talley ho. Two Frescos. They're dropping tanks and turning south."

He banked hard left, going for the MIG's six o'clock.

Unable to turn inside, Wolf fell into a trailing position.

"Reaper One, this is Red Crown. We hold two bandits ahead of you and two bandits coming up behind."

"Roger that," Spencer radioed.

Joey said, "I have the Frescos on radar. They're at three miles. Either one's a good Sparrow shot."

"Can't," Wolf said. "Spencer's in the way."

"We got two MIGs coming up our ass, Wolf. Better hurry."

"I know." *Come on, Spencer, shoot.*

Spencer called, "Fox One," and a smoke plume traced his Sparrow shot at the leftmost MIG, the leader.

Wolf watched as Spencer's missile tracked the lead MIG. At the last second, both MIGs broke hard right and down—the missile missed. Instantly, the MIGs reversed, turning south again, but closer now.

"I'm switching to Sidewinder," Wolf said, tracking the right-hand MIG.

"The range is good."

Within seconds Wolf got a headset tone, the IR missile sensed a heat source. *Was the source Reaper One? Come on, Spencer. Shit or get off the pot.*

"Reaper One, this is Red Crown. Two bandits fifteen miles at your six. Closing fast. Must be Fishbeds."

"Fox two," Spencer called.

A Sidewinder streaked away from his plane toward the lead MIG, and Spencer yanked his aircraft up into a climbing turn.

Wolf fired. "Fox two." His Sidewinder corkscrewed then settled down for its race to the second MIG.

The lead MIG broke right, crossing in front of his wingman, who turned with him. Both Sidewinders followed the MIGs into their turn.

"Come on," Wolf muttered.

The trailing MIG's tail blew away in a small fireball. The doomed airplane pitched up and rolled. A moment later its canopy blew off. The pilot ejected as Wolf's fighter flashed past.

Spencer's voice roared over the radio. "Wolf, break left."

Wolf jerked his plane into a six-G left turn. A missile detonated behind him; fragments pinged against his plane's belly.

"Reaper One's well above us," Joey called. "Coming down and left."

"Got him."

Wolf held his tight turn, sliding into a loose position off Spencer's wing.

"We took some dings," Wolf said. "We lose anything important?"

"Don't ... think ... so. And I've got nothing on radar now."

"That's 'cause we have two Fishbeds off to starboard," Wolf said. "They're diving for the deck and bugging out."

"Reaper One, this is Red Crown. I hold three bandits heading northwest and an Air Force strike coming in from the southwest."

"Roger that," Spencer answered. "We smoked one of the Frescos, and the two Fishbeds did their typical blow-through."

Reaper One turned southeast and came out of afterburner. Wolf followed.

"Whoee," Joey said over the ICS. "That was fun. Who got the kill?"

"We did," Wolf replied. "Spencer's missile split the difference and went between the two MIGs. No doubt about it, amigo. It's our kill."

The two F-4s went into a *Thatch weave*, doing gentle turns in opposition to make a weaving pattern through the sky, each pilot checking the other's six o'clock.

Crossing the beach, Spencer came up on UHF. "Reapers are feet wet."

"This is Red Crown. We confirm one MIG down. Good work."

Wolf and Joey entered the debrief room in time to hear Commander Spencer tell the Intel debriefer, "Yeah, I smoked that Fresco. A Sidewinder right up his ass. Wolf will confirm my kill."

Spencer turned and stared at Wolf. "Won't you, Lieutenant?"

"Sir?" *He's got to be shitting me.*

"Won't you, Lieutenant?"

"Yes ... sir," Wolf said. "Right up the ass."

California

The Chevy pulled over onto Haight Street's unpaved shoulder and coasted to a stop. Henry Spanner let the motor idle for a moment before he turned it off.

"This must be it," he said. "Buena Vista Park." Henry waved his left arm out the driver's open window. "This is what they call Haight-Ashbury. Hippie heaven."

He tucked his map away and stared at the scene before them.

"Jesus," Grant said, "look at those kids. Must be a hundred of them. They look like grunion flopping around on a beach." He sucked in a deep breath and coughed. "And get a whiff of that air. Don't breathe too deep or you won't be able to drive."

"This may come as a shock to you, Grant, straight-laced naval officer that you are, but I've smoked a bit of the weed myself."

"I'm not easily shocked anymore, Henry. And given the people you hang out with, I'm not even surprised."

Henry turned and stared at his brother. "What do you mean by that crack?"

"Haven't you noticed? They're a bunch of queers."

Swallowing hard, Henry said, "They ... we ... prefer the term *gay*."

Now Grant stared. "I see."

"Do you, Grant? I thought you'd have figured it out long ago. The bachelor brother who didn't date much. How'd you miss it?"

"Never paid much attention, I guess. It's not important."

"Yeah, Grant, it is. We need to get this cleared up between us."

"Look, Henry. I'm quite familiar with homosexuality. God knows we have enough of it in the Navy. Matter of fact, the agents of the Naval Investigative Service are called queer chasers ... behind their backs, of course."

Henry pushed open the driver's door and got out. He stood for a couple of seconds then slammed the door and went to a nearby tree.

Three teenagers lounging nearby rose and moved away.

"I'm not a cop," Henry called after them. Then, much softer, he said, "Just an old queer."

He sat down and put his back against the tree.

Grant walked over and sat cross-legged in front of his brother. "I'm sorry, Henry. I guess I didn't react all that well. You're right ... I should have figured it out. Hell, I should have been supportive, you're my brother. Truce?"

He held out his hand.

Henry paused, then reached out and shook his brother's hand. "I'd hug you, but you'd—"

"Don't be an ass, Henry. Now, what say we get on with the search?" He released Henry's hand and stood up. "I've got a dozen copies of Robin's latest photo in the car. Let's see if any of these potheads remember seeing her."

Yankee Station

Roger said, "Okay troops, here's my second column."

He settled onto an empty wardroom chair and laid a typewritten sheet of paper next to Terry's dinner plate.

Terry glanced down at the document while pushing a forkful of mashed potatoes into his mouth. A tiny bit of potato escaped the fork and fell onto one corner of Roger's paper.

Mike, seated across the table, stopped mopping up gravy remains with a piece of bread. "You look like hell, Roger. Is writing that difficult?"

"I've had trouble sleeping. Personal problem."

"Crabs or cooties?"

"Neither, thank you. I have a girlfriend back—"

"Ah, the ultimate problem," Terry said, focusing on his potatoes.

Mike reached across the table and tapped Roger's column with his fork. "What's it say?"

A small bit of gravy attached itself to the paper next to the potato droplet.

Terry sighed, turned to the paper, and read it out loud.

"Quote ... Aboard USS *Valiant* in the Tonkin Gulf, by Roger Brackett.

"Those few Americans who have an idea of what it's like to fly off an aircraft carrier and attack enemy targets probably gained that understanding from a nineteen fifty-four movie ... *The Bridges at Toko-Ri*. In it, Navy pilots have to risk everything to destroy a set of well-defended bridges the enemy needs to perpetuate its aggression.

"The movie was based on a true story ... life had become art.

"In the film, Bill Holden succeeds in dropping his bridge, but his jet is hit by shrapnel and is leaking fuel. Holden tries to make it back to the relative safety of the open sea, but he can't quite clear the last ridgeline. He crash lands on a barren piece of Korean dirt where he and the crew of a rescue helicopter die in a hail of communist gunfire.

"Early this morning, before dawn, the crew of a Navy A-Six off USS *Valiant* struck one of the bridges in a complex called, not Toko-Ri, but Haiphong, another unfamiliar name in yet another likely pointless Asian war. They too took a hit and tried to nurse their shrapnel-damaged plane to safety as it spewed fuel into the night air. This time the effort succeeded.

"In a feat that technology didn't allow in the Korean War, a jet tanker blasted off the carrier, met the inbound plane, and pumped gas into the crippled bird all the way to the carrier's ramp. The wounded A-Six landed with less than a minute's worth of fuel remaining.

"Sometimes when life becomes art, art then returns the favor. But not this time ... unquote."

Terry handed the paper back to Roger. "Looks okay to me, but I don't think our Government is going to appreciate your use of the term pointless Asian war."

Roger laughed. "Sorry 'bout that. My editor will love it, and that's what counts."

"Okay," Mike said. "Send it."

Chapter 18
Day Ten

California

The screen door to the porch jerked open and Charley's frail body appeared in the dark opening. Back-lit by a nearby streetlight, he appeared almost as an apparition.

"Hey, little bird. You got any money in that blue purse of yours?"

Robin said, "You got the last of it yesterday."

"Shit." He let the door bang shut behind him and strode over to the chest of drawers parked against one wall. He yanked open the top drawer and searched under a stack of magazines. "Come on," he said. "You too, Raven. Get your dead asses off the couch. You're coming with me."

Raven didn't move. "Where?"

"Where there's money. I'm tired of this shitty town. We're going to L.A. and we need travel money. Come on."

He pulled a switchblade knife out of the drawer and flipped it open. He ran a thumb along the blade then closed the knife and stuck it in his hip pocket.

"I'm not going anywhere," Robin said. She put her lit cigarette down in an already-full ashtray and stood up. "I like it here."

Charley turned and slapped her—hard.

Robin fell against the scarred coffee table and banged her head. Dazed, she sat up rubbing the side of her throbbing head.

"Get up," Charley ordered. The knife appeared in his hand, and the blade sprang open with a soft *click*. "Get up you little bitch or I'll cut you."

Stepping to Charley's side, Raven put a hand on his arm. "Come on, Charley, she didn't mean anything. We'll do what you say." She took Robin's hand and tried to pull her up. "That's right, isn't it, Robin?"

"I—" Robin struggled to her feet using Raven's hand and the coffee table for support. Still unsteady, she nodded and in a very small voice said, "Yes."

"Okay then," Charley said. He closed the knife and put it back into his hip pocket. "But don't ever talk back to me again, you understand?"

Robin whispered, "Yes."

Charley picked Robin's cigarette out of the ashtray, stuck it into the corner of his mouth and strutted toward the door.

Raven and Robin followed.

Robin stood a bit behind Raven, closer to the alley's entrance. They both watched the doorway to Hooligan's Bar across the street. Several men came out in pairs or groups and went on their way.

Charley was waiting for a loner.

The loner came out at eleven thirty, tripped and caught a lamppost for support. The man stared at the two women standing near the alleyway across the street. He gave a little wave and came over to them.

"Hello, pretty girls. Whatcha doin' out here so late? Lonesome?"

Raven said, "Waiting for someone."

"For me?"

Charley stepped out of the dark alley and put his knife blade against the man's throat. "Yeah, sucker. For you. Don't move or I'll cut you." Charley's free hand found the man's wallet and took it. "Now, get that ring off."

"That's my wedding ring. Please don't take it."

The blade pressed against the man's flesh. "Do it."

A trickle of blood oozed out of the man's neck. "Okay, okay. Please don't hurt me. Please."

He struggled with the ring.

Once the ring slipped over the man's knuckle, Charley yanked it the rest of the way. He slipped the ring onto his own finger then stepped away from his victim. "Now, you—"

A police squad car rolled around the corner fifty yards away.

Charley snapped, "Get back into the alley."

The two girls backed into the shadows.

Grabbing his victim's jacket collar, Charley tried to pull the man along, but the victim broke free and stumbled into the street, waving his arms at the police car. "Help me ... help me ... I've been robbed."

The squad car swerved and braked to a stop, its headlights aided by a spotlight that blossomed and pivoted toward the alley entrance.

Charley yelled, "Run," and ran past the two girls, disappearing into the dark alley.

The spotlight found Raven and Robin, throwing tall shadows against the brick wall behind them. A cop appeared on the far side of the squad car, gun drawn.

He sprawled across the hood, aimed his weapon at the girls, and yelled, "Freeze."

Both girls froze.

Raven swore to herself.

Large tears ran down Robin's ashen face.

Yankee Station

Commander Jansen tacked a large chart up on the corkboard at the front of the VA-66 ready room. The assembled aircrews could see over their CO's shoulder that the map depicted the broad swath of mountains where North Vietnam met China. The wavy border separating the two countries was highlighted on the chart with yellow marker.

Jansen stepped back, and it was possible to see that two black lines bracketed a railroad track; it came out of China and meandered down a narrow canyon leading to the delta and Hanoi. A small black circle surrounded a bridge on the rail line just a few miles south of the Chinese border.

"That," Jansen said, tapping the bridge with a wooden pointer, "is our target this afternoon."

He paused as a ripple of chatter spread around the room. "Note the target's proximity to China ... three miles. That's one hell of a lot less than twenty-five, and I've been informed that this mission has the personal interest of the President of the United States."

A voice from the back of the room asked, "Johnson?"

Titters of laughter followed.

"LBJ himself," Jansen said. "The President thinks now is a good time to take out that railroad bridge while all the attention is focused on Haiphong." He paused, a grimace on his face. "And I understand he's going to be up on our strike frequency, listening."

Someone asked, "Why?"

"So if anyone bombs China, the President knows who to have the CIA kill."

Nobody laughed.

"Okay," Jansen said, "let's get on with it. We'll have four A-Sixes with ten Mark-eighty-threes apiece as strike birds and two F-Fours from each fighter squadron flying cover for us."

Another voice. "Why no A-Fours?"

"The FRAG (Fragmentary) order called for A-Sixes and F-Fours. Could be because we can go faster than the A-Fours, but I'm guessing it's because the President likes our navigation capabilities."

"Lucky us."

The strike leveled off at seventeen thousand feet and went feet dry well north of Haiphong. Jansen set up a slight weave to keep some 85mm gunner from getting in a lucky shot.

Mike, flying as Jansen's wingman, cruised a few hundred feet to the right and slightly behind the strike leader. The other section of A-6s was off to their left several hundred yards in a modified combat spread. The fighter planes flanked them a couple of thousand feet higher.

On ICS, Mike asked, "How far to the Chinese border?"

Terry checked his computer. "It's about fifteen miles north of us, but we're getting closer to it all the time. Three minutes to target."

Two minutes later the bridge came into view, tucked down in a canyon. Mike leaned forward to get a better view as the flight descended to fourteen thousand feet. Another steel-truss job.

A stream of static erupted over the UHF, followed by a cough and then, "Banner Lead, this is your President. How far y'all from the target now?"

Terry said over the ICS, "Crissakes ... that's LBJ all right."

Jansen answered on the UHF. "We're approaching it now, Mr. President."

"Y'all sure you're on the south side of that damn border?"

"Yes, sir. I'm certain."

"Good. I want y'all to make your runs parallel to the border, one plane at a time."

"Sir, that'll give the enemy a—"

"I said one plane at a time. And make damn sure nothin' crosses that border into China, understand?"

"Yes, sir."

"And how many bombs y'all gonna drop at a time?"

"Ten, sir."

"Ten? That's too many. You drop one or two at a time, hear?"

"Yes, sir. Okay Banner flight, string it out. Set up a racetrack pattern like you would at a practice range. Make your runs to the west, parallel to the border. Drop two at a time. Check in to confirm."

"Two."

"Three."

"Four."

"Lead roger. We're at the target, Mr. President. I'm rolling in for the first run now."

"Terrance, this is the dumbest thing I've heard of," Mike said. "Check the Master Arm on."

Terry moved the Master Arm switch. "We're hot. You know, at least it's quiet up here. No sign at all of flak or SAMs."

Mike said, "Watch out for MIGs," then rolled into his dive and focused on the bombsight as its pipper tracked across the autumn landscape toward the bridge.

Jansen's two hits blanketed the bridge in a cloud of debris. The hanging dust indicated calm surface winds, and Mike took that into account.

Watching the altimeter unwind, Terry called, "Seven thousand ... six thousand ... five thousand."

Mike pickled and pulled out of the dive as their bombs arced across the chasm and into the dust cloud masking the bridge. He started a climbing turn to the left to join the racetrack pattern behind Jansen.

President Johnson said, "Well ... Y'all hit anything yet?"

"Hard to tell, Mr. President, there's too much dirt and rock in the air to see the bridge right now."

"Well, y'all keep poundin' it, heah? I got important *bizness* elsewhere. An' be damn sure y'all don't sling any bombs into China. All I need now is another goddamn war on mah hands."

An audible click was followed by a moment of quiet static and then silence.

Ten minutes later Jansen dropped his last two bombs then called "Winchester," and went into a final circle around the bridge at fourteen thousand feet. The other three A-6s came up off their final runs and cut inside Jansen's turn radius to rendezvous.

Terry asked, "Can you see the bridge from your side?"

"Yeah. The dust has pretty much blown away."

"Is it down?"

"I think so," Mike said. "Hard to say. You know how those steel-truss bridges are."

"Yeah, I do. What a goat screw this war is."

The strike took up an easterly heading and climbed. The four fighters did a protective weave overhead in case any MIGs showed up.

After several minutes of silence, Terry said, "I'm thinking of quitting."

"After your tour's up?"

"No. Right now."

"You're kidding."

"Dead serious. Like I told you, Judy's afraid I'll get killed and leave her alone with the baby."

"Terry, that's normal. All the wives are ... well, maybe not mine."

"I don't know, Mike. If this was—"

"A necessary war?"

"Something like that." Terry stared at the terrain drifting by far below. "At least we got a nice view of the fall foliage today. It's sure pretty up here. Like the Appalachians."

Vietnam

Bowie spent the entire day lying in a crevice partway up a thumb of limestone that provided a view of the terrain to the south. He gambled by moving in daylight after the encounter with the farmer, but he figured to distance himself from that place in case the man brought back friends—armed friends—to see the green-black bear.

He awoke at sunset feeling refreshed. He was hungry, but that wasn't much of a problem. He'd learned at survival school that a man could go for more than a week without food before it caused serious problems. Three days was nothing. And now he had a full canteen. He drank, then squandered a bit of water washing the grime from his eyelids and ears.

Once darkness settled in, Bowie scrambled about on the rock to improve his position, then sat still, listening with his newly developed auditory skills. Rustling in some trees a good hundred yards away was likely a bird. Scratching sounds farther up his personal piece of karst had to be a beetle. Then he heard a civilized sound: sporadic small-arms fire.

Bowie made his way down the rock, paused to listen again, then headed south at a trot.

The moon burped out of the Tonkin Gulf at what Bowie figured was about 0300. It was a mixed blessing. He was close to the action now, maybe too close with the moon up, but his immediate choices were limited. He decided to seek cover and hope the skirmish lines, if that was what they were, moved north and rolled past him. He found a shallow depression and covered himself with broken branches.

Twenty minutes later a dozen dark figures emerged from the tree line fifty yards to the south. They moved closer, fanning out. Their *black pajamas* identified them: Viet Cong.

Damn. Bowie began to sweat. He tried to make himself smaller.

Fifteen yards away, the advancing men went to ground. One of them took cover behind a dirt hummock then pulled two hand grenades from a pouch and set them on the ground next to his right hand. The other sprawled behind what appeared to be a large ant hill. This one lay his rifle in front of him and aimed it at the tree line. Then they waited.

All of them waited.

The minutes dragged on for Bowie. His leg itched. A bead of sweat dribbled off the bridge of his nose into his left eye and stung like hell. He didn't move.

The nearest VC did. In slow motion, the man reached back and scratched his ass.

Bowie had to smile despite the situation. Then he heard the rustling of branches. Whoever was coming was here.

A moment later a soldier in camouflage emerged from the trees and knelt on a knee. He stayed in that position for a few seconds then rose and motioned those behind him to come on. A U.S. Marine stepped into a swath of moonlight and was leading his men right into a VC trap.

Jumping up, Bowie screamed, "Ambush!"

The lead Marine dropped to the ground and a cacophony of small-arms fire erupted. Muzzle flashes turned the night blinding white.

The VC directly in front of Bowie twisted to face him and slung his rifle around. The muzzle winked even before the barrel finished its arc.

Bowie lunged sideways in an attempt to avoid the man's next shot and collided with a broken tree stump. He sprawled on his belly and looked up in time to see the VC's head splatter from a direct hit.

A dark shadow raced at him from the other side of the stump and Bowie rose to meet the charge. His last thought was surprise that the blow to his side didn't hurt.

After the fire fight, the Marine patrol moved into the kill zone and checked each of the black-clad bodies. One of the VC tried to rise and took a bullet to the chest for his trouble. A young black Marine moved to Bowie's side, rolled him over, and reared back in surprise.

"Jesus, Sarge. You gotta see this. We've killed a brother."

Virginia

Breakfast meeting with some constituents over, Jason Fox and Annie Hill stood in the doorway of an Arlington restaurant watching a mass of young people heading toward the Pentagon.

"Good God, Annie, look at them. They're like ants, all ovah the place. What in hell are they doin'?"

"They're protesting the war again, Jason. You know, that thing in Vietnam you support. Stopping the communist hordes and all."

"It was a rhetorical question, Annie. You don' have to be a smart-ass about it."

"Sorry, boss. I sympathize with them. Most of the males you see are draft bait and they're scared to death."

"One would think they'd be proud to serve."

"You didn't."

"Ah was too young for Korea ... and ah'm too old for this one. You know that, so quit tryin' to harass me."

"You're thirty-three, Jason. The Army won't draft you, but I bet they'd take you if you enlisted. Now *that* would demonstrate the depth of your support for the war."

Leading off toward the parking lot, Jason said. "Come on, we'll have to detour to get back to the office without bein' mobbed."

"I don't think they'll recognize your Grand Prix."

"They'll recognize me. Ah was on CBS news last week, remember? And mah picture's been in the Washington Post twice recently."

"You're right. I forgot you're a media personality now. Sorry."

"You really are becomin' a pain in the ass, Annie."

"I'm just in a good mood, Jason. I'll behave. Honest."

Jason held the passenger door open for her. "Ah guess ah'll have to give you some slack since you're goin' to be a mommy. When's the event?"

He walked around to the driver's side and got in.

Annie waited until Jason was seated then answered, "Next May, according to the doctors ... if nothing goes wrong."

"Nothin' will go wrong," Jason said.

He pulled out onto the street then stopped while a gaggle of scruffy-looking kids in tie-dyed shirts and torn jeans flowed past the car. One of them looked at Jason, grinned and made the V peace sign.

Grinning back, Jason answered with his middle finger.

Yankee Station

The little glowing hands on Terry's Navy-issue wristwatch told him it was almost midnight. He hadn't slept, and now he gave up.

Soft snores from the top rack told him Jeb was not having the same problem. The man could sleep through anything, and then after he ran through three or four songs on his guitar, he'd put the instrument back in its case and close his eyes. That was all it took. Nighty-night.

Terry slid out of bed, eased his pull-down desk open and sat on his gray-steel chair with the green plastic seat. He turned on the small desk light and pulled out his box of stationery. Paper and pen ready, he began to write.

Dearest Judy,

I can't—

Chapter 19
Day Eleven

California

Grant said, "Pull over here."

Henry brought the car to a stuttering stop on the gravel strip that bordered Buena Vista Park. "Look Grant, I think it's time we looked elsewhere. We've been combing through this love-fest for more than a day now and don't have a damn thing to show for it."

"She's somewhere around here," Grant said. "I'm sure of it. That sleaze-bag we talked to yesterday said he thought he'd seen her."

"He probably also saw pink dinosaurs. God, he was high. How do they function like that, the sex and everything? And can you imagine the diseases being spread around here?"

"You're not good for my morale, Henry. Let's hope we find Robin before it's too late. Come on … let's talk to that blonde surfer type leaning against the tree over there. At least he's vertical."

Grant crossed a small stretch of grass, Henry trotting to keep up, and stopped in front of the boy.

Maybe twenty, Grant thought. *Certainly no more. And wasting his miserable life. Why the hell isn't he in uniform?*

"Morning," Grant said, faking a smile. He held up Robin's photo. "Have you seen this girl?"

"Let's see your badge," the boy said.

"I'm not a cop. I'm her father."

"Oh." The boy pushed away from the tree, took the picture, and stared at it for a moment. "Yeah, man. I see the resemblance."

"Have you seen her?"

"Yeah. She hangs with a choice chick name of Raven. Robin and Raven. Bitchin' cool."

He handed the photo back.

"Where?"

The boy looked around. "Not here, man."

"Where does Raven live … man?"

The boy turned and pointed north. "Old yellow house two blocks over. Broken shutter. Can't miss it. Charley's place."

"Charley?"

"Yeah. He rents it. You gonna take Robin home?"

"Yes."

"Right on, dude."

The boy leaned back against the tree and stared off into space.

Grant turned to Henry with a broad smile. "Come on, Hank. Let's go get my baby girl."

He made long strides back toward the car.

Henry trotted alongside. "Hank? You haven't called me that in years."

"Well, if I can be a dude, you can be a Hank."

"Hate to tell you this, Grant, but dude is not a complimentary term. It means you're square, a geek ... someone not in the know."

"By God, the kid got that right."

The porch creaked, protesting the weight of the two men. Grant added to the assault by banging on the screen door.

The front door opened a crack, and one bleary eye looked out. A thin voice asked, "You a cop?"

"No. You Charley?"

"Why you want to know?"

"Humor me." Grant jerked open the screen door. "You Charley?"

The eye retreated a few inches. "Maybe. What you want?"

"I've come for Robin."

"Don't know any Robin, man."

The door closed and a lock clicked. Holding the screen aside, Grant raised one foot and kicked the door open. Old wood splintered, and the door banged against the inside wall. Charley sprawled on the floor.

Grant stalked into the room and stood over the man, glaring down at him. "You damn well do know her. Where is she?"

"Don't know, man." Charley stared at the legs in front of him. "She's gone."

"Gone where?"

Charley crabbed backwards, scrambled to his feet, and backed up against a dresser. One hand fidgeted against the open top drawer. "Left yesterday ... with Raven." His eyes wandered around the room, unfocused. "Said they were going to Hollywood."

"Hollywood? How?"

Giggling, Charley said, "Hitchhiking, man."

His right hand reached into the open drawer.

Close behind Grant, Henry said, "He's lying."

"Screw you," Charley said.

He pulled his switchblade from the drawer and flicked it open. His eyes focused now. The tip of the knife made little circles in front of Grant's face.

Henry stepped to one side, his brother's revolver in one hand. He cocked the gun and held it at arm's length, aimed at Charley's head.

"Drop the knife, asshole."

Grant stepped back. "Henry. What in—"

"Stay out of this, Grant."

Charley dropped the knife.

Henry leaned forward, the gun closer to Charley's head. "Now, *man*, where ... is ... Robin?"

"The cops have her." Charley sagged back against the dresser. "City cops."

"The cops? What for?"

"You'll have to ask them."

"Now I believe him," Henry said, stepping back a few feet, then easing the hammer down and lowering the revolver. "Let's go, Grant. You first."

A bit dazed, Grant backed to the door and stepped outside.

Henry stopped in the doorway and waved the gun in Charley's direction. "If the cops don't have her, asshole, I'll be back," then he turned and hurried down the porch stairs.

Grant was waiting. "Henry, I think I've been underestimating you. I left the gun in the glove compartment. Why'd you think to bring it?"

"Because," Henry said, "I've spent more time around scum than you have."

He handed the gun over, butt first.

"Daddy!" Robin ran across the small cell and hugged Grant Spanner through the bars. "I'm sorry ... I'm so sorry," she said, pressing her tear-streaked face against the bars, eyes closed and sobbing.

"I'm here, baby," Grant said. He reached through the bars and held her close. "Everything's going to be fine now." He kissed Robin on the forehead. "It'll be all right."

Henry stepped up alongside Grant and looked at the girl still curled up on a rack against the far wall. "You the one called Raven?"

Raven sat up. "Yes, sir."

"Okay," Henry said. He turned to Grant. "You stay here ... I'll go see about getting these two out on bail."

Yankee Station

Captain Franklin scanned the arc of sea off to port with his binoculars and chuckled. "Haven't seen much of that Russian trawler lately, have we, CAG?"

He let the binoculars drop down onto his chest.

"Nope," CAG said. "But he's just over the horizon. Saw the bastard out there last time I was up. Made a low pass over him and you should have seen the crew scramble to get under cover."

A sailor appeared in the hatch behind the captain's chair. He snapped to attention and said, "Permission to enter the bridge, sir?"

The OOD answered, "Permission granted."

Under the watchful eye of the Marine guard, the sailor stepped forward and handed the captain a message folder. Red stripes across it accentuated the TOP SECRET label.

"Thank you, Sparks. Does this need an answer?"

"No, sir."

"Very well. You can go."

"Aye aye, sir."

The sailor turned and left.

CAG moved aside while Franklin pulled the message from its folder and read it.

"Orders from the admiral," Franklin said. "*Valiant* is to extend ops today until twenty-two hundred then go to a new schedule, ten hundred to twenty-two hundred, starting tomorrow."

"That's odd," CAG said. "We're—"

"There's more. The Pentagon has ordered an immediate halt to any bombing within ten miles of Haiphong."

Franklin handed the message to CAG.

"Jesus Christ," CAG said. He scanned the message. "We finally got those buggers run out of missiles and ammo. *Now* is the time to pick those bridges to pieces, not stop."

"You have a strike going in any minute, don't you?"

"Yes, sir." CAG glanced at his wristwatch. "They should be rolling in right about now."

"Guess it's too late to call them off," Franklin said. "Oh well."

"Yeah. Sorry 'bout that." CAG stared off at the horizon for a moment. "I hope somebody up the line feels real bad about this."

"Amen."

"What an everlasting shame," CAG said. "We've lost three airplanes, three pilots and a RIO in the last few days, and for what? Yes, the bridges are closed, but not to the point where they can't be repaired in a few days."

"And the other carriers' losses have been even worse than ours," Franklin said. "How long you figure before Uncle Ho and company have the bridges up and running again?"

"Some in no more than a week," CAG said. "This order had to come from the President himself. Goddamn politicians."

"Can I gather from that remark the rumor is false; you're not related to Senator Stennis?"

CAG looked around then whispered, "You can, sir. But please don't pass that around. The rumor gives me an edge."

Franklin laughed. "I'll keep your secret, CAG. Now you better go change some target assignments."

"Aye aye, Captain. But my heart's not in it. Damn."

Roger spread his latest column out on the green felt and went over it again. His editor might nitpick the thing and screw it up, of course, but Roger liked his own version of perfection whenever he could get it.

> Aboard USS *Valiant* in the Tonkin Gulf
> by Roger Brackett
>
> I attended a burial at sea yesterday, a sad, magnificent, tragic event hewn from centuries of naval tradition. A young airman, Albert Crowder of Tuscaloosa, Alabama, was killed on *Valiant*'s flight

deck a few days ago when a nose wheel broke off a landing aircraft.

It's tempting to call it a freak accident, but that would be misleading. The ship is a monster of moving parts, most of them dangerous, and accidents are natural byproducts of human error and material weakness. So far this cruise, *Valiant*'s crew has suffered two deaths and seven serious injuries, not counting casualties attributable to the air war.

In this case, an F-4 fighter plane came aboard with its nose cocked off a trifle, too little to see without the benefit of the camera that records all landings. But the pilot's pass was a bit less than perfect, and the nose wheels suffered an unusual stress. One of them snapped off, sailed up the flight deck, and struck young Airman Crowder. The blow killed him.

It's also tempting to say that the dead man was merely in the wrong place at the wrong time. That, too, would be misleading; he was exactly where he was supposed to be, caring for one of the aircraft tied down on deck. Doing his duty.

USS *Valiant* is at war, and the captain decided that burial at sea was appropriate. So, at the appointed time, all operations ceased, and the ceremony took place on one of the huge elevators jutting out from the ship's side at hangar-deck level.

Representatives from every division and department were present in ranks on the hangar deck, looking crisp in the Navy's summer white uniform. An honor platoon made up of Airman Crowder's friends was in attendance, and a seven-Marine firing detail stood by on the elevator.

The ship's executive officer was in charge. At his signal, everyone was called to attention, and the ceremony began. The bosun's pipe sounded; then a deep, somber voice came over the ship's 1MC speaker system: "All hands bury the dead." Then, after a pause, "Half-mast the colors."

Four pallbearers brought Airman Albert Crowder's body to the elevator on a stretcher draped with the American flag, stars over the heart. They placed the stretcher on a bier located next to the deck's edge.

The ship's band played the Navy Hymn while a strong tenor sang the words:

> *Eternal Father, strong to save,*
> *Whose arm hath bound the restless wave.*
> *Who bids the mighty ocean deep,*
> *Its own appointed limits keep.*
> *Oh hear us when we cry to Thee,*
> *For those in peril on the sea.*
> *Amen.*

The ship's chaplain read from the scripture and then led a solemn prayer for the soul of the departed. When the chaplain was finished, the pallbearers tipped the stretcher seaward. The body, wrapped in white, slid off the stretcher, out from under the flag, into the blue ocean.

Weighted down, the body sank into the depths. As it descended, the chaplain read the benediction, the Marines fired a twenty-one gun salute, and a bugler in the band played taps.

I cried ... and was not alone.

Two members of the honor guard then folded the American flag into the familiar triangle and presented it to the captain. The flag and one of the shell casings from the gun salute will eventually be delivered to Mr. and Mrs. Crowder.

With that, the executive officer dismissed the detail, and USS *Valiant* went back to war.

Roger signed his name at the bottom, slid the few pages into a manila envelope, and made his way to the ship's post office.

Chapter 20
Day Eleven Continued

Yankee Station

Whenever the ship's business allowed, Captain Franklin made it a point to take his evening meal in Wardroom Two. He was surprised to find he liked the formality of the event, and it allowed him to get to know the officers serving under him.

The commanding officer, executive officer, and department heads all had traditional silver napkin rings with their position title engraved thereon in fancy script. The more junior officers also had silver napkin rings, but no engraving; their names appeared on a band of white tape that circled the ring.

According to custom, the rings were only used for the evening meal. Aboard *Valiant*, officers picked up their rings, napkins inserted, from the sideboard and placed them where they wanted to eat, with the result that friends and peers grouped together.

Franklin changed that, instructing the wardroom stewards to place a napkin and ring next to each plate on a random basis. This led to some confusion prior to dinner as officers searched for their rings, but it had the intended effect of forcing them to mingle. Senior officers found themselves chatting with ensigns and junior lieutenants whom they might otherwise never meet, especially in a nonworking environment.

And the captain insisted his own ring be included. But the *buck,* a tall silver goblet with gold naval aviator wings attached, was always placed next to the napkin ring with CO engraved on it. The buck marked the position to be served first, and the stewards well understood that democracy goes just so far on a naval vessel.

Tonight, over a dessert of plum pudding, Captain Franklin was regaling those near his dish with the story of how he got his nickname. The rapt, or maybe not so rapt, audience included the Catholic chaplain and the supply officer, both senior commanders, plus a junior lieutenant and two ensigns.

Captain Franklin described, in some detail, how the cockpit portion of his shattered plane slid up the deck into the *barricade*. He had to digress to explain the old straight-deck carriers had as many as thirteen cables followed by a large net to snag any plane that failed to catch one.

The ship's executive officer appeared at Franklin's elbow. "Excuse me, Captain, I need to speak to you."

"Privately?"

"Yes, sir."

"Very well," Franklin said. He made a wry face at his listeners. "Excuse me, gentlemen, it appears duty calls."

He rose and followed the XO out of the wardroom. Lance corporal Del Jackson, on duty as the captain's guard, left his position by the door and followed a few paces behind.

The XO paused in the passageway, looked around to make sure no one but the Marine guard was near, then said, "We appear to have a budding race riot on our hands."

"Oh damn it," Franklin said. "What's up?"

"I got a tip from one of the stewards. A small group of black sailors has gathered in the foc'sle, and they're plotting to beat up Seaman Frost, that white sailor Parker hit with the chipping hammer."

"In God's name, why?"

"Because, among other things, he called Parker a nigger."

"Yeah. I know."

"Apparently Seaman Frost is a racist loudmouth, and this group is out for some revenge. With your permission, I'll get a Marine detail and arrest them."

Franklin leaned back against the bulkhead and stared at his shoes for a moment.

"No," he said. "Go ahead and get your Marines, but keep them back from the foc'sle. "I want to head this off ... if I can."

"What do you have in mind, Captain?"

"I'm going to go talk to them."

"Alone?"

"I'll take the corporal here with me."

"Jesus, Captain. I don't know—"

"If things turn bad you can always bring in the rest of the Marines."

"If it isn't too late."

Franklin started up the passageway, heading for the bow. Corporal Del Jackson followed just three paces behind.

Two fore-and-aft passageways, one on the port side, one to starboard, ended at hatches leading into the ship's *forecastle* (foc'sle). This was a large space in the ship's bow containing two windlasses, one for each of the two huge anchors that hung out of the hawse pipes. Several yards of anchor chain lay on the deck with each chain leading from its windlass to an opening to the chain locker below. It was usually a quiet place, sometimes used for church services.

The starboard hatch was closed, but not dogged. Franklin pulled the steel door open. A single fluorescent light on the space's aft bulkhead lit the place in a dim glow, enough to disclose eight black sailors in Navy dungarees huddled beside the starboard windlass.

All eight sailors turned to face the hatch. One by one, they froze and became a tableau.

No one spoke.

The sound of aircraft being moved on the flight deck above blended with the slapping of the bow as it drove through the waves. Franklin stepped through the hatch, took several paces forward and stopped.

Corporal Jackson followed, then moved to one side and snapped, "Attention on deck."

Moving in slow, deliberate increments, the sailors came to positions approximating attention. Several fists clenched.

Franklin moved forward again until he was about ten feet from the first man then ordered, "At ease."

No one moved.

"Who's the leader here?"

The men stood still, eyes locked on the captain. No one spoke for several seconds.

Then a stocky man with the single chevron of a petty officer third class stenciled on his short-sleeve shirt stepped forward and in a low, husky voice said, "I am."

"What's your name, sailor?"

The man paused. "Roberts."

"Don't bullshit the captain. The stencil on your shirt says Robbins."

"That's what I meant."

"That's what I meant, SIR."

Several of the men stirred, one reached into a pocket.

Corporal Jackson put his right hand over the holstered .45 on his hip and moved enough so that most eyes shifted to him.

Robbins looked over his shoulder at the men behind him and shook his head. Turning back to Captain Franklin, he said, "That's what I meant ... sir."

"Good. I hear you men plan to beat up Seaman Frost. It upsets me if harm comes to one of my men. I think you can understand that."

Silence.

"Care to comment, Petty Officer Robbins?"

"No, sir."

"Then let me put it this way, if some men were to beat up Seaman Frost, what would be the reason?"

"That white racist asshole stood tall over Grover and called him a nigger. So Grover, he did what any righteous black man should do. But you sent the white asshole to sick bay and stuck the black man in the brig. And you call that justice."

"I see."

"I don't think you do ... sir."

"Yeah, I do. Seaman Frost isn't your real problem, I am. Back in the world you'd settle this in some dark alley. Black honor restored and everyone except poor Frost could feel justice had been served. But we aren't back in the world ... we're here ... where I am responsible for justice. You're right ... Seaman Frost does act like a racist. So do others in the deck division. It's a serious problem, and I've instructed the first lieutenant and the bosun to fix it."

"Hah," one of the men muttered. "Fat chance."

"Look," Franklin said, "a black man named Martin Luther King, Jr. gave a speech four years ago urging racial peace and harmony. You may have heard of it. People call it the 'I have a dream' speech."

Several heads nodded.

"Well," Franklin said, "Mr. King was striving for racial harmony for a large country and possibly the world. I'm trying for it on one ship. Will you give me a chance to work it out?"

Robbins paused. "As I see it, sir, we got two choices ... do what you want or go to the brig ourselves. We'll do it your way."

"Good."

"But we won't wait forever ... sir."

Mike broke hard left to avoid the stream of tracers racing up through the darkness ahead. "Damn it. Some of the bombs didn't come off. I can feel it."

"Wait a sec," Terry said. "The weapons on station five are still there." He broke out his Navy-issue, L-shaped flashlight and played its beam over the faulty rack, outboard on the starboard wing. "The MER looks okay. Must be a bad electrical lead in the pylon."

"Wonderful." Mike turned the A-6 toward the nearest town. "Recycle the switches, and I'll try another pickle. If it works, we'll wake up Vinh."

Terry cycled the master arm switch and those associated with station five. "You're hot."

"Roger."

Mike mashed down the pickle ... nothing. He then turned the plane east. A minute later they were over water.

"Banner Five-zero-one is feet wet, switching." Mike changed radio frequencies. "Wigwam, Banner Five-zero-one has six Mark-eighty-twos on station five that won't come off. Our state eight point five. Request instructions."

"Stand by, Banner."

Terry asked, "Think they'll have us drop the whole rack in the water?"

"They sure as hell won't let us bring the bombs back aboard."

"Banner Five-zero-one, this is Wigwam. Your signal is Bingo. Danang is one-six-five degrees, one fifty-two miles."

"Wilco. Banner Five-zero-one is switching to Danang approach control."

They turned south. "So," Mike said, "that answers your question. If we can get the Marines to hustle the download, we can still make the last recovery. I have no desire to sleep over in grunt city."

"I have Danang on radar," Terry said. "Steering's good."

Thirty minutes later Mike taxied 501 up to the sand-bagged bunkers and steel hut that comprised the Marine A-6 line shack at Danang Air Base, a Republic of Vietnam airfield nestled on the coast 85 miles south of the DMZ. A couple of floodlights lit up the immediate area and the dozen rather scruffy-looking A-6s parked nearby. Some Air Force airplanes could be seen through the gloom in the distance.

A Marine in green fatigues gave them taxi directions that brought 501 to a halt right in front of the hut. He crossed his wands to indicate *hold your brakes* and then slammed yellow wooden chocks in front of the two main mounts.

Terry said, "Homey, ain't it?"

He reached up and put his ejection seat on safe.

Mike did the same to his seat then opened the canopy. "Makes me glad I went to sea."

The Marine on deck swung down the A-6's built-in ladders, pulled out a handful of red-flagged safety pins, three for the landing gear and four for the MERs, and proceeded to install them.

Terry and Mike went through the A-6 shutdown procedure. Then they unstrapped and climbed down.

A smiling Marine officer in green fatigues emerged from the hut. "Howdy," he said. "I'm Captain Josh Riley. We got a crew on the way to take off your hung ordnance. Come on in and have a cup of good Marine coffee. How much gas you want?"

"Pump us up to twelve thousand pounds," Mike said.

"Done," Riley said. He turned to the approaching crew of Marines and said, "You got that, Gunny?"

"Yes, sir. Bombs down, gas up, twelve thousand."

Riley held the door open while his guests entered the hut; then he took two mugs featuring squadron symbols down from a shelf and proceeded to fill them with a liquid that looked as if it had once been coffee. He turned and called to a Marine private slouched over a small desk in the far corner, an open *Playboy* in front of him.

"Foster, go get our guests some donuts from the *gedunk*. The chocolate ones with sprinkles."

"Yes, sir."

The private stole another glance at the magazine, then stashed it in a drawer and headed out the back door.

A large poster on the wall caught Mike's attention. It showed an A-6 with Marine markings flying down a dark canyon. The words below read, *Yea though I fly through the valley of the shadow of death, I shall fear no evil, for I am the meanest motha' in the valley.*

Mike and Terry sat down on folding chairs in front of a battered wooden desk situated in the middle of the room. Dozens of cigarette burns scarred the desktop, and half a dozen playing cards were jammed under one leg.

Riley handed over the two cups and settled down behind the desk. "I'll get the gas chits filled out. We're the poor cousins, remember, so we have to charge you for the fuel. Sorry 'bout that."

He bent over the paperwork.

"No problem," Mike said. "It all comes out of the same bucket if you go up the food chain far enough. How are your A-Sixes doing?"

He took a sip of coffee then made a face at Terry.

"We're in tough shape," Riley said, not looking up. "It's a real bitch getting parts up here, especially the electronic stuff. Right now we're running about twenty percent full-system availability. How's yours?"

"Somewhat better," Terry said. He set his coffee cup down on the desk. "Maybe fifty percent right now."

"God ... we'd go ape if we could get that high. Here." He slid a five-part set of fuel chits over to Mike. "We damn near beg the supply people down at Saigon for some help, but all they ever say is, sorry 'bout that."

"That's tough," Mike said.

He pressed his ballpoint pen down hard enough to get his signature through to the bottom of the stack, then tore off his copy and stuffed it into a pocket.

The back door banged open and a cardboard box preceded the enlisted runner into the room. The private lifted the cover and held the open box out to Mike.

Mike picked up a mass of chocolate and multi-colored sprinkles that might hide a donut underneath then peered at it.

Terry selected the one with the least chocolate, examined it, then bit off a small piece. "It's good," he declared. "Real fresh."

The private grinned and offered the box to Riley.

"We got good cooks," Riley said. He took two donuts and stacked them on the rim of his coffee cup. "They bake every evening soon as it cools down."

Leftover donuts in hand, the private went back to his desk.

Riley scanned the paperwork once more then stuffed it into the center desk drawer. "Want some more coffee guys?"

"No thanks," Mike said. "Don't want to need that damn relief tube on the way home."

"I know what you mean," Riley said. "Though it's not a real problem if you're well endowed."

The Marine sergeant stuck his head in the door. "Everything's taken care of, Captain. They're good to go."

The three officers stood up and trooped outside. Mike shook Riley's hand as he said, "Thanks for the hospitality, Captain. The Navy appreciates it."

"No problem. Come again anytime."

Ten minutes later, as 501 climbed through eight thousand feet en route to the ship, Terry pushed the radar hood away. "Radar's out," he said. "You'll have to use TACAN."

"Got it already. Switch us to Wigwam approach."

They were *Valiant*'s last trap of the day.

The squadron maintenance chief caught up with Mike and Terry in the ready room as they filled out the paperwork for the two flights.

"Well," Master Chief Gronski said, "you gentlemen have a good time at Danang?"

Mike looked up. "They took good care of us, Master Chief. Fresh-made chocolate donuts."

"And did either of you gentlemen watch my airplane while they dropped the bombs and gassed it up?"

"The radar," Terry said. "It didn't work on the way home. They steal one of the components?"

"No, sir. They swung up the plane's nose cone and stole the whole damn radar unit."

Chapter 21
Day Twelve

Vietnam

Nancy Angelides lifted the man's arm, felt for his pulse, and timed the rate. *Sixty-five beats a minute. Better. He might make it after all. God knows, the odds had been against it when they brought him in.*

She lay the arm back down on the white sheet and picked up the clipboard hanging at the foot of the bed.

The arm moved on its own, and Nancy turned, more than a little surprised. The man's eyes were open. Clear and aware. The eyes looked at the hoses feeding fluids into his body then at her.

The man asked, "Where am I?"

"An Army MASH unit. You've been shot."

"American MASH?"

"Yes, Marine. American. Don't I look it?"

"Not Marine ... Navy."

The man's eyes closed, and he slipped back into a deep sleep.

Nancy lifted the clipboard and changed *Unknown Marine* to *Unknown Navy.*

Two hours later, Bowie Jones woke again. This time he saw a middle-aged man leaning over him, fussing with a large bandage that lay across Bowie's side and chest.

"Ah, you're awake," the man said. "I'm Doctor Bennett. You're going to make it."

Bowie asked, "How bad is it?"

He moved his head to look at the bandaged area then winced at the sudden pain and lay his head back down on the flat pillow.

"Take it easy," the doctor said. "You took a bullet on your right side. It broke two ribs and messed up a large hunk of internal meat, but it missed the vital organs. You also lost a lot of blood before the Marine chopper brought you in. Fortunately, you're an easy match."

"That it?"

"That's it. We had to open you up a bit to sew the pieces together, but you'll be fine in a month or two."

"Can I still fly?"

"Ah, you're a pilot. How did a Navy pilot wind up in a Marine fire fight?"

"Shot down. Walked south."

"Jesus, you're lucky you found the Marines."

"Yeah. Lucky. Will I be able to fly again?"

"Don't see why not." The doctor picked up the clipboard and took out a pen. "So, what's your name and unit?"

"Lieutenant Junior Grade Bowie Jones, seven-four-four-nine-zero-one. I fly off USS *Valiant*."

"We'll let them know you're here," the doctor said. "Now, go back to sleep. Your body needs rest."

"Yes, sir."

Washington State

The tapping was so quiet that Marion Jansen almost didn't hear it. When she did, she muttered "Damn woodpeckers," yanked a broom out of the kitchen pantry, and headed for the front door.

A-6s weren't the only flying things to inhabit Whidbey Island, so too did pileated woodpeckers. She and Harold—she refused to call him Dutch—hadn't finished unloading the moving van before she became acquainted with the big birds; one of them attacked her mother's ancient armoire as it sat on the lawn waiting to be moved inside. Marion still didn't know what *pileated* meant, and didn't much care.

Marion threw the front door open, broom at the ready, and looked up for the woodpecker.

The young woman on the front stoop stepped backwards and said, "Oh, dear."

Blinking in surprise, Marion lowered the broom. "Good grief," she said. "I must have frightened you near to death. I'm sorry ... I thought you were a woodpecker."

The woman offered a wan smile. "I hate to bother you like this, Mrs. Jansen, but ... I'm Judy Anders."

"Anders? Terry's wife?"

"Yes, ma'am."

"Oh my gosh," Marion said. "I'm happy to meet you at last. Come in, come in. Welcome to Whidbey Island."

She held the broom with one hand and the door open with the other.

Judy smiled again and stepped past Marion into the Jansen house, really more of a cottage. Once inside, she looked around and said, "Charming place."

"It's vintage Navy," Marion said. "Something from everywhere." She used the broom handle as a pointer. "The couch is from Virginia, the coffee table from Spain. The end tables were carved in Taiwan, and those humongous lamps sitting on them are from Mexico. Harold brought home a Zulu mask from one of his trips, but I refuse to put it on the wall. Too scary."

Marion paused and then laughed. "Harold tells me I talk too much. I guess that's true. Please, sit down. There's coffee in the kitchen ... and tea. Would you like some?"

"Iced tea, thank you. No lemon."

Judy made her way to the overstuffed chair facing one end of the coffee table and settled in.

"No lemon," Marion repeated. She went to the kitchen and put the broom back in the pantry. She caught her reflection in the window pane above the sink as she poured their tea and made a face at it. *So, Judy Anders has come to Whidbey Island. Looking for support from the other squadron wives? Wants to join the clan at last? Maybe. We'll soon find out.*

As Marion entered the room, Judy asked, "Where did that painting of Elvis come from?"

"The Philippines. Harold bought it on the last cruise. It's oil on velvet. Isn't if awful?" She dropped two cork pads on the coffee table and set glasses of iced tea on each, no lemon in Judy's. "It was my birthday present."

"I kind of like it."

"To each his own, I guess. What brings you to the island?"

Judy sipped her iced tea before answering. "I need your advice, Mrs. Jansen. I just—"

"Please, Judy. Call me Marion."

"But you're the commanding officer's wife. I thought—"

"I'm cutting you off again. Sorry. It's one of my bad habits. Look, the regular Navy has a lot of starchy protocol, even among some wives.

But that's not usually the case in our Airedale Navy. So please don't be concerned with my rank, I don't have any. Now, tell me about this advice you need."

"Well, it's about me and Terry. We ... damn it, the short version is that I want him safely home with me, and I'm sure he intends to stay in the Navy, which means flying in this war. I don't know what to do."

"I see," Marion said. "And you want this old Navy wife to tell you what to do?"

"Not exactly. But I'd very much appreciate it if you could help me reach a decision. Does that make sense?"

"Yes, Judy, it does. Let's start with what you term 'your decision.' I take it you're thinking of giving Terry an ultimatum ... get out of the Navy or I'll leave you. That about it?"

"At least stop flying or I'll leave. Maybe I could handle it if he wasn't flying. It's just so damn dangerous, especially now. I want him to live. With me ... with the baby."

"I understand. You ever meet Mike Roamer, Terry's pilot?"

"Once."

"Mike's wife gave him a choice, her or the flying. He surprised her and took the flying. I don't know how he feels about it now, but I hear she's quite depressed."

"They still married?"

"Separated, far as I know. Tell me, if Terry does what you want, will that guarantee you two and the child will live happily ever after, like the fairy tale?"

"No, but—"

"Look, I don't know Terry very well, but I do know my husband. He's like a great many other men in naval aviation. These guys pretty much come out of the same mold, almost interchangeable. Little boys with expensive toys. Most of them would be miserable if they couldn't fly. Yes, a few came in with hopes of having a glorious military career ending with admiral's stripes, but most signed up just to fly as long as they could. Why do you think Terry joined?"

Judy thought a moment. "All he talked about when he was home was the flying."

"I believe it. Same with Harold. Same with the aviator boyfriend I had before I married the art connoisseur."

She laughed and gestured at the painting of Elvis.

"But Terry has responsibilities now. Me ... and the baby. We should come first, shouldn't we?"

"I can't answer that question. I can tell you that I don't come first with Harold. Oh ... he'd tell you I do, and he'd believe it when he said it. But if duty calls, that old warhorse whinnies and gallops away. He counts on me to take care of the family ... and now the other squadron wives ... when he's away. And after he comes home, he'll be a loving husband again ... until the next call."

"And that's enough for you?"

"More than enough."

"And you don't worry he might get killed?"

"Of course I worry. Every one of us worries. But we squadron wives support one another, take care of each other, and cry together whenever one of our men falls. I hear you've been staying with your parents while Terry's away. And that's fine, but you can't possibly have the support you'd have here with us, and my sense is you need that support right now."

"But—"

"You asked for my advice, Judy, so here it is. Move to the island, join our group, and think long and hard about what you want for Terry, not just yourself."

Judy set down her tea and stood up. "Thank you Mrs. Jansen ... Marion. You've given me much to think about."

At the door, Judy turned and asked, "If we stay in the Navy, is he apt to buy me one of those velvet paintings?"

"I'm afraid so," Marion said. "It goes with the territory."

Marion followed her guest and waved as Judy climbed into a rental car parked at the curb.

Back inside, Marion spoke to the velvet Elvis. "If *we* stay in? Maybe she's finally figuring it out."

Yankee Station

Mike liked this new 1000 to 2200 schedule; it suited his night-owl instincts. Briefing for the first launch of the day began at 0900, so even if he was on it, he could have a leisurely breakfast.

He'd begun his second cup of coffee when Roger put his tray down across the table and asked, "You flying today?"

Mike replied, "Don't know. I haven't seen the flight schedule yet. Why?"

"I need material for a column and you seem to be a good provider."

"I try to please. You want exciting or human interest?"

"Hmmm, exciting. I just sent off a human interest one."

"Oh?" Mike raised an eyebrow. "Without showing it to me and Terry? I thought we had a deal."

"It was about the burial at sea. That plane captain that got killed on deck. I didn't figure I needed your blessings for it."

"You're right. How soon you going home?"

"Soon as I can. I'm getting married."

"Serious business. You sure?"

"I'm sure."

Terry slid into the empty chair next to Mike. "You seen the flight schedule, Mike?"

"Nope."

"We're going to Hanoi tonight."

Mike put his coffee cup down. "Downtown?"

"Almost. CINC-PAC-FLEET wants a couple strings of *seeds* in the river just east of the city."

Roger asked, "What's a seed?"

"Sort of a mine," Terry said, "a five hundred pound bomb with a special fuse. After you drop it, tail fins pop out like speed brakes to slow the thing down. It dives into the water or mud and lies there, doggo. When something comes along, man or machine the fuse senses it. You can stroll right up to it with no problem, but as soon as you take a step away ... boom."

"Jesus," Roger said. "What'll they think of next?"

"World peace," Mike said. "I hear they're working on it." He got up and carried his tray to the sideboard. "You better get out your prayer beads, Terrance. This is going to be a wild one."

He grinned as he left the room.

"It sounds dangerous," Roger said.

"It is. The Intel guys say Hanoi has more guns and missiles defending it than any city in the history of aerial warfare."

"Geez, Terry. Aren't you scared?"

"Nope. I'm terrified."

"But you'll go anyway?"

"Have to. Mike's going, and he gets lost without me."

Terry got up and walked out. He wasn't smiling.

South Carolina

Jason asked, "You seen these poll numbers?" His glee was palpable. "Ah'm ahead of Jamie Traynor by six points."

The couple at the next table, the only other diners in the Hog Heaven Restaurant, gave him an odd look.

"Goody, goody gum drops," Annie said. "All my hard work is paying off. Do I get a raise?"

She arched an eyebrow and reached for her wine glass.

"You get to keep your job for anothah two years ... *if* you manage to get me re-elected," raising his own now-empty glass in a mock toast.

"Well then," Annie said, "we better get along to the VFW. The gaffers will be into their fourth beer already, and you know what it's like when your audience is drunk."

"It's bettah than when ah'm drunk."

"Maybe. Hard to tell the difference. Come on, it's almost seven thirty."

"Okay, okay." Jason pulled out a wallet and glanced inside the fold. "Can you get the check? Ah'm a bit short tonight."

"What else is new?"

Annie reached across the table and grabbed the bill. She plunked it down next to her empty plate and fumbled in her bulky purse.

"Make sure to give the guy a good tip," Jason said. "Ah may need his vote."

"I always do, Jason. Here." She handed a twenty-dollar bill and the check across the table. "That's enough for the tab and a nice tip. Put your card on top of it ... maybe he'll remember your name."

"Buyin' anothah vote, Annie?"

"Whatever it takes, Jason."

The rental company's Ford Galaxy was parked across the street. The traffic light on the corner turned green, so they had to wait at the curb for a handful of cars to pass.

Annie hummed a tune, her head nodding in time with the music.

"That sounds kind of familiar," Jason said. "What is it?"

"It's 'Age of Aquarius,' from *Hair*. It just opened Off Broadway."

"Oh yeah, that disgustin' hippie musical. Speakin' of hippies, you hear anythin' more from what's-his-name?"

"His name is Roger, and that paragraph in the Navy message is all I needed to hear."

Jason took her by the arm. "Come on, we can get across now."

He helped Annie step down from the curb and held her arm as they crossed the street.

"I'm not an invalid," Annie said.

"Yeah, but you're pregnant, and ah'm a southern gentleman."

"Come on, I'm not even showing yet." She chuckled. "If I were, you wouldn't be seen anywhere near me."

Letting her arm go, Jason turned toward the driver's door.

Annie stepped over the curb and around a tree root protruding from the patchy suburban grass that lay between the curb and the sidewalk. She didn't see the second root—the one that tripped her.

"Oh!" She landed hard, face down on a patch of bare dirt, her purse under her. "Damn."

"Annie?" Jason ran around the car's trunk. "Annie? You okay?"

Wincing, Annie tried to get up. She collapsed back onto the ground and rolled over onto her side.

Her voice little more than a whisper, she said, "Oh God, I think I'm having a miscarriage."

Chapter 22
Day Twelve Continued

Yankee Station

Commander Jansen laid a chart out on the planning table in the ship's IOIC (Integrated Operations Intelligence Center) and pinned a plastic overlay on top of it. He looked up at the three officers across the table: Mike, Terry and his own B/N, Phil Bloomberg. "CINC-PAC-FLEET wants two strings of seeds in the Red River between downtown Hanoi and the Gia Lam airport."

Terry asked, "Why?"

"Don't know," Jansen said. "With the bridges down, maybe they're flying stuff into Gia Lam and ferrying it across the river to Hanoi." He pointed at the plastic overlay. "At any rate, we have to put the seeds where those two lines are. We'll penetrate through the karst south of Hanoi, then turn north and come in on the deck. First crew takes the northern drop ... second crew takes the nearer drop. Which one you want, Mike?"

Mike gave the chart a practiced look "All those dots marking the flak sites around the place makes me think of measles. No easy way in ... or out." He wiggled his jaw. "I'll go first."

Jansen laughed. "Why'd you pick that?"

"Well," Mike said, "first one in stands at least some chance of surprising them. Tail end Charley is, well—"

"Okay, Mike, you're the *ichi ban*. We launch at twenty-thirty. Remember you have to be above five hundred feet at release to give those BSU-eighty-six retarding fins time to slow down the weapons. Any questions?" There were none.

The night was almost as black as Mike wished it to be. No moon yet. He adjusted the brightness on the plane's VDI (vertical-display-indicator), the television-like screen mounted on the instrument panel in front of him. Besides showing the plane's attitude relative to the horizon, the display danced with multiple layers of faux mountains and passes, all computer generated, as the system tried to lead them through the dark valleys at minimum altitude.

As usual, Mike ignored the fancy parts of the show and flew altitudes he computed ahead of time for each leg of the trip. He wasn't about to trust some new computer wrinkle to keep him out of the dirt.

"Time to turn," Terry said. "Steering's good."

The bug on Mike's HSI swung right to a new heading of zero-four-eight degrees. Mike rolled the A-6 into a hard turn and leveled out on the new course.

They were now southwest of Hanoi, tacking back toward the coast in order to stay behind a karst ridge, away from the enemy's Spoon Rest search radars as long as possible.

Easing the stick forward, Mike began a gradual descent. He checked the altitudes written on his knee-board chart; he wanted to be no more than two hundred feet above the rocks when they went through the mountain pass up ahead—assuming, of course, that Terry's radar navigation put them in the center of the narrow gap.

"We'll be through the pass in twenty seconds," Terry said, his face still buried in the radar hood.

"Roger that."

The A-6 continued its descent through the darkness.

"Okay," Terry said, "we're through the pass. Come left. Steering is to the target."

The HSI bug swung left and steadied on three-five-two degrees, the heading for the seed drop.

They were out of the mountains now and onto the flat delta. Fifteen miles to the fiery gauntlet—twenty-five to the target.

Mike steadied the A-6 up on the new heading and checked their altitude: two hundred feet on the radar altimeter. He rammed the throttles to the stops, and the plane accelerated, stretching for five hundred knots.

Three minutes to target.

The radar-warning light blinked a few times. The enemy was searching for them. Then the warning light started a rythmic beat, and the aural warning came up with its *dedul ... dedul ... dedul*. The radars found them.

They descended. At a hundred feet on the radar altimeter, the warnings stopped, but the North Vietnamese now knew an aircraft was out there—coming.

They arrived over the wandering river, visible in reflected starlight, and Mike went down to fifty feet. Scattered lights ahead on the left marked the looming city of Hanoi, partially blacked out.

Two minutes to the target.

Across town, the west edge of Hanoi erupted in muzzle flashes. They formed a solid wall of winking lights that stretched for over a mile and yanked Mike's eyes away from the instrument panel.

A hundred gun barrels, Mike guessed, *and every one aimed at me.* Orange tracers streaming left to right formed a dazzling umbrella a few feet above the low-flying A-6.

More flak started; this from the right. Fewer guns, but closer. Tracers now zipped past both ways. They were in the gauntlet.

"Stepping the computer into attack," Terry said, not looking up from the radar scope.

Flashes from exploding 37mm and 57mm flak bursts turned night almost into day. Quad-mounted searchlights found their target and finished the job.

Mike abandoned the instruments and went visual. He saw they were approaching a suburban street flanked by two-story buildings; it led straight ahead, toward the target. Without hesitation, he jinked over, took the plane down below roof-top level and sent the A-6 roaring up the middle of the street at five hundred knots.

One minute to the target.

Thousands of antiaircraft rounds streamed at the racing A-6. Low rounds slammed into the buildings on either flank; higher rounds flicked closely overhead and fell back to earth on the far side among other buildings, on the people living there. It occurred to Mike that the North Vietnamese were blowing the hell out of their own city.

But the gunners couldn't touch them.

Then they were out of the city, over the river, at the target. The flack fell behind and, as if someone threw a switch, full darkness snapped back. Back on instruments, Mike pulled the plane up to five hundred feet ... and the computer rippled the seeds off. The A-6 shuddered as the racks kicked the retarded weapons away.

The ICS screamed *deduldeduldedul*. Missile-control radars were tracking them. Up to now they flew for their country; now they were running for their lives.

Terry pushed away the radar hood, looked over his shoulder, and yelled, "SAM at five o'clock. Break right. Break right."

Mike rolled the plane into a nose-down, hard right turn—diving for the weeds. Wings banked past ninety degrees, coming down through two hundred feet in the now-black void, the aircraft under complete control, Mike almost smiled. *Only in an A-6.*

The SAM detonated outside their turn radius, and Mike rolled out heading southeast. The radar altimeter read one hundred feet.

"SAM at six," Terry warned. Then, "Closing ... closing. Pull!"

Hauling back on the control stick, Mike put 5 G's on the plane. The A-6 soared up into the night sky.

The SAM followed them. Despite the high G load, Terry twisted in his seat to track the pursuing SAM.

As they roared up through three thousand feet, he stammered, "Oh s-s-shit. It's got us."

"Not yet." Mike rolled the plane over and pulled max G's. The A-6 whipped over the top of an arc—inverted—and plunged back toward the winding river below.

Whump! The SAM went off close above them, but the missile was still going up, and the fragments missed.

Easing off the G's, Mike rolled the plane upright.

The instruments told a grim story: they were now in a steep dive at low altitude. Mike pulled back on the stick until he felt the plane quiver on the verge of a high-speed stall. He held it there, nose coming up, altimeters spinning downward.

Five hundred feet—four hundred—three hundred.

Fighting the G-force, Terry grunted out, "Another ... SAM ... tracking."

Two hundred feet—one hundred.

The plane's nose rose through the horizon, but momentum still carried them downward.

The SAM detonated above them with another *whump*.

Light from the flash reflected off water only a few feet below as the plane bottomed out; they were over the river again. Both altimeters registered negative altitudes, inside their margins of error.

The A-6 came up out of the river bed in a desperate run for altitude and the coast. Like a scalded cat climbing the wall, the plane ran for safety. Mike stayed on instruments while Terry kept watch over his shoulder.

Climbing through ten thousand feet, Terry said, "They lobbed another one at us, but it blew a ways back. We're okay now."

At eighteen thousand feet, halfway to water, Mike throttled back and set a course for the coast, then laughed. "Jesus, that was some ride."

"We made it," Terry said.

Wham. Wham. Wham. A ripple of 85mm flak bracketed the plane.

The blows rapped Terry's head against the canopy, stunning him. His first thought coming out of it concerned the noise. Air was roaring through the cockpit. *Holes in the canopy?* Then ... *Mike?*

Mike was slumped forward, head on his chest, held upright by his shoulder harness. A drop of blood fell from his chin.

The VDI showed the airplane in a descending left turn, diving at Haiphong.

Terry released his shoulder harness, leaned over, and grabbed the stick with his left hand. He'd flown an A-6 this way before, for kicks, and now the experience paid off. He horsed the plane into level flight on an easterly heading.

Stunned again, Terry sat quite still, considering the enormity of his predicament. The rising moon showed him the coastline passing below, so he keyed the UHF and said, "Banner Five-zero-seven is feet wet. Declaring an emergency."

"Banner Five-zero-seven, this is Red Crown. You've got a lot of background noise. What's the nature of your emergency?"

"Flak got us. Holes in the canopy. My pilot is unconscious ... maybe dead."

After a long pause, "Red Crown copies. Your intentions?"

"Go to Wigwam and eject us both."

"Copy that, your steer is one-one-two, eighty-four miles."

Left hand on the stick, Terry turned to the new heading. "Red Crown, do you hold Banner Five-zero-one behind us somewhere?"

"Negative."

"Understand, Red Crown." Terry let that sink in. "I'm switching to Wigwam approach."

"Roger that, Banner Five-zero-seven. Good luck. Red Crown out."

Wigwam came up on the new frequency. "Banner Five-zero-seven, this is Wigwam approach. What are your—"

The voice changed. "This is CAG. Can you get the bird here?"

"Affirmative."

"Mike still unconscious?"

"Yes, sir."

"Okay, Tight-Ass, you're going to have to save him. You have a silk scarf?"

"No, sir. Mike has one in his flight suit. He wears it sometimes."

"Can you reach it?"

"Wait one."

Terry unzipped the pocket on the right leg of Mike's flight suit. The silk scarf winked in the moonlight. "Got it, CAG."

"Okay. Here's what you do. Run that scarf through the alternate ejection handle between Mike's legs. See if you can hold the two ends together and still keep your hand clear of the seat."

"Stand by."

A few seconds later, "That works, CAG."

"Good. Make damn sure your hand is out of the way before you pull that handle. The seat will rip that scarf out of your hand, but silk means it won't take your arm with it. Got that?"

"Got it."

"The helo is going to have to put divers in the water as soon as Mike hits or he'll drown. Fly the plane up the port side of the ship at five hundred feet. Use the scarf to eject Mike abeam then you get out. Understood?"

"Yes, sir."

"Can you control your speed?"

"We're at cruise power so we should be okay."

"All right. We've got the helos on deck ready to go. Good luck."

Terry bobbed in the water, watching, as a helo crew pulled Mike's limp body out of the water. A few minutes later another helo pulled Terry up and dumped him on its deck.

Wet and exhausted, Terry asked, "Is my pilot alive?"

"Don't know," the crewman said. "Sit tight, sir. We'll have you aboard *Valiant* in a jiffy."

South Carolina

Jason looked up from a tattered *Outdoor Living* magazine when a man in scrubs entered the little waiting room. The stethoscope draped around his neck labeled him a doctor.

The man looked around then walked up to Jason, the only one there. "You the husband?"

"No, suh," Jason said. "Ah'm the lady's employer. She's not married."

"I see. You the father?"

"No, suh. Like ah said—" Jason looked around to see if anyone else might have heard the question.

"Sorry, Mr.—?"

"James. Beauregard James." *Best to be careful here.*

"Sorry, Mr. James. Miss Hill has miscarried."

"Ah was afraid of that."

"Yes, it's too bad. The good news is … there's no reason why she can't have more babies. Her plumbing is fine, but she'll have to be more careful with the next pregnancy. No falling down."

"That is good news, doctor. Can ah see Miss Hill now?"

"Make it brief. She's awake, but very tired and needs sleep." He stepped aside and pointed at the green door behind him. "Third cubicle on the right."

"Does she know?"

"Yes. I told her before I came out here."

"Thank you, suh."

Jason headed for the door.

She looked pale and her hair arrayed across the pillow exaggerated the fact, but Annie managed a weak smile. "Hi, Jason. Did the doc tell you?"

"Yes, Annie, he did. But you can have more babies. That's good news."

"I guess. You think Roger will be disappointed in me?"

"Ah think that red-headed roostah is goin' to marry you as quick as he can so you two can get to makin' lots of babies." He stopped and blushed. "Ah'm sorry."

Annie laughed. "That's okay, Jason. I hope you're right. And thank you for taking care of me last night. You lost a lot of votes by not showing up at the VFW hall."

"Ah called them from heah. Said ah was detained by an emergency involvin' the loved one of a poor boy overseas."

"You didn't."

"Ah did. An' it worked like a charm. That an' the fact ah had the bartendah buy them all a round of drinks."

"How did you manage that?"

"Ah gave him the numbah on your credit card."

"Oh Jason. You just have to get re-elected. God knows, our country needs men like you."

Chapter 23
Day Thirteen

Yankee Station

All other action on the flight deck came to a halt as the visiting Bell UH-1 helicopter fluttered down to a gentle roost next to the island. The engine whined to a stop as the blades swung in an ever-slowing circle. The side hatch slid open and a crewman jumped out then pulled out a little metal step-stool and set it on the deck.

Six USS *Valiant* sailors, each in a different-colored flight-deck jersey, formed a corridor, three on a side, between the chopper and the ship's island. The sailors faced inward and snapped to attention.

Rear Admiral Frank Ruston, pudgy face wreathed in a broad smile, appeared in the helo's hatch. He looked around then reached for the crewman's hand outstretched to help him down. With a grunt, Ruston stepped on the stool and then onto the flight deck.

A bosun's pipe whistled over the ship's 1MC, piping the side, and the six *Valiant* sailors saluted.

The admiral returned their salute and held it as he strolled through the corridor formed by the men. The morning sun twinkled off the two stars on each collar flap. Navy wings, tarnished by age, roosted above his left breast pocket.

Captain Franklin stood at attention a few feet beyond the corridor's end, saluting.

At the last note of the bosun's pipe, everyone dropped their salute, but the side boys remained at attention and the 1MC announced, "Task Force Seventy-Six arriving."

Honors having been rendered, Rear Admiral Ruston and Captain Franklin shook hands. Both men smiled.

Ruston clapped his free hand on Franklin's shoulder. "Congratulations, Spud. Sorry I missed the change of command. I love those things. They don't have ceremonies like that in the Army and Air Force, you know. Only in God's own creation, the Navy."

"It was a quickie, Admiral. We had a war to fight."

"I reckon. Where we headed?"

"I've got coffee in my in-port cabin. Will that do?"

"Works for me, Spud. Lead the way."

The two officers went inside the island, the bosun's mate in charge of the honors detail dismissed the six men, and the flight deck went back to war.

"Re-spot," the air boss announced. "The helo will be lifting in about fifteen minutes."

Spud waited for the admiral to take a seat before he settled in across the coffee table and motioned for Manuel to serve. Once the steward finished pouring coffee and left the room, Ruston pulled a small flask from his hip pocket. He twisted off the flask's cap and poured a little of its contents into his coffee.

"For my heart," he said, grinning, then offered the flask to Spud.

"No thanks, Admiral. I'm driving."

Ruston put the flask away then downed a slug of Irish coffee and wiped his mouth with the back of one hand. "Your boys did a damn good job on the bridges, Spud. Sorry about your losses last night. Is that pilot in your sickbay going to make it?"

"Don't know yet, Admiral. Some eighty-five millimeter fragments penetrated the canopy, and one of them struck him in the head. His hardhat absorbed much of the blow, but he has swelling on the brain. The doctors called it an acute subdural hematoma. They drilled a small hole in his skull and are trying to relieve the pressure, but it's touch and go for now."

"Make sure that B/N gets a medal out of this. Damn fine job." Ruston took another sip of coffee. "I'll endorse a DFC for him."

"I'll get someone writing it up."

"Good. How's the lad doing?"

"He's pissed off. Told me he wants to go back in and bomb the hell out of something."

"Sounds like good therapy to me. Hear anything on Commander Jansen? The missing A-Six?"

"No, sir."

"Listen, if that plane was still flyable, they might have made it into the mountains west of Hanoi. The Air Force operates over there all the time. Maybe they'll pick up something."

"You know the odds on that, Admiral."

"Yeah, I do. How is his loss going to affect the squadron?"

"The XO will take over, of course, and he seems pretty competent, but Commander Jansen was a damn good CO. He'll be missed."

"Speaking of good COs, what was the nature of Grant Spanner's family emergency? Must have been serious."

"Yes, sir. His teenage daughter ran away and is missing. Since his wife died last year, Grant figured he needed to be a father, go find her."

"You know, Spud, almost everyone I know has kids in some form of trouble." He shook his head. "It's the life we lead, I think. We're gone too damn much. Your kids okay?"

"So far, Admiral." Spud knocked on the wood coffee table. "Gail's too young to get into trouble, and Fred is all wrapped up in high school football. Wild horses couldn't drag him away from that."

"Good. My one son, the light of my life, is a damn draft dodger hiding up in Canada. God, it hurts to say that."

He took another slug of coffee as moisture formed in the corners of his eyes. Spud, not having any idea what to say, looked away and drank from his own cup.

"Well," Ruston said, clearing his throat, "to business. What do you need that you're having trouble getting?"

Spud set down his cup and leaned forward. "Faster replacement of the lost A-Sixes, Admiral, they're essential for night work. The XO tells me it took three weeks to get the last one out here from CONUS."

"What else?"

"Aircraft parts, especially systems components for the E-Twos and the A-Sixes. We're at the end of a pretty long supply chain."

"I hear you. Spare parts were the main topic of conversation at that meeting in Yokosuka last week. AIR-PAC is trying to get a bigger slice of the supply pie away from AIR-LANT, but you know how that goes. If it's any consolation, the Marines in-country are in worse shape."

"That's no consolation, sir, but speaking of in-country, any idea how soon we'll be pulled off the line … get a little liberty in port. I've only been out here a couple of weeks, but the crew is going on sixty days now, and they're starting to wink at each other."

Ruston laughed. "I'll see what I can do. Now that we've been yanked away from Haiphong again, maybe we'll see a little slack. My staff is working on getting you into Hong Kong." Ruston drank the last of his coffee and stood. "Let me know how that wounded pilot does."

Spud jumped to his feet. "I'll send you a message soon as we know anything definitive."

"Do that. Let's go. Your air boss is going to want my chopper off his deck."

The admiral led the way this time, Spud and the Marine escort close behind.

Vietnam

Dutch Jansen lay in a crevice near the top of a ridge line some thirty miles west of Hanoi. He'd been there, alone, since about 2130 the night before, grateful to have survived a hell of a ride.

The SAM that hit their A-6 right after weapon release knocked out everything electrical, set the port engine on fire, and caused the plane to shake like a dice cup. Rather than eject right away, Jansen tried to reach mountains, something he and Phil Bloomberg discussed months before. Both decided back then that risking death in a fireball was preferable to the certainty of capture and torture if they bailed out over the delta.

So Jansen turned left, crossing part of Hanoi, for the simple reason that the closest mountains lay in that direction. The trail of flame they left behind must have convinced the Hanoi gunners the plane was about to crash; the flak subsided, and no more SAMs were fired.

They rode that torch for almost a full minute before the shaking increased, and Jansen's ability to control the plane grew problematic. When starlight showed dark shadows below that heralded mountains, and with the aircraft bucking, Phil ejected with Jansen following a few seconds later.

The plane disintegrated in a fireball before either parachute reached the ground, and pieces of flaming metal rained down onto the low mountains.

Jansen hid his parachute in a rocky crack, then scrambled upslope, seeking the high ground. Twenty minutes later he reached the top of this particular ridge and found a crevice large enough to conceal a man. He slipped into it and checked over his survival gear. The water he carried in a small plastic flask was warm, but it seemed like a godsend. He downed all of it.

Along about dawn, Jansen began to pray. Never a religious man, he prayed for God to take care of Marion and Harold Junior. Then he prayed for his B/N to survive. He wasn't sure praying to a Christian God would help Phil Bloomberg, a Jew, but he had to try. Finally, Jansen prayed for the U.S. Air Force to come to his rescue, much as the cavalry did in old western movies.

He figured this ridge had to lie beneath a logical route for any strike forces coming up from Thailand to hit targets northwest of Hanoi. Search-and-rescue forces should be standing by to go after the crew of any strike bird that went down, and Jansen didn't think an Air Force SAR crew would discriminate against a fellow airman just because he was Navy.

So Jansen waited, clutching his lifeline, a little PRC-63 radio capable of transmitting and receiving on the international UHF emergency frequency of 243.0 MHz. The radio had a homing beacon capability, but the North Vietnamese might be all over that in minutes.

No, I have to wait for a close encounter with friendly aircraft.

If any USAF planes came close enough, twenty-five miles, he could get their attention with the radio and then fire a smoke signal to mark his position. Of course the Vietnamese could also hear the radio calls, and then it would be a race between NVN troops and the Air Force SAR forces—a gamble.

But Jansen figured his gambles had paid off so far, at least for him. Phil apparently was not that lucky. A flurry of gunshots a mile or so to the east at dawn likely meant that his B/N was either dead or a prisoner.

The sound arrived as a dull hum in the distance. Jansen poked his head out of the crevice, looked south, and spotted the source: a gaggle of dots low in the sky that grew larger as he watched. Over the next few minutes the dots turned into what Jansen recognized as Air Force F-105 fighter-bombers, known to their pilots as *Thuds*.

When Jansen figured they were within range of his little PRC, he keyed the MIC button. "Mayday. Mayday. Mayday. This is Banner Five-zero-one down on a karst ridge west of Hanoi."

After an interminable few seconds, he got a response. "Banner, this is Blue Hog One. Can you authenticate?"

"Negative. Lost my kneeboard in the ejection."

"What were you flying?"

"An A-Six."

"Navy?"

"Affirmative. You're almost overhead now."

"Okay. Quick, what's the southernmost naval air station in Texas?"

"Kingsville."

"And what does Snoopy fly?"

"A doghouse."

"Congratulations, Banner Five-zero-one, you've won a rescue. Turn that radio off and save the battery. When you hear a chopper, turn it back on and be ready to pop smoke. We'll keep a section handy to cover you."

"Copy that. Banner Five-zero-one out." Jansen clicked off the radio and leaned against the side of the crevice, his legs weak.

The Air Force strike was now north of him, the roar diminishing.

Jansen faced east. If the forces that tangled with Phil were heading this way, he needed to move. He checked his survival vest again, making sure everything was secure, especially the PRC-63.

Twenty minutes later Jansen spotted soldiers about half a mile away, moving up the slope and coming closer. He stood, ready to flee, but paused, listening to a new sound.

Two F-105s came howling out of the north and pounced on the enemy troops below. Four smoke blossoms enveloped the soldiers, and muted *booms* rolled up the ridge.

Then Jansen spotted the chopper. He turned on the PRC and heard, "Banner Five-zero-one, this is Jolly Green Twenty-one. Come in."

"Jolly Green, this is Banner Five-zero-one. I'm about three miles north of you, due west of the bombing."

"Roger that. Pop smoke."

"Wilco."

Jansen pulled one of the smoke canisters out of his survival vest, made sure the smooth end was up, and pulled the tab. A stream of orange smoke boiled out of the can.

"We have you, Banner."

Bullets zinged by Jansen, some striking rocks and ricocheting into the air. He ducked back into the crevice, keyed the radio transmit button, and shouted, "I'm taking ground fire."

"Copy that."

The big banana-shaped helicopter went into a hover half a mile away as two F-105s pounded the slopes east of Jansen's position again.

Moments later the Jolly Green came to a hover thirty yards west of Jansen's crevice and lowered a cable with a horse-collar rescue sling.

Jansen popped out of his hiding place and ran for the sling. He jammed his head and shoulders through the horse collar and waved a thumbs-up at the chopper.

With a mighty *wop-wop-wop* of the blades, the Jolly Green turned west then raced away from the ridge even as the cable hauled one very happy Dutch Jansen into its oversized bay.

The enlisted crewman who pulled him aboard gave Jansen a broad smile and said, "Welcome aboard, Navy."

Chapter 24
Day Thirteen Continued

Yankee Station

Lieutenant Terry Anders slumped into his ready room chair, the one with his name on the headrest. Being in the third row, his presence didn't interfere with the flight briefing that occupied the people up front. Terry could kibitz, but he paid minimal attention—his mind on other things.

The XO stood at the podium, briefing the strike, a pair of A-6s going to Nam Dinh. "Rendezvous at twelve thousand. We'll have a section of Rawhide Phantoms as escort. They'll be —"

Terry tuned him out. Now that his squadron was down to six aircraft, only five flyable, two A-6s at a time was probably the new normal. *Is anything around here normal?* He couldn't see what the target was; maybe the Nam Dinh Catholic church. He didn't care anymore. *Stupid, miserable war.*

The XO's voice droned on. "We'll hook around and roll in north to south. Watch out for that batch of flak sites west of town, and be—"

When, Terry wondered, *should I start calling the XO by the new honorary title Skipper. Was there a protocol for this sort of thing? Did they wait until the Navy reached a formal conclusion about the missing squadron commander: MIA, KIA, POW? That could take forever.*

The briefing ended, the four crewmen straggled back to the locker area behind the green curtain.

As the XO passed by, Terry asked, "What's your target?"

"A suspected truck parked in some woods next to Nam Dinh."

"Have fun."

Squadron duty officer Jeb Wilson marked the aircraft assignments in grease pencil on the back-lit, plastic status board next to the duty desk. He also noted the two go-bird's approximate positions on a diagram of the flight deck.

Their original nine aircraft were listed down the right-hand side of the panel: 500 to 508. The first aircraft in every fighter and attack squadron roster was *double-nuts*, CAG's airplane. The air wing commander was expected to fly with each of these squadrons, so the *00* bird always had CAG's name painted on it. Squadron COs got the *01* birds. All of that was meaningless, however; everyone flew whichever airplane was ready.

The status board now displayed large red X's next to four aircraft: three lost and one with significant damage from the Haiphong bridge run. It occurred to Terry he was aboard when three of the four airplanes earned their red X's. And yet he was still here. *Lucky me. Yeah, lucky.*

Roger Brackett opened the ready room door, glanced around, came in, then eased into a chair next to Terry and said, "How's Mike doing?"

Terry shook his head. "Don't know. I tried to get Doc Jewett to give me a clue, but he's as tight-lipped as the other doctors on board. They look wise and say, 'time will tell'."

"I don't pray very much," Roger said. "I'm not as religious as you, but I said one for Mike last night. Hope it helps."

"It always does."

"You know, I asked Mike to do something exciting yesterday to give me another column. I didn't figure on this."

"Looks as though he did his part. You get your column written?"

"Not yet."

"Waiting to see if he lives or dies?"

"Yeah, afraid so. I've done a little research on the strikes last night, but I have to know the outcome before I write."

"I guess that's reasonable. A bit ghoulish, but understandable."

"Look, Terry, the Intel folks up in IOIC gave me some info they didn't want passed on, but I think you should know."

"What's that?"

"A recce plane went past Hanoi this morning. It took photos of the river where you put those seeds in last night. The pictures showed a bunch of empty fifty-gallon steel drums floating down the river."

"So?"

"To blow up the seeds, Terry. Those mines will sense the barrels and detonate."

Terry slumped in his chair. "So it was all for nothing."

"Looks that way ... sorry."

After a moment Terry sat up. "When you going home, Roger?"

"Tomorrow. The air boss finally gave me a seat on the COD going into Cubi Point."

"Will you carry a letter for me? Mail it in the states?"

"No problem. With luck I'll be—"

The squawk box belched. "Ready Three, this is Doctor Jewett. Terry Anders there?"

The SDO pushed down the squawk box's lever and said, "Yes, sir. Listening."

"Mike's awake," the doctor said. "He's asking for you."

Washington State

The phone rang and Marion flinched. Nobody called her after nine at night unless it was—she didn't want to think about it.

The phone rang again.

She put down the book she'd been trying to read and stared at the black instrument on the night stand next to the lamp.

It rang again.

This had to be the call she'd dreaded ever since the news this morning when the feather-headed announcer chirped, "MACV announced that two Navy aircraft were lost in a daring low-level strike into Hanoi last night."

That could only be A-6s. And if they were from *Valiant*, Harold would insist on being in one of them.

The phone rang again.

Putting her life on hold, Marion picked up the receiver. "Hello?"

"Hi, sweetheart. It's Harold."

Marion began to cry. She tried to speak, but no words came out. She waved the receiver up and down in little motions.

"Honey? It's me, Harold. You okay?"

"Yes," she sobbed.

"You crying?"

"No."

A lie.

"Yes, you are. I can tell. Look, I'm okay. I got shot down, but the Air Force rescued me."

"The Air Force?"

"Yeah. I'll never speak ill of those weenies in light blue again."

Marion managed a small laugh. "You just did."

"Did what?"

"You called them weenies."

"Oh damn. Old habits are hard to break. I'll have to try harder."

"Where are you, Harold?"

"I'm at the Takhli Royal Thai Air Force base in Thailand. You should see the life our Air Force crews lead here. Everyone wears blue Thai-silk flight suits to the officer's club, with white silk scarves. The name tags are embroidered, and the officer's club is fantastic. It's as if Disney is catering the war for these guys."

"Harold, you sound jealous."

"A little, I guess. You okay now? You stopped crying?"

"I'm fine, Harold. Now."

"Why were you so upset?"

"Oh, the news on the radio today was that two Navy aircraft were lost in a raid into Hanoi last night. Everyone knows that means A-Sixes."

"*Two* planes lost? You sure?"

"Yes, Harold. They said *two*. I'm sure of it."

"Dammit. That means Roamer and Anders got shot down too. That hadn't occurred to me. And, honey, Phil didn't make it. Don't say anything until the Navy gives notice, but I'm pretty sure he's either dead or a POW."

"Oh dear. The poor guy. At least he's not married. But Terry's wife is here."

"At Whidbey?"

"Visiting. Looking for housing. I think she's going to ... well, she *was* talking about moving here. But if Terry's down—"

"I got rescued. Maybe they did too. Look, I've got a ride to Danang in a few minutes and I'll catch a COD out to the ship ASAP. I'll try to get word to you as soon as I can about the boys. Okay?"

"I love you, Harold."

"You're just saying that because it's true. How's Junior?"

"He's ornery, like his father."

"Good. Is he handy?"

"No, dear. He took the car to a debate club meeting at the high school."

"He's in a debate club? Great. Look, I have to go, hon. I love you, Marion. Stay well."

"You too. And leave those Thai girls alone. You know—"

The phone line went dead.

Marion lay back down and had a good, happy cry.

Yankee Station

A beehive bandage on Mike's head came down to his eyebrows and ears. His face was pale, eyes closed.

"Okay, Terry. You've got two minutes."

Doctor Jewett stepped back and pulled the drape closed that separated Mike's bed from the rest of post-op.

Mike's eyes opened, and he turned his head a few degrees toward his visitor.

"You look like hell," Terry said. "How do you feel?"

"Like I look," Mike replied. He licked his lips. "I haven't had a headache this bad since I won that gin drinking contest in Cubi last year. The doc says you saved my ass. Thank you."

"All I did was fly the bird back to the ship left-handed and eject you alongside. Piece of cake."

"Yeah, right. A piece of cake. Where's the skipper? I thought he'd be down to see me."

Terry paused. "They didn't come back."

"Oh." Mike paused a moment. "They probably flew into the ground … or maybe the river. I sure as hell hope that mission was worth it."

"Mike … never mind. You're alive, that's what counts right now. The docs give you any idea when you can fly again?"

"Are you kidding? They're arguing about how soon I can get up to take a leak. Even that seems to be several days away."

Doctor Jewett pulled back the curtain. "Okay, Terry. Time to break it up. The patient needs rest."

Terry asked, "He going to be okay?"

"Hell yes. All he's got is a swollen head. You'd think he was a fighter pilot."

The doctor followed Terry out of the critical-care ward and stopped him in the passageway. "Lieutenant?"

"Sir?"

"I haven't told him yet," the doctor said, "but it's doubtful Mike will ever fly again."

"That'll destroy him."

"Oh, come on … there *can* be life after flying."

"Not for Mike, Doc. Not for Mike."

Washington State

The phone rang again. This time Marion tossed her book aside and grabbed the receiver. "You forget something, Harold?"

"Mrs. Jansen?"

"Yes."

"This is Deputy Wilson from the sheriff's office. I'm sorry, but your son's been involved in an auto accident."

Marion's life went into slow motion. She sat up in bed and swung her legs over the side. "Is he okay?"

"He's been taken to the Oak Harbor hospital, ma'am. I don't know his condition."

"Is he alive? *Is he?*"

"Yes, ma'am. He was the last time I saw him."

"Thank God."

"Yes, ma'am."

Vietnam

Nancy Angelides said, "You have a visitor."

She lifted Bowie's chart from the foot of the bed and began to make notes on it.

Bowie looked past his nurse. A tall Marine in khaki stood inside the curtain that separated Bowie's bed from the rest of sickbay. Silver eagles gleamed on the man's collars.

The colonel smiled and said, "Good morning, Lieutenant. The doc says you're well enough for a chat. How do you feel?"

"Not ready to wrestle gators, Colonel, but I can handle a chat."

"Good." The colonel came alongside the bed and held out his hand. "I'm Bret Samson. Those were my Marines you saved the other night."

Bowie shook the proffered hand. "Glad to be of assistance."

"I understand you were shot down and walked south looking for rescue. That right?"

"Yes, sir. My A-Four got smoked by a thirty-seven millimeter gun up near Vinh, and a company of North Vietnamese soldiers moving south captured me. The asshole in charge decided to take me along. Several nights later I escaped and ran south. I was hiding under a brush pile when those VC came out of the trees and set up their ambush. Pretty soon I saw Marines come out of the tree line, so I yelled a warning. That's all I remember until I woke up here."

"And you saved some damn good Marines. We don't know which side shot you, but we're grateful for the help."

"How'd the firefight turn out?"

"Seven dead VC and one wounded Marine ... and you, of course. Listen, Lieutenant, the doc says they're putting you on a flight to San Diego tomorrow. You're going to be at the Balboa Naval Hospital until you're fit for duty again. I've alerted the Marine liaison office there to make sure you get whatever you need. Anything. That understood?"

"Yes, sir. Thank you."

"No, Lieutenant, thank you. Semper Fi."

The colonel grinned and left.

"I'm impressed," Nurse Angelides said. She hung up the clipboard. "The only time we see a Marine colonel around here is if they're bleeding or visiting one of their own."

Washington State

Marion Jansen paced the tiny hospital waiting area adjacent to the intensive care unit: twelve paces to the far wall, twelve back. She glanced at her watch for the second time—three minutes to midnight. She was reversing course when the door labeled *No Admittance* opened and a man in green scrubs came through the opening.

"Mrs. Jansen?"

She stopped. "Yes."

The man said, "I operated on your son's leg. He'll be okay. He has facial bruises, two cracked ribs and the broken leg, but they'll heal."

Marion's knees gave way and she sank to the floor. She wanted to cry again, but there were no tears left in her.

Chapter 25
Day Fourteen

California

William H. Jaeger, currently the older member of the venerable law firm of Jaeger and Jaeger, came out of the judge's chambers through a side door. He waved at his clients to stay put and then disappeared into the men's room across the hall.

"Jesus," Henry said, scrunching up his nose, "you'd think he could hold it long enough to tell us what's going on."

Grant said, "He's old. Give him some slack. You'll be there soon."

"Yeah, I've been aging pretty damn fast lately."

Several minutes later, Mr. Jaeger came out of the men's room and joined his two clients in the waiting area at the end of the hallway.

"Sorry, had to pee. I thought the judge would never stop talking."

He sat down across from Grant and motioned for Henry to move closer. Henry moved his chair around and leaned forward.

"What did he say?"

"Wait a sec," Jaeger said. He pulled a yellow legal tablet out of his briefcase and set it on one knee. "Okay, here's the deal." He consulted his notes while Grant and Henry fidgeted. "Since Robin is still a juvenile the judge is willing to drop the felonies if she pleads guilty to the misdemeanor charge of disorderly conduct."

Grant sat up straight. "Now wait—"

Jaeger held up a hand. "She'll be released to your custody and be on probation until she's eighteen, which is ...." He ran a finger down his notes. "In three months, if I have the date right."

He looked up at Grant.

"That's correct."

"Okay. Once she turns eighteen, she can petition the judge to have the misdemeanor conviction purged from the court records."

Henry said, "That is a damn good deal."

"I'm a damn good attorney," Jaeger said. "And I play poker with the judge once a month."

"But," Grant said, "will she have a criminal record?"

"If the judge agrees to purge, the conviction will disappear from this court's records. The police may or may not destroy the record of her arrest. Now, Captain Spanner, you want to accept the deal?"

"Yes, sir. Is there a fine?"

"Oh yeah. Thanks for reminding me. Two hundred dollars."

"I'll pay it," Grant said.

"Thought you would."

Raising a hand, Henry asked, "What of the other girl?"

"Now that's a different matter. She's over eighteen; therefore, the law considers her more responsible for her actions."

"But all she did was stand there," Henry said. "The lousy bastard used her ... used both girls ... as bait."

"Willing bait," Jaeger said. He consulted his notes once again. "The judge will let her plead to the same misdemeanor charge, but she'll get two years probation and a stiff fine."

"How stiff?"

"A thousand dollars."

"Jesus," Henry said. "She can't pay that, and from what Robin told us, I don't think her so-called parents will."

"Well," Jaeger said, taking a sudden interest in the ceiling fresco, "she stays in county jail until someone does pay."

Looking at Grant, then back at Jaeger, Henry said, "I'll pay it."

Jaeger peered at him. "Why?"

"Do you mean ... are my intentions honorable?"

"Exactly."

"Mr. Jaeger, women don't appeal to me. Surely a San Francisco native such as yourself can understand my situation."

The attorney smiled. "I'll let the judge know."

Henry looked at Grant. "Care to comment? You surprised?"

"Hank, I'm no longer surprised at anything about you."

Yankee Station

The COD, coming in on a special run from Cubi to Danang to USS *Valiant*, trapped aboard thirty seconds after the last go-bird launched. The taxi directors brought the waddling utility aircraft out of the wires, spun it around, and parked it aft of the island, clear of the angled deck.

CAG didn't wait for the props to finish spooling down. He yanked open the plane's side door and called out, "Welcome home, Dutch."

Commander Jansen hopped out of the COD wearing a bright blue Thai-silk flight suit with gold wings embroidered on the left breast. A white silk scarf was draped around his neck, the ends tucked inside the blue jumper. Besides the Air Force presents, he wore a huge grin.

"Jesus Christ," CAG said, pumping Jansen's hand. "You look like a New York pimp."

"Well, CAG, you should see how the other half lives," Jansen said. "It's out of this world."

"Yeah. And they have real long runways too. Come on. The boss wants to see you on the bridge. We both want to find out what happened."

"Wait a second, CAG. I called my wife from Thailand. She heard on the radio that the Navy lost *two* aircraft at Hanoi last night. What happened to Roamer and Anders?"

"They took an eighty-five hit that knocked Roamer out. Anders flew the plane back here and ejected them both alongside. Anders is fine. Roamer was touch and go with bleeding under the skull, but he'll make it. You can see him after we brief the captain."

"CAG, we need to get a message to Whidbey. The wives know the lost planes had to be two A-Sixes. They'll be having fits."

"I'll take care of it. Right now, Captain Franklin wants to see you."

He turned and trotted toward the island.

Captain Franklin spun his chair around and burst out laughing. "What in hell is this, CAG ... the tooth fairy?"

"No, sir. This here be the angel Gabriel. See the gold wings."

"I'm from planet Takhli," Jansen said. "Take me to your leader."

"You'll have to settle for me," Franklin said. He reached out and shook Jansen's hand. "Welcome to earth. By God, you do look pretty." Then his mood turned somber. "We got the message that you'd been rescued, but Phil Bloomberg is still missing. What's the story?"

"We didn't get much flak, I guess their gun barrels were too hot from firing at the first A-Six. But a missile nailed us right after the seeds came off. The port engine torched, and I started to lose control of the airplane. We made it to the mountains west of Hanoi, then ejected. I landed near the crest of a ridge ... Phil touched down about a mile east of me. I heard gunfire from there at dawn and have to assume he's either dead or a prisoner."

"And the Air Force picked you up?"

"Yes, sir. About midmorning."

"You're lucky. Did CAG tell you about Roamer and Anders?"

"Yes, sir. I hope the mission was worth it."

Captain Franklin looked at CAG.

"I'll fill him in later," CAG said.

"Yeah," Franklin said. "Do that. Okay, Dutch, you better get down to your ready room and say hello to your crews. They've been waiting for you."

"Aye, aye, Captain."

Franklin spun his chair to face forward as soon as Jansen left the bridge. "Damn shame."

CAG nodded agreement. "Yes, sir."

Franklin raised his binoculars and peered at the Russian trawler cruising toward them. "Ivan is getting feisty again. You figure that A-three tanker has any excess fuel it needs to dump?"

The VA-66 crews, except for Mike Roamer and those in the air, were waiting in Ready Three. The clapping that started when their CO stepped through the door turned to whooping and cheering as Jansen posed in his fancy silk flight suit.

Once the welcome celebration died down and the crews dispersed, Commander Jansen pulled Terry aside. "You did a hell of a job, mister. How's Mike?"

"Doc says he'll make it, but he'll probably never fly again."

"Does Mike know?"

"Not yet."

"Christ, that'll break his heart. Of course, it might save his marriage."

"Hadn't thought of that," Terry said. "Kind of ironic if it happens that way." He paused. "Look, Skipper, you're going to need a new B/N. How about me?"

Now Jansen paused. "I heard you were on the verge of turning in your wings. Change your mind?"

"Yes, sir. I'm so pissed about this worthless war I've decided to make the Navy a career."

"Come again?"

Terry laughed. "Well, sir, I figure B/Ns are going to wind up running the A-Six program, and I plan to excel ... all the way to admiral. And maybe the next time some hare-brained politicians decide to send us into a shitty quagmire like this, I'll be in a position to stand up and howl about it."

Jansen smiled. "Truly a noble goal, young man. God knows the current crop of flag officers didn't make much noise. But what about *your* marriage? Look, Terry, I'm aware of the situation with your wife. Hell, we all are. Aren't you afraid she'll leave if you stay in?"

"I was, sir. But things are changing. She used to worry about what would happen to her ... now she's worried more about me. And I'm convinced she's got the makings of a good Navy wife. All she needs now is a little more confidence, and she'll stick with me."

"She may have already reached that decision, Terry. I called Marion from Thailand. Judy's in Whidbey Island, she seems to be looking for housing."

"My wife's at the base? Looking for a house?"

"That's what I hear."

"Thank God."

California

Spanner seemed relaxed. He recognized the feeling, even though it was a long time since he felt that way. It all comes back, he mused. *Like riding a bicycle.*

He raised his wine glass and said, "Here's to you, Hank. You done good."

Henry raised his own glass. "*Salud y pesetas.*"

The two girls came back from the restroom giggling. They breezed past the maître d' and left several restaurant diners smiling in their path. Robin gave her father a fleeting kiss on the cheek as she passed by, then giggled some more as she sat down.

Spanner chuckled. "What's the kiss for?"

"For being you and for rescuing us from Charley."

Raven asked, "What's going to happen to him?"

Henry snorted. "Do you care?"

"No way, merely curious."

"Actually," Henry said, "it looks as though he got away. The cops got a warrant based on your testimony to the judge, and they searched the house where you've been living, but they came up dry. Charley and the other girls apparently lit out for parts unknown. One of the neighbors said they were headed for Death Valley."

"A good place for him," Spanner said.

Robin asked, "What's going to happen to you ... to us?"

"I've got orders to the Pentagon, honey. I figure to be there for two years. I'll be up for admiral by then, and all bets will be off. If I make it, I'll get new orders. If I don't make it, I'll retire."

Robin looked perplexed. "But what—"

"About you? Well ... you can go back to USC, of course. But you'd have to stay with your Uncle Henry."

"Oh no," Henry said and made a face.

"Or ... you can come east with me. We can get an apartment in D.C., and you can attend Georgetown University. I hear it's a pretty fair school."

Beaming, Robin said, "Let's do that."

"Good," Henry said. "And what about you, Raven?"

"The judge says I have to get a job and report to my probation officer once a week. I guess that takes care of *my* next two years."

"You have any job experience?"

"After high school I spent a couple of years as a singer in a little night spot back home. Mostly ballads. That's it."

Henry leaned forward. "A singer? Interesting. I have a little booking agency in Long Beach, you know, finding gigs for the local talent. I could use someone to help scout out the right venues. Sounds as if you could fill that bill. Interested?"

"I can't, Mr. Spanner. My probation officer is in San Francisco."

"I know an old lawyer who can get the judge to transfer your probation to my neck of the woods. I'll call him first thing in the morning."

Yankee Station

The sound of guitar chords made their way through the steel bulkhead, a warning that Jeb Wilson was pickin' again. Terry hesitated, but opened the door to his stateroom anyway; he needed his stationery.

Jeb sat on the side of his bunk stroking his guitar, humming while he experimented with chords.

Terry sat at his desk and reached for his stationery box. "What's that you're playing, Jeb?"

"Writin' a song."

"Country?"

"Blues."

"Oh yeah?" Terry opened his stationery box; it contained half a dozen envelopes but no writing paper. He'd forgotten. "Why blues?"

"Fits my mood."

"I understand," Terry said. He jammed the stationery box back into the desk drawer. "What triggered this bout of creativity?"

"Got a letter from my older brother, Seth. He's a fighter pilot on the CINC-PAC-FLEET staff." Jeb coaxed a new chord out of the guitar. "Couple of weeks ago Seth caught a MAC charter flight from Hawaii to San Francisco International. He was in uniform. When he got into the airline terminal, a woman shouted 'baby killer' at him. Then some guy tried to spit on him."

"Your brother beat the crap out of him?"

"He ran away; Seth didn't bother to chase him."

"Damn hippies."

"Seth said they both looked like regular college kids. The guy even had on a necktie. I guess it's just that kind of war, that kind of year." Jeb strummed some more and went back to humming.

Leaning back in his chair, Terry asked, "You got any words to that song yet?"

"Just the chorus."

"Let's hear it."

Jeb played a few chords then sang, "Here I'm fightin' for my country, while my country's fightin' me. This year's so damn depressin'... that I'm bummed as I can be. But there ain't no point in bitchin' ... I got nothin' more to lose. Just another pissed-off victim of those sixty-seven blues."

Terry applauded. "Amen brother. By the way, you got anymore stationery? I'm all out."

Chapter 26
Day Fourteen Continued

Yankee Station

The fried fish and chips featured in the Wardroom One buffet line didn't appeal to Terry. He asked one of the stewards behind the counter for scrambled eggs and corned beef hash with a side of rye toast. The eggs turned out to be overcooked, so he smothered them with catsup.

Not wanting any company, he looked over the half-dozen tables for an empty chair among other empty chairs. He'd come from IOIC where he saw the last recce sweep past Hanoi showing normal river traffic where they placed the seeds. *All a waste. Roger was right.*

Roger pulled a chair out across from Terry, dumped his canvas travel bag on the deck, and sat down. "Stopped by to say adios. There's a COD leaving for Cubi Point on the last launch, and I'm on it."

Holding out an envelope, Terry said, "Here's the letter I mentioned."

Roger stuffed it into a slot on the side of his travel bag. "I'll mail it from Hawaii tomorrow."

"Thanks," Terry said. "I'm sorry you're leaving. I was beginning to like you."

"Beginning?"

"I'm a slow learner. You say good-bye to Mike already?"

"I tried. They won't let me in. I wrote him a note and left it in his mailbox down in your ready room. Will you take it to him?"

"No problem. You finish that last column?"

"Yeah. I left a copy with the note. I'd as soon be gone when you guys read it." He stood up and stuck out his hand. "Good luck, my friend. I hear you've got a new pilot. Take care of him."

"That's my job." Terry stood and shook Roger's hand. "Give my regards to Broadway, and a fickle finger to the Pentagon."

With a little wave, Roger picked up his bag and left.

Terry sat back down then pushed away his unfinished dinner. He wasn't hungry.

Jansen was leading the next morning's first strike, so Terry worked up a plan for it then wandered the hangar deck. He paused at the elevator bay and stared out at the darkened sea.

Lightning flickered far to the west, over North Vietnam. The ship was quiet now, the last recovery of the day over. After a few minutes he made his way down to the ready room.

Two flight crews were struggling out of their sweat-stained gear back in the locker area. The SDO was working the phone to maintenance control, trying to get a status report for the next day's schedule. The bulletin board claimed the evening movie was *Who's Afraid of Virginia Woolf?* There wouldn't be many attendees.

Terry pulled Roger's note to Mike out of his mailbox and stuffed it, unread, into a pocket. Sickbay was his next stop. The long piece of paper sticking out of the box had to be Roger's last column from Yankee Station. Terry took it to his seat in the third row and ignored the quiet chatter behind him as he read.

>Aboard USS *Valiant* in the Tonkin Gulf
>by Roger Brackett
>
>Throughout World War II, American GIs storming bomb-blasted beaches or fighting their way into battle-gutted towns were often surprised to be welcomed by an odd bit of graffiti: a caricature of a bald man peering over a fence, along with the words, *Kilroy was here.*
>
>"What the hell?" they'd say. "Who's this guy, Kilroy?"
>
>But those young soldiers soon got the joke, and were apt to leave their own version of *Kilroy was here* when they moved on to other battles and found new scorched walls upon which to write. Kilroy seemed to be an appropriate stand-in for every anonymous GI, those kids from America's heartland who never saw the ocean until they were on it, but who slogged across every beach and into every enemy hamlet, always under fire.
>
>Tell you what. Find someone in their forties and ask them what *Kilroy was here* brings to mind. Right off,

they'll say, "World War Two."

The American ground troops in Vietnam have their very own adage, at least as appropriate, at least as ubiquitous: *"Sorry 'bout that."*

Spill salt on someone else's eggs in the mess hall? *Sorry 'bout that.*

Bump into a buddy during a firefight and spoil their aim? *Sorry 'bout that.*

Shoot your best friend in the foot because you panicked when the sniper opened fire? The appropriate words are, of course, *Sorry 'bout that.*

And when you're standing over a fallen comrade who will never, ever open his eyes again? What you whisper is, *Sorry 'bout that.*

It's all-purpose, you see. Always appropriate. And good manners.

I'm going to need those words myself. You see, I'm about to tell you something you won't like: we're going to lose this war.

Those scrawny little North Vietnamese are going to beat us. Not because they're more powerful; we are. Certainly not because they have better equipment; we do. And not because they're braver; there is no monopoly on that virtue in this war. No, they're going to beat us because they're smarter than we are. *Sorry 'bout that.*

You think I exaggerate?

The North Vietnamese built a paper-maché airplane on a runway to get us to waste bombs, aircraft, and lives attacking it. We did ... for a time.

Our present administration kept key bridges around the North Vietnamese port city of Haiphong off-limits for years while the enemy used them to bring in, unmolested, megatons of air defense weapons. Then the President sent in Navy strike aircraft to drop the bridges. It took them several days, flying against heavy antiaircraft fire, to put the bridges out of commission. Many good aircraft and brave men were lost doing it.

Then the President put the bridges back into off-limits status. The North Vietnamese are repairing them as we speak. The bridges should be operational again in a few days.

Last night some targeting geniuses somewhere up the chop chain sent two of America's most sophisticated aircraft, flown by four well-trained men, to put extremely complex mines into a river near downtown Hanoi, a city armed with more antiaircraft weapons than any other place in the history of warfare. The mines were laid, but both aircraft and one of the men were lost. This morning the Vietnamese floated empty fifty-gallon drums down the river to detonate the very expensive, very clever mines. Empty barrels defeated the best tactics and technology we could muster.

They're smarter than we are. *Sorry 'bout that.*

Terry folded the paper and put it in his pocket with Roger's farewell note to Mike. Then he pulled the column back out and stared at it.

"You're wrong," he said. "There's no way the United States is going to lose this war. Maybe we should, but we won't." He crumpled the paper up and dropped it in a wastebasket near the door. "You're wrong, Roger. Sorry 'bout that."

A magazine lay on the metal table parked alongside Mike's bed, folded as if half read. A glass of ice water stood near it, a bendable straw leaning against its lip. Signs of progress.

"You must be healing," Terry said. He put Roger's note down next to the magazine.

"One day at a time. What's that?"

"Roger's farewell. He's on his way to the states."

"He leave another column with you?"

"Didn't give me one when he said good-bye." *Not really a lie.*

"I thought maybe he'd write up our last mission. We did a hell of a job, you know. Low, fast, duckin' SAMs in the dark. And all that flak. Only an A-Six could handle what we did."

"You never flew better, Mike."

Terry eased down onto a metal stool near the foot of the bed.

"Yeah." Mike looked at the ceiling for several seconds. "The doc told me, Terry. I'll never fly again."

"Did he say why?"

"Yeah. I might have a seizure someday. Can you believe that? Maybe tomorrow, maybe years from now, maybe never. They've got medication for it, he says, but no more flying."

"I'm sorry, Mike. I know what it means to you."

"It's the only thing in my life I ever did well. I was a mediocre student, second string at sports, not much of a ladies' man. But I could fly, Terrance, I could really fly."

Tears formed in Mike's eyes.

Terry looked away. "Any idea what you'll do?"

"Been giving that some thought. I'd like to teach. Ground school stuff. You know: navigation, aerodynamics, meteorology."

"In the Navy?"

"Don't think so. Maybe one of those civilian Embry-Riddle schools. They've got one in Fort Worth."

"Goin' back to Texas?"

"I know some people in Dallas."

The curtain swung back. "Times up," the orderly said.

"Yeah," Mike said. "My time is up."

Washington, D.C.

"Annie," Jason demanded, "what in hell are you doin' here?"

He stood behind his desk, she in the office doorway.

"I work here, remember?"

She walked to Jason's desk and tossed a handful of papers into a wicker basket that once held cookies from a South Carolina favor seeker. A small photo of someone's *innie* navel was attached to the basket. A different basket bore the photo of an *outie* navel, but that basket was empty.

"You just had a miscarriage," Jason said. "Go home."

"Will you be quiet." Annie glanced over her shoulder; the door *was* closed. "The whole damn world doesn't have to know."

"Sorry," Jason said, somewhat subdued. He motioned her closer and whispered, "Go home."

"No." Annie said. "I'm fine. They released me yesterday evening, I had a good night's sleep, and I'm ready to work. We need to go over your schedule for the rest of this week, you're overbooked."

The door opened a crack and Naomi's face appeared. "You got a call, Annie. From Manila."

"Manila?"

"Yeah. Must be your boyfriend."

"Take it in heah," Jason said. He stood up. "Ah'll wait outside with Naomi, make sure she doesn't eavesdrop."

Naomi made a face and disappeared.

Jason followed her out and closed the door.

Annie picked up the phone on the first ring. "Roger?"

"Hi, Annie. I love you."

"Roger?"

"Yeah. How many men call you and say 'I love you'?"

"You'd be amazed, Roger." She laughed. "Some of them pant a lot too."

"I'm not into that ... yet. I haven't gotten an answer from you. Will you marry me?"

"Roger ... you need to know. I—"

"I know everything I need to know. I love you. Marry me."

"I had a miscarriage," Annie said, the words jumbled together.

"You lost the baby?"

"Yes."

"You okay?"

"Yes, fine."

"Then will you marry me?"

"You still want me? Even though—"

"Of course. Will ... you ... marry ... me?"

"Oh Roger. Of course I will. I love you too. Now more than ever."

"In Hawaii? Tomorrow?"

"Hawaii? Tomorrow?"

"Yeah. I've got a flight from Manila to Honolulu in the morning. I checked the Pan Am flight schedules. You can catch one from Dulles to Hawaii with a short stopover in Los Angeles. We can get married tomorrow evening on the beach at Waikiki. Sunset. The surf pounding. You and me."

"You're nuts, Roger. Why the rush?"

"I've learned a few things in the last couple of weeks. One of them is that life is short … grab what you want. And I want you. Right now."

"Where will I meet you?"

"I've booked a room at the Royal Hawaiian."

"The Pink Palace of the Pacific?"

"The one and only."

Annie stood up. "I'll be there. I love you, you big goof."

She hung up the phone and flipped through Jason's rolodex, looking for Pan Am's phone number, singing while she searched:

"*Tiny bubbles … in the wine.*"

Epilogue

Rolling Thunder rolled on. By the end of 1967, the Pentagon had dropped more bomb tonnage on Southeast Asia than had been used on Europe in World War Two, and a CIA study claimed that the air strikes had cost the United States $9.60 for each $1.00 of damage inflicted on the enemy. Forty-five percent of Americans believed that sending troops to Vietnam had been a mistake.

But U.S. Army brass claimed that North Vietnam and their Viet Cong allies were now incapable of conducting meaningful military operations. There was "light at the end of the tunnel." Then early on the morning of January 31, 1968, the enemy struck in what came to be called the Tet Offensive. It was a military disaster for the communists, but a political win for them: American will to support the war folded.

Robert McNamara, Secretary of Defense, cost-effectiveness maven, and architect of the war, resigned February 28th. A month later, President Lyndon Johnson announced he would not run for reelection. His favorability rating at the time was about thirty-five percent. His war polices rated even lower: twenty-three percent.

And America was filled with hate. Civil rights icon Martin Luther King was assassinated on April 4; Presidential Candidate Robert F. Kennedy was gunned down on June 6th. The Democratic Convention held in August turned into a bloody street battle between Chicago police and anti-war demonstrators.

Then on November 1, 1968, just prior to the election, Rolling Thunder was halted after three years and eight months. Bombs no longer fell on North Vietnam; U.S. air strikes were focused on close-air support and supply line interdiction in South Vietnam. *The enemy's guns and missiles moved south also, and American aircrews continued to be shot down, imprisoned, tortured.*

Republican candidate for President, Richard Millhouse Nixon, claimed he had a plan to end the war and garnered 301 electoral votes, an easy victory. As it turned out, Nixon's plan to end the war was to turn the fighting over to the South Vietnamese. He called it "Vietnamization." In June of 1969 he began to withdraw U.S. troops.

In April of 1970, President Nixon sent American soldiers into Cambodia in an attempt to cut off enemy supply lines. *American pilots had been quietly bombing that country for more than a year.* The consequence was a bloody civil war there that brought the murderous Khmer Rouge communists to power. The move also stoked American unrest. Student demonstrations at Kent State got out of hand, and the National Guard was called in. Members of the Guard shot and killed four students, an event that fed other demonstrations across the land.

On March 30, 1972, the North Vietnamese sent waves of infantry and armor into South Vietnam in what came to be called the "Easter Attack." In retaliation, Nixon ordered his aviation forces to resume bombing North Vietnam (without the restrictions imposed by the Johnson administration) and sent B-52 bomber strikes against Hanoi.

In October, race riots broke out aboard the American aircraft carrier *Kitty Hawk* and the fleet oiler *Hassayampa*, two ships supporting flight operations against North Vietnam. Nineteen black sailors aboard *Kitty Hawk* were ultimately found guilty of assault.

By December, North Vietnam was ready to parlay, and in January 1973, the United States, South Vietnam, North Vietnam, and the Viet Cong signed a cease-fire agreement. But the "civil war" in Vietnam continued, and on April 30, 1975, North Vietnamese forces captured Saigon. The last Americans to leave that city had to leap aboard helicopters on the roof of the United States embassy.

Many American junior officers who fought in the Vietnam War vowed to make sure their country never again fought in that half-hearted manner. Army Major Colin Powell, one of those men, went on to become a four-star general and Chairman of the Joint Chiefs of Staff. His 'Powell Doctrine,' forged from the memory of Vietnam, called for waging war only when absolutely necessary, and then only with decisive force and a clear exit strategy.

Since that war, U.S. forces have fought in seven significant conflicts: Grenada (1983), Panama (1989), The Persian Gulf (1991), Somalia (1993), Bosnia (1990s), Afghanistan (2001-present), and Iraq (2003-present).

Doesn't look like we learned a lot from Vietnam. *Sorry 'bout that.*

Tucson, Arizona, 2010

About the Author
B.K. Bryans

Brian was a teenage cowboy on two southern Arizona ranches before he became the young horse wrangler for a film company shooting western movies for television at the Old Tucson movie set.

After two years at the University of Arizona, he entered the Naval Aviation Cadet Program in Pensacola, Florida, and became a carrier-qualified jet pilot at age twenty. As a naval aviator, Brian flew 3,669 hours in thirteen different types of aircraft, made 652 carrier landings (163 of them at night), and flew 183 combat missions in A-6 Intruders during the Vietnam War. He was awarded the Silver Star, the Distinguished Flying Cross, and thirteen Air Medals. He went on to command Attack Squadron Thirty-Five (VA-35) aboard USS *Nimitz*.

While in the Navy, Brian earned a B.A. in Mathematics and an M.S. in Operations Research & Systems Analysis. Besides his flying tours, Brian served as aide to the Senior Member of the United Nations Armistice Commission in Korea, aide to the Commander of the U.S. Seventh Fleet, and Chief of Special Studies for the Joint Chiefs of Staff. He retired from the U.S. Navy as a captain.

Brian then worked as a consultant and software developer before serving as a manager with the Arizona state government. He is now retired again ... and writing.

About The Cover
Moonlight Intruders by Craig Kodera

Craig Kodera painted **Moonlight Intruders,** the artwork used on the cover of *Those '67 Blues*. He approaches his various art subjects from a contemporary point of view, yet his style also encompasses the traditional. Many of his art pieces hang in several museums, including the permanent collection of art at the Smithsonian Institution's National Air and Space museum, Washington. D.C. His art clients include Northrop, Bell Helicopter, Federal Express, McDonnell Douglas Corp., Airbus North America, San Diego Aerospace Museum, American Air Lines, and the C.R. Smith museum.

Recent awards for his work include the 2001, R.G. Smith Award for Excellence in Naval Aviation Art, and the Best of the Best Award, Aviation Week Space and Technology magazine for the year 2000.

Craig is the Charter Vice President of the American society of Aviation Artists, a member of the Air Force Art Program and a member of the Los Angeles Society of Illustrators.

As a former Air Force Reserve Pilot, he logged over 1300 hours flying time in a Lockheed HC-140H Hercules for the Air Rescue Service. While serving with Strategic Air Command, he flew a McDonnell Douglas KC-10A Extender. In 1986, he began flying with Air California then stayed on as first officer after the airline was acquired by American Airlines.

He is a graduate of UCLA with a degree in mass communications and a minor in art history.

The Moonlight Intruders print, as well as other limited edition prints by Craig, can be purchased from The Greenwich Workshop, www.greenwichworkshop.com.

Printed in Great Britain
by Amazon.co.uk, Ltd.,
Marston Gate.